Fat Time and Other Stories

Also by Jeffery Renard Allen

FICTION

Song of the Shank

Holding Pattern

Rails Under My Back

POETRY

Harbors and Spirits

Stellar Places

FAT TIME

and Other Stories

Jeffery Renard Allen

Graywolf Press

Some of the stories in this collection first appeared in the following publications: "Circle" in *Fifth Sunday*; "Fat Time" in *Granta*; "The Lucky Ones" in *Konch*; "Heads" and "Pinocchio" in the *Oxford American*; "Testimonial" in the *Scofield*; "Orbits" in *American Short Fiction*; "The Next Flight" in *Tin House*.

Permission acknowledgments for lyrics quoted in the text appear on page 283.

This publication is made possible, in part, by the voters of Minnesota through a Minnesota State Arts Board Operating Support grant, thanks to a legislative appropriation from the arts and cultural heritage fund. Significant support has also been provided by the McKnight Foundation, the Amazon Literary Partnership, and other generous contributions from foundations, corporations, and individuals. To these organizations and individuals we offer our heartfelt thanks.

Published by Graywolf Press
212 Third Avenue North, Suite 485
Minneapolis, Minnesota 55401

www.graywolfpress.org

Published in the United States of America

ISBN 978-1-64445-239-4 (paperback)
ISBN 978-1-64445-240-0 (ebook)

2 4 6 8 9 7 5 3 1
First Graywolf Printing, 2023

Library of Congress Control Number: 2022946507

Cover design: Adam B. Bohannon

Cover image: Derived from Jack Johnson, photographed by Otto Sarony, 1908

In memory of my mother, Alice Allen (1930–2020)

Blessings, blessings yeah
I see elephant tusk on the bow of a sailing lady
Docked on the Ivory Coast
Mercedes in a row winding down the road
I hope my black skin don't dirt this white tuxedo
Before the Basquiat show and if so
Well fuck it, fuck it
Because this water drown my family
This water mixed my blood
This water tells my story
This water knows it all
Go ahead and spill some champagne in the water
Go ahead and watch the sun blaze
On the waves of the ocean

—FRANK OCEAN ON JAY-Z'S "OCEANS"

Contents

Fat Time and Other Stories

PART 1

Water Brought Us

Testimonial

(Supported in Belief/Verified in Fact)

Who could have imagined, only five minutes to save your son? A roar heard in open sunlight. Fear felt together. The net (noose) tightening. Some breakdown in communication. A wrong turn. Life a warning. God no guarantee. Move now at breakneck speed. Many places to hide and none. Indeed, I could camouflage myself in reeds and thickets. Lather myself in mud and lie down in the rocky riverbed. And they might pass me by. But even if I could disappear, no hiding place for my son. For what if they overtook me, caught me? In such circumstance, his fate linked to mine. Trapped.

So I slicked down his body with water—hurry up, hurry up—from the oily stream where we greased our guns. Secured a breathing mask to his tiny face, still pale in color and sun-deprived from the fresh womb. Enough concentrated oxygen to keep him alive a half day or more. Then I tethered a cow to a tree so that it would not pull away once the painful work began. I started to ease my son into the cow's anus with two hands a lot like the way we loaded a long shell into one of the big guns. The cow tensed but, to my surprise, offered little resistance. I slapped the hard round buttocks and sent the animal off at a slow trot, knowing that it would not run far.

I dropped down into my hiding place.

Those of us—the men, only the men—who survived awakened to a world covered in white clay. Ground leaf branch and tree covered with the white stuff of witness. We ran about in every direction at once, like shy birds hard to catch. As we soon discovered, it was no accident or miracle that we had survived. They had deliberately spared us. Dead littered the contested flexible boundaries of our town. They had ripped apart each male child. Pieces of skin tissue organ scattered over the fields like some strange harvest. Patterned rows of spinal columns like newly planted trees. Lengths of intestines like dew-whitened vines. Tufts of hair on the breeze. Twigs of bone under our surveying feet.

Unidentifiable.

I could not find the cow.

No piles of fleshy shit. No tracks. No trace. Nothing.

We marked out a circle and worked through the night to dig a collective grave, our fierce spades slicing into the earth and flinging freed dirt into the air, our mouths spitting red tracers of talk and tobacco into the sky. We gathered what we could into boxes and baskets and buried it, then came with our weapons and stood around the steepled dirt. Uttered their names.

Some wept. Others remained silent. (Sad faces, silent petitions.) Some burst into hymn while others danced our calamities. (If a man dances alone he will not dance for long.) Tired, the older men handed over their dance to the younger. Many of us would start marking this day with an annual return to the grave—wanting to attach some definite meaning, some magical intent to our loss. Others would enact something secret—and probably offensive—behind closed doors and shuttered windows. Any ritual leaves out too much.

All of us would dream at night about the return of our sons—barely recognizable creatures, disguised, terrifying us out of our senses. Lookalikes in a deathly masquerade. We returned to our shops and jobs, mourning taking over our habits and thoughts. The murdered boys lingered on in the beautiful thought of revenge.

One night many years later, when I was an old man, I drifted about my house, restless, under some desire that failed to find appropriate satisfaction—food, coffee, books—so I decided to make a round through the woods—insomnia calling me forth, sheep by sheep—familiar territory even in the dark, navigating less by sight than by feel. I soon reached the outskirts of the sleeping town where I decided to stand guard. What was at stake? The war had come and gone. So my actions were a thing pre-done, anticipatory, a thing re-done, commemorative. Many such nights before. A drowsy spectator of star and moon in bright relief against dark sky. An old man wandering until the tug of sleep pulled me home.

Wandering this night, invisible brush and leaves a dark chorus filling the air with the disembodied chirps of crickets. I heard another sound. The movement of a shapeless animal? No. More like—I'm certain—shoes crunching leaf- and vine-covered ground, heels snapping dry branches in two. I stopped and stared into the dark. Saw nothing at first, only tree-jammed dark. Then a form broke the night, burst into vision like a lantern. A man. Growing larger the closer he came. So tall he had to walk stooped forward to keep his head from tangling with the branches. Dressed sharp as a tack, as if he'd just come from a dinner party. I didn't think to raise my rifle. Instead I backed away. From this man. Little more than white flesh on a pole. Never having earned the richness of color that was his birthright. Who I knew to be my son. Smelling of shit.

He sat down on the log, bowed his head, ran his fingers over the abandoned bark. Seen with single intention. A restlessness in every inflection of his body. Lost and needy. I tried to hide my fear. What he might do to me? Who he might have become? Would he spit accusation in my eyes? (Innocent. I tell you. Innocent. Tell him. I would never summon a ghost. I let go long ago. Forgive me.)

I speared the rifle barrel-first into the soil, then sat down at the other end of the log. We sat for a spell, him at one end, me at the other. Shared space. A family affair. I gave him water from my steel canteen but he could not swallow. I spoke the words of a father, but he could only stammer. So I remained quiet. Unasked questions. Watching my dejected son. His hands balled into fists, clutching something hard-earned and unsayable. I took his shoulders into my hands, though I was afraid of his skin. Afraid for him too. What would the others make of his return? Would they be jealous? They whose sons had not escaped the coffined clay? Would I need to hide my son again?

"I'm dead," he said.

An orphan. Cut off. Sweet child of original darkness. The black sanctuary of a cow's ass. Purity outraged. Here again. His past virgin territory he could never inhabit. Birth a category of facts that can never be repeated.

I spoke no reply. And we sat the silence of anxious vigil.

Fall

"I am truly a drop of sun under the earth."

—Frantz Fanon

I tapped him on the chin with my machete, in a dark room lit only by the sound of our hissing lanterns, sharp light and sharp blade causing his eyes to pop open, the muscles in his face straining in recognition and urgency. He tried to lift his head off the pillow, black liquid dribbling down his chin, but I gestured with the blade to indicate that it would do him little good to move, to speak. So he eased his head back and let his face lie on the pillow, taking in the seven men squeezed into his bedroom. Perhaps fear had placed us all in this room together.

I unbuttoned my shirt, exposing my chest and abdomen to the air. I let him stare into my skin. What he saw reflected there caused him to say my name like I was someone. The eight of us, we were all breathing. Was this what we'd wanted all along?

You have every right, he said. But whatever I took from your kind never did me a bit of good. Just look around you.

I looked around me. Then I stood quietly and listened, but there was space around his declarations. Every word started to vibrate into a loud muddled echo as if I'd shrunk down into something small inside the chamber of his ear.

There's a way of forgetting and forgiving. There's a way of stepping back. But I don't want to know the world in that way anymore.

I gave him a simple nod.

I won't cast judgment, he said. You have become something more.

I dragged my machete one slow inch at a time across his throat so that the room lit up with his pain, slow lights shining on every object.

I kicked the front door open and we went out into the night, the moon wide and spreading across the sky like batter in a hot skillet. I handed the machete to Nsembo so that he could wash the blood off. Once he did so, we—the seven of us—all sat together on the ground around the yard in the slanted moonlight. We spoke quietly, inconsequential chatter, our bodies close, merging into a single voice, another round of life, sufficient to the day.

Just a week ago, I wondered what this moment would be like. In anything's undoing, we might imagine some notion of ourselves. But you cannot know what it will be like for another. I wish I could tell you that the killing started because I had reached a tipping point—another abduction, another disappearance, another maiming, disfigurement, murder, rape—but I cannot. It started because God spoke to me in a dream.

I can't think of the night it happened as notable or peculiar. Beside my wife in bed as on any other night. Thinking. A year since the four girls vanished, their clothing abandoned in the deep field of intensified grass surrounding the ruins of the old church. The church had been razed generations ago during the time of our ancestors. So many battles fought. In the heat of combat, our ancestors had suffered and endured many wrongs. Thirsty, I thought water then found myself sitting under a tree with a cup in my hands so suddenly that I almost dropped it. I took a sip and considered the sky, determined to remain calm. I heard the buzz of a distant sound and saw a sharp light descend through the trees, through all the branches, down to the swollen roots. The light started traveling across the ground toward me until listening took the place of movement, light pouring inside me, swelling me from within, causing something to whirl out to the edges of my body, light echoing in such a way as to allow me to gaze on multiple extensions of myself. But I reached a limit, could replicate no more, and started to retract, skin snapping return with such force that I pulled the dark sky close to me, so close that I wet the tip of one finger and touched a star.

I sat for a while on my bed feeling around the edges of the dream. Though much was uncertain, for the first time in a long time, I knew exactly what was required of me. But I required something of God in return, that he would keep me through it all to the duration.

Now, emboldened by my mission, I told myself, No weapon formed against me shall prosper.

Why do men begin crusades that can have only one outcome? Perhaps revolt has flared in many of us from the very beginning, for me and those like me, my brethren *zeru zeru*, the world has always been dangerous. The blacks hunt us for our body parts and our fluids and remake themselves from us, breathe light and air through us, the *zeru zeru*, albinos, a select people. Desired. Buked and scorned. Under attack. New bruises rising upon the old bruises.

What the blacks don't know, mourning allows our lives to pass more slowly than they should. Tears release latent poisons and in so doing protect and replenish the skin in our life lived in darkness, constantly on guard. Outcasts, we must touch everything before the sun comes up. Wait for the black beyond the windows before we go outdoors into the dull facts of evening. Mothers/wives/daughters busy with their fires and pots. Sweeping yards. Hanging heavy wash on lines. Gathering wood. Honest muscle work through the night hours. The blacks claim that we are weightless, skinny and frail and weak, they say, no strength, no energy, they say, people who tire easily in this life without sun.

But they have not heard our voices pouring out of doors and windows in air thick with a haze of charcoal heat and the smells of slow-cooked stews. Each evening this fit of beginnings: a bite to eat, a mouthful of bread, a meal to rush through.

The night after the dream, I was just outside the village working our slender plots without feeling time at all. No more alone than usual. I could see the windows of our village glinting gold in the distance. And the flash of metal here and there. Something long forgotten but familiar seemed to hover about the uneven roofs. Then my wife, Feliata, was standing there with me, her hand touching my arm. Slender in her dress and her feet stuck in a pair of plush pink slippers with fake pink fur that I had given her for Christmas a few months earlier. She always conducted herself like a woman of means. Each day she wore a different dress with a metal or leather or bone complement in a necklace, earrings, bracelet, and anklet, and with rings on all her fingers.

She placed a *kanga* on the ground and smoothed it into a square, then laid out an assortment of food. I sat down, and she took her place across from me. She said something to me, then bowed forward—her small head with its small sculpted braids—as if from the weight of the words. Prepared a bowl of porridge for me, with sugar mixed thick and pieces of ripe bananas sticking out like thumbs.

We sat across from each other eating in silence in the moonlit-stained air. I still couldn't shake off the dream, but I could feel Feliata's awareness of it. What would I say? My silence always worried her. She would sometimes ask me what I was thinking and look me full in the face and wait for an answer. Not that I had anything to hide. Just that, when I talk, she pays too much attention.

I started talking, each thought falling into the next. I didn't try very hard to explain.

I said, You know when something really touches you, that burning feeling inside.

A sudden rush of blood under her skin. (There's always a better way to approach a contentious topic.) Look, I don't care where it comes from, she said. Me, I take what I'm given. She fingered a pinch of *ugali*, rolled it into a ball, then dipped it in the stew.

I picked up my cup and drank. The juice was green and pleasing. I smelled the soil and the crops sleeping underneath, the aroma of the bottled-up yams. I shaped a ball of *ugali* and ate it, only for the food to stay too long in my mouth, sticky white aftertaste. What did she take me for? She'd spent most of her life with me. Had I not always carefully pondered my actions? I'm not right, not perfect, not well. Who among us is? We are hunted, forced to live in darkness, how can one not be a little crazy or crippled? I expressed my dissatisfaction, wife or not.

She stuck out her red tongue. What do you see there? she asked. Then she took my words apart, took everything I had said apart, every sentence broken. Couldn't restrain herself.

I bent forward to listen more closely, trying to turn my anger under. No single feeling escaped the whole.

Feliata edged thin and delicate toward me, all the pores in her face distinct. Beloved, she said, don't hate me.

I finished my meal, put my empty plate down, and continued to sit and let my heavy bones breathe the black air. Feliata called out to me, standing now in the symmetrically aligned field, tool in hand, each muscle ready to swell, each bone ready to bend. These dry hours of work. A shovelful of earth, a handful of seed, cleaves and cut places. A shovel or rake in every movement. Breaking earth. Big clouds of black dirt flopping about.

This is shitty work, Feliata said.

I touched her and felt her hard flesh start to loosen up. Tempted now, all my old thinking still underneath, my mind wanting to return to the me before the dream, before his hand had reached out and touched me. Why had God decided to entrust this important task to me? Perhaps because, so far as our children were concerned, Feliata and I had been more fortunate than many, illness rather than murder claiming three of our offspring before any of them were old enough to walk. The first baby drowned in a splash of milk. The second went with sunlight leaking from his wounds.

And the third one passed away with explosions of sky in her eyes. Lives never to be. We mourned just long enough, as we all do, every day.

The land is overwhelming and unapologetic. Our forearms hurt. Our backs. Legs. Still, I need to be in it, for the labor feels like a way of reaching back. A way of reminding myself where I'm not, where I could be. We were sweating, breathless, the air traveling in and out. We worked until our strength thinned out. Feliata gathered up the pots and pans into a neat bundle. She jutted her chin at me, and I gathered up the tools, then I took her hand in mine, and we started back for our house. Her way of walking.

He chose the old rattan armchair for himself and offered me to take one of the other chairs. He said all the proper things one is supposed to say to an elder—Uncle, please place your feet on my back—then sat docile and polite and waited for me to speak. The silence fit the distance of his life from mine. Two decades ago, his parents had managed to hide him beneath a cabbage before their attackers drew down on them, me and the others safe in high grass, listening to them repeat the noise of their fear. Now the color red in the palms of my hands was calling for blood.

I had thought myself there, at Nsembo's. Had grown sure of my plan, Nsembo the one person I knew I needed to set that plan in motion. He was anchored. In the darkness before me I saw his features, alive and glowing—part of his hair this way, part that way, as if shaped by the tosses and turns on his pillow; the few sparse hairs that sprouted on his chin, his large ears with thick lobes, his long mottled red neck—his outline scrawled in grainy light coming from the one kerosene lamp on the high stool in the corner behind him. His house exhaled an odor of varnish. Sufficient unto himself, Nsembo put considerable effort into pride of place, seemingly unaware that his house offered him no safety from the blacks who hunted us. Was it this that I could give him?

I could taste what I wanted to say but couldn't say it. If I could, I would have spoken in a language other than the air rushing in and out of my lungs. Instead, the breath fell out of my voice, my plans racing ahead faster than I could speak them. The good thing, after the telling I felt light, a chestful of space. Then I noticed that Nsembo was still looking at me, his gaze black and steady, awed and astonished. Had I said too much?

He brushed something off the knee of his pants, one leg then the other. With his forearms resting on the chair, he turned his head and torso about looking for something. Fetched a bottle and held it out to me.

I shook my head.

I'm sorry, Uncle, but it's all I have.

No worries, I said.

He took some for himself, held the open bottle of soda to his lips. I should not have looked more closely but I did, the orange stain on his mouth, more that made me sick for my own.

He took another sip then just held the bottle as if he didn't know it was there. Uncle, he said, I appreciate your faith in me, but who am I to decide?

I slid my foot into a patch of light. But don't you see how it would be, you with me? I asked. Iron sharpens iron.

He eased back into his chair, his long body softening the stretch of his posture. The dark was changing. Still, I saw in his bright eyes and the clench of his jaw that he was willing to join me even if I was wrong. But I needed him to have a hand in choosing. Needed to hear him say the words.

The violence began its shape as silence and continued as silence that hollowed into us for a while, time spilling out in all directions. We concerted a plan. Nsembo would prepare a dinner the next day in the clearing for the twins Henry and Hark and others who were the most likely to join us.

I did not wait to hear anything else but turned away from the house with the noise of my own breath as a guide home. The next time he sees me, I thought, no part of the self that he knows will remain.

The following evening, I passed the long backs of men and women in the fields, Feliata among them, and set off down a back road of my youth. Kikwete and I had walked this path more than three decades ago. We had found ourselves standing side by side watching the elders collect our foreskins off the ground, watching them rinse the blood off, then place them in a basket to take to market. (The blacks say that the skin has a sweet taste.) Then Kikwete moved off into the deep branches and leaves, and I followed him, trees crossing the air a hundred feet above us. We found our way through exhausted space to the clearing. He eased himself onto the ground, and I did the same, distance between us. (How much space did we take up?) The elders had prepared a salve to dull the pain in our groins, but our members still felt like they were on fire, so we sat on the ground fanning ourselves, time rushing around us.

These motherfuckers just like to cut people, Kikwete said.

Some foul shit. Did you see the way that one fat bastard was laughing?

I saw him. Kikwete's chest heaved with a restlessness of breath as though the air itself were suffocating him. Damn, he said. His features shriveled up in pain, and some unseen weight threw his head back, face pointed at the sky. Then the misery of it all clouded the space around me, no words left.

So we stayed, two huddled bodies, the ground beneath us, the only sound crickets counting the seconds and wind leaking through the trees.

Here is something you won't believe, he said.

What is it?

I heard a flutter of wings above.

I'm going to give my life to the church, he said.

Okay, but why would anybody want to do that?

No good reason, he said. It's just that I think my season is upon me. He puked on the grass.

After that day, he began to go off to the clearing for hours at a time with Bible, pencil and paper, a heel of bread, and a thermos filled with tea. He rose quickly through the ranks of the church because of both his willingness to take action for God and the living and his ability to fellowship with the dead. He kept his traveling bag on a chair next to his bed in anticipation of the trips he'd take each night into the underworld, the past, or the future, or other people's dreams. Many evenings he entered his office at the church with entities still clinging to his shoulders.

Given the cruel order of our lives, he pleaded with us to burden him with our worst thoughts and fears rather than be alone with them. He could withstand it since, God's blessing, he rarely held anything in his mind. (I knew him as well as any other, but here I sensed a half truth, suspected that rumination was responsible for his thinning hair, his bald pate. As he bent over his Bible at his desk, spirits would act out on the stage of his yellow scalp the passages he was reading.) Whenever we suffered a barbarity, he sought to reassure us.

The more sins, the better, he would say. When a woman is taken captive and has her head shaved and her eyebrows cut off and all her hair cut off and her nails pared, then she might be taken to wife.

Such were the workings of grace. After putting in his hours at the church, he would join us in the fields, sweat for sweat.

I was now there in the waiting place to tell Nsembo and the other men that one of our own, Kikwete, must be the first to die. This was where my mind went. Heard them before I saw them, six men secret but loud in the clearing. Moonlight mobile around them, the yellows and reds of their bodies difficult to grasp, knives of darkened light. They were busily talking, drinking, and playing cards. Laughing and interrupting one another, falling into one another's arms, body branching into body, making a clatter with their bottles and cups.

They caught my noise, turned in my direction, and saw me. All talk stopped, and so did I, returning their gaze in the changing sound of night.

Come on, fellas, Nsembo said. One last hand. Carefully and with ponderous movements, he shuffled the cards.

I stood there silent, waiting for my confidence to return before I took a place on the ground in the circle across from Nsembo, my every muscle tense, ready to persuade or bargain or defend. The moment offered so much.

Nsembo poured another round for everyone. The wine cooled my glass. Then heat in my mouth, heat in my throat. The other men drank theirs quickly and demanded more.

Nsembo squared the deck, shuffled the cards, dealt. They began the hand, flinging cards to the ground, cursing and teasing. The men didn't look up from their cards. Stalled, I sat there losing myself to the minutes, the light growing heavier. I felt the ground grow under me. Went down in my weight.

Bellyup won the hand.

This cocksucker, Jomo said.

Me, Bellyup said, I can't lose.

That's because you got that lucky wife at home, Mr. Newly Wed.

Yeah, Miss Lucky. I need some of that luck to bring me back alive.

Tell me.

Smiling around the words. Then they started laughing so hard that one of them almost puked. Bellyup flashed his eyes at them, but he had nerves to spare. Younger than the other me, he stood somewhat in awe of them, had even cultivated a middle-age paunch from his wife's good cooking. In this slowed-down time, I again became conscious that I was looking at the men who would help me fulfill my God-sent mission.

Didn't nobody tell you? Luck ain't free. It'll cost you. A pretty penny.

Well, shit. I got money. I can pay. Nelson rattled the coins in his pants pocket. But she don't want none of me.

Bellyup shook his head indicating that they had gone too far, but before he could act, Nsembo made a great show of scattering the cards across the ground. Then Nsembo stood up, shoved his hands in his pockets, his eyes lit.

What can I say? Jomo said. You know how we are. But so what? The braids shining around his head curved toward the twins Henry and Hark seated on either side of him.

Then don't let me stop you.

No, don't stop me. All I got is sweat and time.

Nsembo wanted to say something—I could see—but, maneuvering carefully, he thought better of it and just took the words, gave no quarter, already one step ahead of Jomo, wanting to move on to important matters. He signaled toward Nelson, who, all long muscle, took to his feet and went around the circle collecting the glasses. I held on to mine. Would not let go of it. (I was waiting for the right moment.) Nsembo came to stand next to me where I sat on the ground. And there above me, he drank wine right from the bottle—he'd saved the last for himself—wiped his mouth, then put his hand on my shoulder. Something in his touch. I tried not to move. Gathered myself. Piled up three breaths, four.

The muddy light grew heavier. I held out my glass to Nelson, glad now to be free of it. A belief in words grew upon me. I felt them coming out of my mouth, took the men through it, the words dragged up from the bottom of my lungs in an effort to turn the others all one way. I relaxed, the words coming easier. Looked from face to face until I stumbled back into the consciousness of my own talking. Was my verbiage actually necessary? Hard to say since I thought of my place there as a calm arrival, everything already mapped out, a clear series of steps, each gesture enclosed the next. All of this has happened. I don't have to tell them everything. Let them fill in what I leave out.

Wow, Jomo said. Don't you say some shit. He cut his eyes at me.

His face was too much for me, but I told myself that he was not ugly, that his face had character.

Watch your tongue with these jokes of yours, Nelson said. I believe our brother is telling us the truth. People are capable of making up such stories. He made a motion with his mouth as though he were swallowing his own mustache, his own face, self-cannibalism.

Jomo looked at Bellyup. I saw moonlight eddying around his hands. What about you? he asked.

I could feel Bellyup flutter, but he stared straight ahead without expression, his arms circled around himself as if he were counting his ribs under his sweaty shirt. He seemed so purely physical. Although, thinking back in time, I fully remembered the season of his long fever those many years ago, no ease in remembering. Don't think that I can't see through you, he said. My life is worth no more than others.

Jomo shrugged.

Bellyup looked at me, his elbows at odd angles on his knees.

I heard the chain of expectation move around the circle, arriving at Hark and Henry, who were thin and flat like two pages from a book.

What the fuck do I know about your signs? Hark said. He was looking into my eyes.

Hey, Henry said. Your body is not yours.

Hark turned to face his brother.

The niggers can take it anytime they want.

So let them take it.

You don't know what you're saying.

What has my life been? Henry said. I know exactly what I'm saying. Then to us, he said, He believes he can do what I can't.

I could see clearly the way his hands moved as he tried to explain.

I never said that, Hark said. So you're a mind reader now? You think you know everything.

No, but if you want to know how much darkness is around you, you need to measure it.

Go on and talk. I might as well not be here.

I have a hard time with you.

The twins went on like this, one pushing words forward with his hands, the other waving the words away. The two men so alone to the rest of us that we just watched and listened with a mixture of disapprobation and fascination and pity while they chattered through Nelson's frowns and Jomo's curses and the breath held between Bellyup's teeth. After a time, Nsembo returned to his original place in the circle, then squatted down and pressed an indentation into the ground with the side of his hand. He shifted his weight, then he started to brush away the dirt as if unearthing something. By such means he drew our attention, one by one. Slowly he turned his head, throwing his gaze into us.

Look, he said. Your time is yours, the little that's left. But I'm not in the mood for talk. He folded one hand in the other.

We waited for him to continue.

His mood seemed to soften, his face oddly gentle. You know, I'm trying to understand the difference between kneeling and falling. In both the head goes down. His voice called back an echo, as though some unseen presence were bearing witness to the truth of what he was saying. My whole skull was vibrating. Whatever else he said soon lost itself in the bend of sound.

In this silence, I weighed what to say next, trying to imagine the bits left out. (How does one thing part from another?) I had to fill in the blank space between me and the other men. Then a thought came up in me, and I said it. Put the point strongly. I had to. A different brain seemed to be at work.

Like the others, Jomo was looking at me. The one thing different, I could see something settling in his gaze: he was with me, in agreement. He took a breath so deep that it lifted his shoulders, then he got out three words: One more woe. The words drifted away on his breath.

Nelson clutched his thin beard. Tugged at it, elongating his body then letting it snap back. Why not? he said. As long as we don't turn back. No going back. He explained how it would work. Said the places and names right in the air. Made sure he got it all said.

Jomo pushed his chin out. Kikwete, he said. I'll let him see me.

One idea inspired another. Pushing into the mind. I heard them. I listened to them and was encouraged in my reasoning, able now to think of things unrelated to the place where we were. And I felt relieved despite the dark questions that none of us could answer. Were we really going to wage war against the blacks? Surely this was a death mission, even if God had willed it.

And there was Bellyup, a kid looking at me. One who looked at me and looked away.

Light seeped up from the ground in the circle between us, bringing us back to the reality that our plans had made us forget. We all scooted backward. Jomo was the first to hotfoot into a standing position.

Hark rocked forward and strained upright. Henry spun in place and gradually spiraled up like an accomplished ice skater. Each twin assumed a lopsided stance, one curving left, the other curving right, like two sides of a peeled banana.

Nsembo pulled himself up, Nelson not long behind them. And there was Bellyup; his hands that he'd been holding in front of him fell open, hanging now as if broken.

The seven of us stood looking into the pond of light.

Shouldn't we pray or something?

That's what we've been doing.

A few days later, Kikwete returned from a visit out of town. As always when he left on a trip or came back from one, a ring of curious onlookers gathered around him in afternoon light at the main square, their voices rushing up loud on his chest, back, and shoulders. I stood from a distance in the flaring heat and watched this familiar drama, observed Kikwete, a sturdy and perfect form above his admirers at a lumbering seven feet, give a shudder of uneasiness, trying to get on top of his feeling. He was not the kind of man to sing his own praises. Still, he managed to shake the day's travel from his head and smile from his sparse short beard—each hair separated from the next—and surrender to their outpouring. But where to begin? Who to hug? Whose hand to shake? Whose baby to take into his arms? Were it within his power, he would have stretched his skin to cover them all. In his enthusiasm, he found a compromise: kissed who he could, touched a few others, and said that it was good to be home.

He stepped toward me, changing the air. I moved to take the single piece of luggage he was carrying, a small well-worn portfolio thickly plastered with pages from Bibles from every church he had visited over the years. He shook my hand. (How different can the touch of two people be?) He was easier with me than with anyone else in the village and placed the greatest confidence in me, leaving me in charge of the church whenever he was away.

That night, we all sat down at his table to a special supper that Feliata prepared to celebrate his return, greeted by the housegirl with blue flowers sprinkled throughout her hair to mark the occasion.

Kikwete said the blessing: As this day is given.

This is what he taught us about the world.

We settled into our meal, fleshy hunger, the housegirl the first to move toward her plate as if pulled forward by her overbite, then Feliata with a spoon in each hand as was her way. Kikwete didn't throw himself at the food but looked at it, smelled it, admired it, before tucking his napkin in place under his chin. Soon we were all in, absorbing the invasive smell of spices and biting into fatty tender goat and yams soft with sap. I could taste the smoke that charcoal and fire had woven through the meat.

Across the table from me, Kikwete's starched clothes made a sound every time he leaned forward to scoop another helping onto his plate. Bald on top, his ring of hair like something hovering over him.

He gave us the highlights from his recent trip (a forest and a zoo). Told us a funny story about the pastor who had hosted him, twelve children, thirty-six grandchildren, seventy-two great-grandchildren. Told us that he had already received and accepted an invitation from yet another congregation (as always, he would need me to make the arrangements). Word of an elevator in this church. We heard all that he had to say and wanted more. The housegirl, untroubled, smiling and laughing with us. In that moment Kikwete able to take us somewhere far from the horrible arrangement of our lives.

I looked across the table at Feliata with vague focus and felt something well up in me, the new distance between us. Now I had no assurance.

The housegirl took our empty plates away and brought fresh ones. I looked at the housegirl's face. She saw me look at her but said nothing. We enjoyed several bricks of cake, our fingers sticky with sugar, frosting, and crumbs. Eating done, we worried the food from between our teeth with toothpicks.

The perfect dinner.

I heard the door bang, and the housegirl heaved into the room with a bucket of water, which she hauled over splashing to the table for us to wash our hands. Her shoes sounding rough against the floor, her dress a whirl of blue above her skinny legs. The fluid force of her young body moved something in me. Still in her teens, but the violence of time on her limbs and face and in the cramped teeth inside her small bird's mouth. No way anyone could fix what had been done to her.

Kikwete and I pushed up from the table and stepped out into the yard, where we sat drinking tea, satisfaction on both our faces, the house angled dark behind us. No sound but the wind in the blackened trees and the reverberations of crickets. He asked for a report about the church. I told him as much as I could until my voice dried up.

He was gazing at me openly, the way I'd often seen him look at me for close to four decades. The skin puckered skin beneath his eyes. Tell me, he said. I want you to tell me. Everything. His usual way of coaxing me out of my silence.

Even in this moment, I was what he worried about. (Well he should worry.) He always said I thought too much. (I had done wrong in my life.) What he wished for me: that I would think less.

Taken by his concern, I put my whole mind to holding back what God had revealed to me. What could I answer?

When day broke the seven of us pushed our way out across the familiar fields into the long reach of morning. Something to see the way the sun shocked the trees. (Sun does only what sun can.) The machete's handle curved smooth against my palm. Comfort in knowing when a thing is on its way. The doors seemed to open by themselves. It took us little time to pass through the house, the walls of the hallway wet and slick and stained with blotches. No time to slip into his room. To circle around the bed.

Kikwete sat up under the sleep-stunned sheets, whole bodily attention. The mercies of God, he said. He held himself that way for a moment, then eased back onto the mattress and the pillow, the glistening shape of him.

I angled down and sat beside him, my thighs slanted across the edge of the mattress. Sat looking into the color of his face, working my way up to words. The slow speed of the senses. The weight of my watching. Aspects of his skin I'd not noticed before. How did he see me? In his eyes a slight gleam of disappointment, but something else too. What orders should I give these men crowded into the room? So many shoulders, so many hands. Nothing in my past had taught me what to do next.

I spoke in a whisper, bending so close that I could smell his thoughts along with the odor of the oil he used for his ablutions. Balanced minds, we spoke for a long time, him thinking alongside me, my machete on the chair next to the bed. What element held true in both of our worlds? I sensed that he had puzzled a way out of his predicament. Why he would not say so, I do not know. His decision was his. Perhaps I had never stopped counting on this possibility because something in me wanted to save him.

What can I say? he said. The truth's in you. Here we are, halfway through life, and everything I've learned fits in the hollow of my hand. He made a fist.

I nodded, although not in complete understanding. What would I measure myself against once he was gone?

Nothing we can do now, he said. So much on his face. I yearned to share something of his sensations and perceptions, something of the difficulty of my decisions and concerns.

His hand rose to touch mine. I know where the worry goes, he said. My seeing became so slow it seemed to disengage. I dragged my machete across his throat.

Silently, I spoke to God: Fix me so I won't worry much.

Without hurrying, we went through the house room by room looking for weapons. A rusted revolver and an AK-47 in one closet, three banana clips in another. A door swung open and there was the housegirl crouched down like a sprinter ready to lunge in near darkness, her dress skimming her smudged ankles, her face full of questions. How had I forgotten about her? How had we all? Scornful of our presence, she sucked in her cheeks, then turned her head, releasing a movement of shadow, a small fury, her possible runner selves.

Nsembo stepped into the closet with her and pulled the door shut. Shaken by his swift action, I did not intervene to save the housegirl. I submitted. What could I raise against him? I heard Jomo behind me, a thin rasp of air escaping his lips. He pressed past me and was suddenly across the room trying the doorknob. It would not turn. He banged on the door. Yelled at it, and when he received no response, jerked his head around and looked me straight in the eyes. I had to speak. I said nothing. Topsy-turvy, he tried the knob again, turned about the room still alive with the housegirl's scent, his words hitting up the wood, falling on things. Everything in the room seemed to be in movement.

I could hear it all. Movements of air. Clicking. Clucking.

Clattering. A waggling. A warbling. Little sentences. Strips of light slanting through the curtains. Jomo's voice breaking with the force of his shouting. A difficult listening. Fear passed into my sweat. I felt heavy, I felt dense, no good answer to any of it.

And there was Nsembo, working his way backward from inside the closet, pushing the door shut, turning toward me. I knew the expression on his face. The confidence. The ease. The excitement. No need for me to open the door and check on the girl. Was that the moment I felt something turning? His head went into a gesture that was part nod, part promise, part warning. What was being made clear to me? What further aspect of himself would he select to remind me of who he was?

Jomo appeared before him direct and without hesitation, challenge in the forward inclination of his body. Nsembo landed a hand lightly on his shoulder with an amplitude of gesture. Jomo jerked away. Without any retort, Nsembo turned and went into the kitchen with a purpose in mind that I could see from his bearing, Nelson and Bellyup behind him. We trailed after them, found them tarrying by the cupboard. I heard a cabinet open, another slam. Jomo darted me a swift look. Were we thinking the same thought or did we, at the least, recognize each other's reasons? Nsembo came and put glasses in our hands. We took up positions at the table. He poured a round of Namaqua, and we touched glasses and drank. The unexpected thickness of the liquor on my tongue followed by a swelling of thick warm insulation throughout my body that caused my skin to press tight. Twice I heard something spoken next to me before I could catch what was being said. I intercepted a glance between the twins, Henry and Hark. Then felt Jomo stirring next to me. Looked at him and saw his eyes fierce above his tilted glass in long gleaming focus on Nsembo. I could taste his wine in my mouth like extra saliva, spit. He lowered the glass and twirled it in his hand, his face set. Had I read him wrong?

Heads flung back, we drank a second round then a third. Taken by Nsembo's beaming face. In whose plan were we all?

A bit unsteady with the wine, we turned for the front door. Before I could move, Nsembo's hand crept onto my shoulder, squeezed my arm. His eyes looked slightly unsure. He whispered, I'll try to pretend you're okay until you tell me different. No man is infinitely strong.

We took to the hills, shoving our bodies through the light under a bowl of blue sky, a light we'd nearly forgotten in our nocturnal existence. Everything in the world stood ready to give me its secret. We swayed under the weight of a new world, trudged along but efficient and purposeful, always going up, this new world tilted and too bright, the earth under our feet thick and trembling at our speed. Faltered, hunchback with a sack of weapons or water or food or supplies secured between the shoulder blades. Too tired to stop but stopping nonetheless to gather second wind, seated on slanted ground, hands rubbed our bodies back to life. I would secretly study them. What brought them so vividly before me? A spell. I saw how they looked at each other, how they were assessing things, some shade of difference in their glance, their gestures, in the way we pinched our cold *ugali* and fussed with our mushy beans. The way Nelson rotated a ball of *ugali* with his stained thumbs before popping it into his mouth. And how Jomo drank water as if it required all of his attention. The way Hark put his head on one side. And how Henry twined his fingers together or put his hands on his knees. The way Bellyup kept his legs crossed and his ankles tightly together. Something oddly dislocated in the way Nsembo sat. And how did I see myself? Was I still in that elevated state that I now know immediately follows a murder? A spell.

Carrying such thoughts into the slow swing of dusk. The sun blazed into a blackout of vision. We walked watching a twisted horizon. Something came into appearance, dim shapes that merely hinted rather than were. Everything looked like a body in the waning light. Soon the day burned out and we could make out the shapes. Houses scrawled by light up the mountain. We sat down, the heat around us clinging and sticky. A surly bubbling, murmuring in our ears. We watched in silent pleasure, getting a measure of the village, while we counted the moments between the disappearance of one light and the next. How much killing could we do in one night?

The first house we approached was strange to me in the half light, neat and desolate, surrounded by a high concrete wall that was secured by an iron door adorned with intricate patterns and inlaid with colorful shells and pieces of glass. Bellyup stooped down and surveyed the lock, a slight sensible figure. He snapped his handkerchief free from his pocket, draped it over the lock, and held it in place with his splayed fingers, then maneuvered tools from his pocket with his free hand and started to work them invisibly inside the keyhole.

Our flashlights shined white spiders in the dark, light and heat crawling across the floor and walls. It was a subdued home, mute, the wallpaper shabby and beginning to peel, with a few furnishings of heavy sturdy wood too big for a room this size, and a portrait of the family on one wall inside an ornately carved frame. The simplicity struck me. It was as though they wanted to show that they were not alive.

Are you there? I heard someone say.

A flash of movement. They came wading half-asleep into the room, falling over themselves, bodies fluid and elongated like the flickering candles they held.

We were surrounded by objects and chairs, but the objects made no difference to me. The candle, the wax, and everything else I saw burned in like the edges of myself. And there were all the other houses, each one set like wax in hard pure moonlight. Glimmered. God and I would never forget.

What were the things we needed to bury? We buried them, two mounds rising from the earth like shut eyes swollen on a face.

Task done, Nsembo sat down on an old wooden chair that threatened to break every time he shifted his weight. How had he found the resource for it, the digging?

One of us spoke: You realize that this is the greatest night we've all lived?

We each acknowledged that this was so.

I felt light, almost happy. Just to hear it in their voices. Perhaps it really was within our power to see differently.

Nsembo drew up a plan, his hand moving in the light-spotted darkness. Spelling out the details, he was as resolutely factual as he had been when he dug the graves. We listened for a long time, seldom interrupting, seldom asking a question. I could find no error, and I did not want to anticipate him, so I just watched the words turn on the ground, then in the air, but I could tell that Jomo was more interested in Nsembo's tone than in the information. It was as if he heard a signal from my mind.

We took the remainder of the night to sleep, me only fitfully. Was it the mosquitoes that hung in the air and on skin? Once awake, I lay and watched through black branches the moon cross the sky and disappear. I asked my Father to be with me. He reassured me, told me that he already was, that he was guiding my hands.

At daybreak I crawled out of the stiff blankets and, leaning hard into the morning, went over in readiness to where the others lay with heavy-lidded eyes. But something caught my attention before I could act. I saw a bird rise from a tree and swoop across the sky, only to loop back and return to the branch. A second bird tried to outperform the first. Eventually dozens of them, dipping and cutting across the sky, then settling down in precise lines on every branch of the tree. Then someone was pulling me up, drawing the blanket and our new cache of weapons we'd taken.

It was work to carry everything: a trident, a mail, a fully loaded silver revolver, a crossbow and assorted arrows with tips either broken or missing, a rusted samurai sword, a musket, and a harquebus with powder horn, flint, wadding, and shot. My companions were irritated by having to keep in step with my irregular gait. Dazzled in the sun.

We started across the mangrove at low tide, maneuvering through a ganglia of trees twisting out of the soggy seabed, our shoes sucking into the mud, bringing our own life, past a seagull perched on a rotted *jahazi,* then a second *jahazi* submerged under the wet black like a sleeping crocodile. Once on the opposite shore, we started a steep climb, shoulders thrust forward and noise coming from our lungs until the trees broke above us and the sky appeared. We had reached the top of a ridge overlooking a cultivated valley. Low walls sectioned the field into plots. Cattle weighed down with long horns rested in the shade of trees. Old tractors sat rusting like rotting dinosaurs. The valley awakened, every voice a moving body, the long backs of men and women wading through tasseled tops of maize glistening with their sweat.

Our attention was drawn to a large house in the distance, spectacular in its symmetry, and made all the more impressive by an extraordinary grove surrounding it, a brown-green extension of the physical silence of the house. An old and massive baobab tree stood near a side porch, dwarfing the house with its sprawling tributaries of branches and roots. Hard, in fact, to distinguish where house ended and tree began.

Taking no chances, we set out for the house by staying above the valley, drifting in the warmth of our bodies, soon finding ourselves descending into sun-drenched branches, each swollen mango above us inked with the owner's thumbprint. We stood looking into the long grove's pull. Who did we belong to? Had we become things of the light? I was calm, almost relieved at the prospect of action. A chair glowed alone in the middle of the grove. Then I could see a man was seated in the chair, bent over, feeling about in the oversized grass, playing with the dirt, sifting it slowly through his fingers. At length, he used those same fingers to clear clumps of shrub and weed and homely brush from the ground, tear at vines and nettles. A benign figure, his hair pushing wet and white from his skull like some unwanted substance.

We edged through the silence toward him, too quickly perhaps. He turned his head, and seeing us, his face popped alive in surprise. Jomo pointed the AK-47, but his aim was off, as the man ran with all he had toward a shoddy barrack.

He was in the doorway when the twins reached him. They shoved and pushed and dragged him back into the grove under a constellation of mangos. He held himself straight in his strange heavy clothes, his wide shirt open at the neck, shoulders too big for him, his long hands at his sides, the fingers straight, a regaining of something. For the better part of a minute, he stood there looking at us, a sure gaze. Looking at me, he said, Ghost, why do you have that rifle? You got some tall explaining to do.

The daring and defiance that rose up in his voice surprised us. We went quiet, only the sound of the sun shining through the trees, each one of us filled with light. He seemed to grow as the seconds spread. I felt us moving apart, acknowledgment that we didn't belong there.

Then a crackling in the branches above us. A body plunged through the trees in a long white streak and thudded into the ground like something called down from heaven. A woman with colossal wings. She landed wrong-footed, no easy matter to stand but once she did, she stood adjusting her feet, getting the balance right, before wobbling toward the barrack, hardly able to run. The twins set off after her.

A great rush inside my lungs. Left standing and staring at her appearance, the man tried to decide which way to run, but we triangulated automatic rifles on him, a flash of metal. The blast lifted him off the ground in a kind of high jump, and the body landed where it had been.

And the white-winged woman given over to speed, gunning through the open cage of a pergola from which cashew apples hung, a curved nut protruding from each fruit like an overgrown toenail. Gunning for the baobab tree, the twins panting behind her, making a tremendous effort but stumbling and falling, losing ground. How long before she escaped the heavy canopy of trees and took to the sky? She cast a glance back over her winged shoulder, saw the twins on the verge of overtaking her, shouted, Rape.

Startled, unsure, the twins allowed their legs to slow into a lazy trot, like athletes who had conceded a race. Still running, she somehow managed to bend over and grab the hem of her dress with both hands, then peel the dress up, lift it over her head, and fling it away. Shouting, Rape. Again and again. Putting distance between her and the twins. Her feet blurred from speed, like someone spinning logs underfoot. Something went through me. I could hear my voice coming from afar. And it seemed to pull something from the other men standing near me. Mechanical sounds. Abrupt clicks. Soon bullets were flashing around her like ravenous flies. The point was made. She stopped running midstride and stared straight ahead as if an invisible man were holding her back. She stood swaying gently from side to side, sweating and thinking, light on every part, wings twitching. She turned and started back, a shape coming up through the pergola, undulating, shaped by the air that carried it. Her body alternating between white and yellow as if the light had stripped her of color. Brown then green as if she were walking through the trees or the trees were walking through her, interchangeable with the landscape, the grove.

And then she came toward me, slow and deliberate. Even from a distance I could see the fierce intentness on her face. The twins, Henry and Hark, followed her with exaggerated slowness, one on her left, the other on her right, both listing from side to side, their breath coming out in short pants, counterpart to her own. A dry wind shook the trees. The afternoon heat was bad, but the harsh light was worse. The twins' faces were flushed through effort and rage. One removed his shirt trying to cool off. The other used the woman's discarded dress to fan himself. I realized that the light inside the grove had shifted, changed as had the twins. The chase had transformed them. They no longer looked alike. Each one now possessed a face of his own, redefined. Even in stature and build they had become distinct.

Flanking her, they made a show of escorting her back to our group when in actuality she moved of her own accord. In fact, she was moving toward me, came so close that I thought she would walk through me. But then she pulled up just short of my chest, my chin, and stood there, fresh sweat, blazing eyes. I stepped back to keep a certain distance between us. No easy thing.

She folded her wings over her breasts. A slight catch in the air.

You see, Nelson said. Redness came up through his face. This is what we're up against.

Her face opened entirely to me. And she continued that way, watching something move in my skin. Who was I responsible to?

I picked up her dress and held it out to her. She kissed her teeth in disgust but took it, raised her arms over her head, the fabric curving in the air, and shook it on, careful to insert her wings through the slots in the back. I took in the sheer material and colored embroidery on the edges of the sleeves and pockets. Was I only then noticing the pattern or had the garment grown the design during the chase?

She stood before us composed, making a smart impression. I let the sight of her enter me, although I tried not to look at her too closely or too long. She was a head taller than any of us but was quite wide, heavy, thick-hipped and ungainly with a long waist and long legs. I noted her large thighs and thick wrists, her small fine hands. An overall effect of solidity through piecemeal compromise. Her face like her body had components that seemed to hesitate between ugliness and beauty, shining smooth, sleek, and shapeless beneath black dreadlocks that spread across her skull like a miniature version of the grove, each lock a curved trembling wing, anxious for flight.

I nodded, hoping that nonverbal communication might draw a meaningful response from her. (Did I smile? Did I laugh?) But there she remained—mute, impassive.

A flicker of irritation. Right then, looking at her, I experienced an intense feeling of misfortune. I set my thoughts in order. Then: Place yourself on the ground next to your husband.

Seconds of air. She opened her mouth, revealing the gap between her teeth. She did as I instructed, slowly pushing her face into the earth as though to hide from the sun. She knotted her fingers into her husband's. She must have smelled the grass and soil. How much did this count?

She said, I won't miss this place one bit.

I shot her once, a body shivering in broken bits of noise, dead and shimmering in the sun.

In no time we were inside the house. The heavy front door swung open by itself, then the inner door opened to a blast of cold and the roaring of an air conditioner. I could see my breath in the chill before me. We entered a long low-ceilinged room with a brick floor and four evenly placed doors in each wall. We took the first door, which creaked open into another long room with twelve doors. And so it went. Slapping down hallways to more and more rooms and doors. Bumping into furniture in our haste, our hurry. The one, the many: in every window and mirror space doubled. (So many mansions in my Father's house.) Each portal dark up until the moment we stood before it as though awaiting us, our light (the light inside us) breaking the dark.

Presently we entered a room where a glass-paneled credenza covered one entire wall, the shelves loaded with porcelain plates and bowls and carved figures, animal and human. The twins poked around, examining objects. The windows let in green-tinged light from the mango trees outside, which brought to my attention a woman sitting at a desk at the far end of the room. She looked up and saw me, her eyes subdued by an embarrassed expression as though she were in some strange house and not her own home. I took in her features. Her face covered with big black freckles like watermelon seeds. It was a face that at first sight meant nothing to me. She moved uneasily in her chair but managed a trembling stance. I walked over to her, a giant above a shrunken being.

Words were already issuing from her mouth. I don't mean to speak harshly, she said in a quiet voice. She lifted her chin toward me. I know you. And I know your wife. From the church.

Thoughts had time to form and pass while I stood breathing

fast and watched the yellow-green sunlight splintering through the curtains. Stood seeing beyond the glass—blaze and glow, the sky bleeding pink then violet, rustling trees tousling big smudges of color—waiting for my breath to settle, for this feeling to go away. She said something about church and trees that I didn't hear for my musings.

She peered past me and registered an interest in the other men. Things were said. Voices filled the room, achieving a kind of height. I couldn't catch all the words, only heard Nsembo talking quietly and easily to her with a deference I had never seen in him before. She shook her head, held up her hands, then fell back into her seat as if the exchange had exhausted her.

Her actions left us all wound up in silence. I could feel the other men standing behind me. It was for me to make everything right. The church she'd said. My wife she'd said. Perhaps we shared something, but I remained unconsoled by her facts (pleas?). I crossed the room—her hair and makeup styled, her clothes neat and clean, her fingernails and toenails perfectly shaped—and found myself talking to her louder than I meant to. She settled deep into her chair as if she were alone in the room, completely to herself. Not to be outdone, Nsembo popped up beside me, muttering under his breath—give him his due—then louder, picking up where he'd left off. She said nothing, showed no signs. Lit, he leaned in and stared down at her, striking a little burn of panic in my chest, pushing me to think fast and clarify, explain. I touched him hard enough to get him to retreat.

She looked up into my face. I tried to hold her stare but my vision wouldn't settle. I know why you came here, she said. You have the right. Your kind has been rebuked and scorned. And someone has to pay. Power is given by the hand of God. There's no hiding from that. But I'm no good at suffering alone. Her voice sounded flat, drained of whatever emotion it had before.

I said something I should have had the sense not to, the x-y-and-z of it, but the words ran through her. Perhaps I could hear her but she could no longer hear me. She went on.

How long can this last? We're all dirty, polluted. Every single one of us. The sea is the same from the surface to the bottom. We have to start over, start again. She turned her face one way then the other, her red hair standing out against her brown skin. I hope you will find a way, she said. I mean it. I really do. She moved a little in her seat. Everything stood as it was. For a moment we were both quiet enough for sound to return, for me to hear the low distant buzz of the air conditioner, the cold air rushing in an effort to find us. I did not need to move or speak or do anything else, only stand there in the comfort of my own silence and sink into the dream of her talk. It should have been easy for me to envision what she was calling for, to give in to that vision of a new life. Had I not already seen it in the dream?

I was still turning this over, listening to the others making noise behind me, when Nsembo worked his way in, muscled his weight under her arm, and pulled her up out of the chair. Again I intervened, actually pushed him aside. I saw the way he looked at me, but I didn't hold his gaze long enough to allow it to do damage. I turned back to the woman, who was cocked forward with her palms flat against the desk for balance.

Sister, remind me of your name.

Midwin, she said. Then, thinking twice, she corrected herself, Mamma James. I heard in her words and saw in her eyes that she wanted me to know that she was a mother.

Mamma James, why don't you come take a walk with me?

Nsembo passed me the machete.

I want to walk with you. I would prefer that. But I don't want to cause any trouble for you. She swayed above the desk, looking at me full of expectation and confusion, then plopped down as before in the chair.

I took a moment to glance over my shoulder at the others—clustered about the room, eager and alert—keeping the machete low against my side. I didn't like the way they were looking at me. The twins slipped back into their shirts.

Brother, I'm sorry. I am not to ask for even one little thing, especially seeing that time is short. But maybe I could? Maybe if we are all in agreement? She looked past me and eyed the others.

Now what? I heard someone say.

Maybe she wants his hand in marriage.

Laughter.

We are all in agreement, I said.

Little did she know, I appreciated the feeling of being pulled. I would decide when it was too much. I had never thought of myself as someone to be feared. Now I knew myself as someone to be feared.

Brother, thank you. How am I to thank you? She was already digging around inside one drawer of the desk.

Sister, what is it that you require of me? What can I do? I said.

She removed two vials of oil from the drawer, uncorked them, smells I knew, frankincense and myrrh. She wanted to live again.

It was my turn to say something.

She widened her eyes. Am I asking too much of you? I'm afraid I'm asking too much. Will you refuse me?

Would I? We had never really lived in this world.

I set the machete on the floor. With both hands cupped, I accepted one bottle then the other. In an equally ceremonial manner, she tilted her head forward, causing her red dreadlocks to fall and extend like tiny ladders. I smeared a dab of oil across her forehead, smeared a second dab. That done, I placed my palm on the crown of her head where her hair was neatly parted in the middle. I liked the feel of her scalp. She angled her fingers together in front of her face (nose and mouth) in prayer, and soon I heard the word weakening on my lips. A few moments in my mouth twisted around a verse, and I felt something ease inside me, shift, a feeling I couldn't fully comprehend because, before I finished the prayer, she touched the oil on her forehead as if checking to see if her resurrection had already begun.

Amen. I stooped and picked up the machete, my hand still perched like a small bird on her head.

She opened her eyes, stood up to leave, causing strands of red hair to pull loose and stick to my palm. I wrapped my arm around her, and she sank into my shoulder, her face scrunched up and focused. Nsembo looked at me.

I said to him, It's settled now. Just stay here with the others.

It seemed that he'd anticipated this response since he turned away and waved some signal to the other men before I finished speaking. I felt the whole of her body leaning into my chest, and I leaned into her as we started for the door we'd come through.

No, she said. This way. A shortcut. She gestured toward another door. And by such means she led me through the house, letting her body move with mine with unexpected ease, two shapes advancing between immovable planes. In one room we walked over a thick Persian rug, my attention rushing forward to a cordless chandelier hovering beneath the ceiling like a UFO, and a heavy-framed painting of a foot on a wall, objects that reminded me of nothing of my life back home. Was I in a different world altogether? We had gone a few paces in an adjoining room when she pulled away from me and started to run. I caught at her shadow, but she was already out the front door. Then, just as quickly, she snapped inside the baobab tree as if pulled by a string.

I stayed there for some time considering her disappearance.

When I tracked down the others I found that they had started in on the cider press.

We don't have that luxury, I said. She got away.

I watched their faces while they talked.

We have to go back, I said. I had not known my decision until I spoke the words aloud.

He's right, Jomo said.

We each took a turn at grooming ourselves: a bath in a porcelain tub filled with hot water from a faucet, a shave with an electric razor, followed by deodorant and cologne and a suitable change of clothing. The twins cooked a simple meal on the stove. We sat around the table and ate and drank, our thoughts hovering apart, ignoring the sounds of the air conditioner as best we could. A few minutes passed before anyone said anything. It seemed to me that Nsembo was trying to show interest, partly to be polite and partly for other reasons. I directed my mind toward Feliata, thinking of the day when our last child was born. Thirty minutes out of the womb, the baby was still crying. Feliata looked at me.

This one is not like the others, she said.

Still, different or not, we went along with custom. Feliata cut the baby's bush of hair on the seventh day so that it wouldn't suck up all the baby's blood.

The hills rose and fell, and so did we. The light walked from roof to roof, and birds yanked up and down in the sky like serviettes. We stood to the day slanted, skirting one village or another, until the moon came into focus above our heads, the sky still white, the air almost pink, each of us somehow brighter in the illuminated dark. Settled down for the night, a ragtag-looking bunch, our edges blurry as if we were melting, disappearing. Heavy breathing and sighs. What were they feeling? Little could I tell. Wished I could read their minds and glean what they were feeling about me. Doubt? Had their faith been shaken? Exhausted as sleep twined around us.

Birds occupied my imagination, birds sitting cross-legged on the ground to parlay with bats. Then I heard my voice coming from afar, opened my eyes, and saw Nsembo running and whispering toward us. I followed him to the rise and angled myself to watch. Stuttering curses. Tripping and stumbling. A misstep that sent someone tumbling. Branches snapped and men in fatigues came out of the brush, their elongated shadows behind them, about twenty in all on an economy of force mission. What had I inflicted on us? We grouped in the long night as best we could, coiled in a fist of time, their physical presence around us, enough to make the ground feel lopsided. More hours opened up, and they continued to search, but the grass was high enough to hide us.

At dawn, we took up our fatigue and lack of sleep and pushed our way out of the grass, achingly aware of our bodies. We needed to make it back to the mangrove before high tide, hurrying in the ever-weakening light against a sun dropping lower and lower in the sky. Reached the mangrove, wet heat and sucking mud, and started across with foamy water washing around our ankles. Little fish nipping at our feet. Then, just like that, the last of the light left the sky and the sun sank sizzling into the ocean, causing the water to explode upward. I saw the waves pull someone's lumbering frame below the surface of the water before we all went under, clawing at the water, the dark echo of waves.

Wobbly, I dragged Jomo from the water, then willed myself to go back for Nsembo. I took turns pumping each man's chest, downward motion that spurted streams from the pores of their skin. Fully drained, Nsembo yanked upright, power in the movement; his eyes popped open. And, taking the world in, the expression that came over him was unmistakable: disappointment. Jomo sat up, made a quick inventory of his body, then drew me in his line of sight. His appreciation was enough for me. More to accomplish, he removed his clothes and knifed back into the water, betraying a natural kinship for the ocean, then came out the water with three fish that he flung onto the ground, their triangular gills fluttering. At that moment I didn't want to be anywhere else.

Jomo made a vague gesture at the fish, indicating that I should prepare a fire. This would be our last satisfying meal. We had no choice but to resume our march on Fort Pigeon, a geography away, so we did, alert, senses young and bright, skin sensitive to every sound, the color of the growing grass, a movement in a tree, a figure in a window. Could hear and feel the fast pull of life around us. We scrounged what food we could. On the third or fourth day, the sky lowered, and rain drummed down so hard it drowned out our voices. We passed through fields foaming with weather, difficult to see anything ahead, so we settled down across from each other by a fire burning in the rain. Nsembo prepared tea, and I sat and held my cup as if it held my thoughts. Water in our sleep. Water when we awoke. We held expectations for the next day but the rain never let up. Sliding along the muddy roads, sinking with each step, mud up to our knees. Shoving through slick trees that hung in wet loops around us. And still it rained. At times, the rain slowed down to catch its breath and gather more water. Our meals grew further apart. How many hours? How many days? Until the clouds finally pulled apart and a red sun catapulted into the sky, water rushing down into the soil with a gurgling noise.

We could dissolve the miles while hiding in plain sight, the best approach we figured, and so we tried, our shadows slanted ahead of us, black strings pulling us toward our destination. Words too, speaking ourselves into motion through a long day of light, appreciating the hours—we're still here—our thoughts moving in time, forward and back. At one point we thought we saw something come over the top of a rise, and we stopped and hid, a good place to settle down, cool down into sleep, until the morning.

During the night, I felt something wet press into the back of my knee, and I broke into a run, a fumbling reach in the darkness, hounds barking. Jomo scrambled up a tree, I went up another, trapped where they wanted us. Nsembo stood his ground. They asked him his name, and he gave it along with some choice words. One soldier took a step toward him and hit him so hard with a truncheon that it flailed loose from his hand.

They shot Jomo out of the tree, a thud into dirt. Beneath me three red hounds moving in a slow calligraphy, teeth, flank, paws, and tails, their teeth white against the color of the soldiers' black uniforms. I raised my hands in a take-it-easy gesture before climbing down from the tree of my own volition, hounds leashed, in check. The soldiers assembled around me, smelling like liquor and sweat and dogs. I took their stares into mine, not that it mattered: their faces all looked the same to me. They told me to kneel, and when I refused they were on me, trying to put their fingers inside me, through me, were above me pushing their weight, heavy logs forcing me down into the blackened earth.

I awakened to the sound of metal buzzing through air and the feeling of speed moving through me. I was in motion somehow although facedown against glass with my arms curled up under me, a dark tarred road gleaming up at me. Light red and thick around me, inside me, pouring from me. Taking in my surroundings, I determined that I was enclosed inside a transparent glass container, a glowing rectangle, on the back of a truck. I caught the efforts of passengers in adjacent vehicles to catch sight of me. They would look in my direction only to tighten their eyes against me, pure brightness, illumination. Speed a factor too. The truck flew over the shoulder of the road, while the other vehicles slithered along a broken crumbly single lane, motion and gravity something different for us in this hare and turtle race.

I crawled into a seated position. I could feel light vibrate inside my chest. Was I powering the truck, become source? With a simple hand gesture, the driver, a thickset broad-shouldered figure inside the cab, caught my attention. He tried to make eye contact with me in the rearview mirror only to catch my hesitation, my reluctance to acknowledge him. He smiled. Told me his name.

Good for you, I said.

Uncle, as you know, our blessings are rare. But here I am with you. I lay myself at your feet.

I said nothing. Nor did he for some time. Both hands tight on the steering wheel, he kept his gaze fixed on soapies playing on a thin television mounted to the upper windshield on the passenger side, showing little concern for the drive, just an occasional glimpse at the road.

Uncle, he said over his shoulder, there's so much I want to ask you. I mean you no disrespect. It's just that my burdens are more than average. You see, my wife won't let me watch at home. Something caught his attention, and he allowed the truck to slow down. Made the necessary adjustments, then pedaled back into full speed. And, as you can see, I'm a poor man. That's no small matter. I get to watch on the job and, the kicker, the electricity is free. Two birds with one stone. He shifted in his seat. But, uncle, if you will talk to me, I will listen.

I wasn't listening anymore. He didn't try to force the issue, just kept watching the screen.

We streamed by wooden and metal signs sunk into the ground

naming villages and towns and counting off the distance from the capital. Soon emerged in the haze on the horizon. A few minutes later we entered its narrow streets cluttered with brick buildings evidencing no calculation or craft. Roofs glimmered in the heat, longing to be higher, skyscrapers. (The incompetence, corruption, and filth. The hope.) People surged in and out of shops. Others, exhausted after a day of labor, walked with haggard breath as if they were passing air from one person to the next. Dozens stopped to gawk at us in dark curiosity.

We parked outside a government building on a cobblestoned street lined with palm trees, soldiers swarming out to take charge of me in a whir of noise and metal. They rushed me through a revolving door and dispatched me to a brightly lit room cooled by an overhead fan, where they sat me down at an oversized table with heavy chairs around it.

Gray hair and beard, a well-dressed man entered the room, white gloves squeezed onto his hands and a stethoscope around his neck. Carrying a stool by one leg like a fowl headed to slaughter, he caught my gaze then placed the object down before me and let his clamped face relax, showing teeth, smile and notsmile. He told me that he was a doctor from a private hospital, speaking slowly, his words dragging along as if he was either retarded or thought that I was. Perhaps he expected me to be enthralled. *Private hospital.* He lowered himself onto the stool, pinched my wrist, and looked at his watch, lips moving, counting silently. For long minutes this doctor from a private hospital took time to consider my injuries before treating my wounds with store-bought disinfectant, then fumbling around in his side pocket and producing a small golden needle, which he used to stitch me up with silk thread.

As soon as he left, another man entered the room, his walk a bit stilted. In one motion, he sat down on a chair across from me, filling the air with cologne and deodorant. He introduced himself and moved to take my hand into his. The proximity of his body caused our knees to knock together under the table. Why would I want his touch?

I'm sorry, he said. Sometimes I overvalue myself.

You? I said.

I watched his thin frame, his round shoulders. Something both new and agitated about his form like a growing chicken. No appearance of a bureaucrat. Also his odd way of sitting with his arms crossed on his torso and his hands buried inside his armpits. Still, he was wonderful to look at in his immaculate uniform unlike any I had seen, although I was not one to be taken in by appearances.

I will suffer your slights and suspicions, he said. I don't believe in hiding. There are worse things.

I nodded. It was a good turn, I said, thinking to cut the conversation short and send him on his way.

But how did you do it? In this country all we know is misery and hardship and poverty and fear. But here you are, somehow.

I stepped through a hole in the world. But now the fun and games are over.

He bent his head down a little. Listen to what you're saying. I came to counsel with you, but you don't want to speak to me. Who could hold that against you?

He had all that to say, watching me intently, taking on the guilt of his kind.

Then he said, A panther hunts when its belly is empty. That much I know, understand. Yes, but not in this country. No, not here.

I was learning all of his voices. At least he kept his voice low. He had that much to say for him.

Friend, I said. I'm glad that you came to see me and sit with me. Now I hope you can put all the worries out of your mind.

Waves would pull me out of sleep each morning. I would hear their beating coming from far away, rise from my cot and walk over to the window, and see through the iron bars all the birds moving in light together, their wings thrashing against the air. Off in the distance the sun a tremendous vertical blaze rising out of the sea, which sprawled under *jahazi,* their white sails defined against the pastel colors of the new day. I could see sought-after fish sliding under the water, and the great fins of sharks circling too close to shore. Although the sea had no chance of reaching me, it felt uneasy for me to be so close to it, waves pulling me out of sleep, trying to pull me through the window.

These sounds overlaid by other sounds, what passed for barking seals that turned out to be little black goats in the courtyard seven stories below, which was hidden from the street by a fence and flanked on three sides by colonial buildings boasting iron balconies. The guards would enter my cell and take pleasure in seeing the sun chase me about, first one panel on the floor then another and a third until light filled the cell from top to bottom. I moved through the heat like a man walking underwater, tiring easily, groggy, half-awake but restless. The light would flicker, bright and dim all at once, and I would open my eyes and find that my wife had come for a visit. With me seated on my cot, she would sit on the floor, her legs stretched out and folded at the ankles, while we ate whatever food she had prepared. I sensed she had questions she wanted to ask me. We engaged in small talk instead, mostly about the past, the said and done. Am I remembering correctly, how she seemed far away, refusing to look at me, turning her face away whenever I caught her gaze, how we would speak quietly, our words overlapping, weighing ourselves on each other? It was only when she stood up to leave that she rose out into the woman I recognized, became her old self again.

After a few months or a few days, a journalist from the national newspaper came seeking an interview. Although he was a small slight man like some rare mushroom pushed up from the earth, I could not stop looking at his finely tailored dashiki with rows of gold stitching around the neck and cuffs, and a plants-and-blossoms print that grew larger and larger as he approached as if the flowers were growing out of his torso. His hair sat black and thick on his head like a porkpie hat. And his hand was energetic in shaking mine. Thus he presented himself before me where I sat bent forward on my cot warming a cup of tea in my hands.

Here we go again, I said. You're hoping to get something out of me?

I will take down your words exactly as you say them to me. Would you rather leave it to them? When he spoke his goatee moved from side to side like seaweed. You're the only one left who can tell it.

I gave no indication that this fact surprised me, only stretched my back straight, feeling my spine resume its proper alignment. In time, I would learn that Nsembo, Jomo, and the twins had been hung to do the least amount of damage to their bodies, blood, urine, semen, saliva, and shit collected in sterile jars, and pus suctioned like snake venom from their putrefying wounds before the corpses were auctioned.

He took a notebook from his side pocket. He didn't open it, only kept it flat in his left hand. He asked me if it was true that I was the author of the insurrection. I nodded but said nothing, taking time to gather my story.

How suddenly the faces fall away, events already shifting to the back of my mind. Where did what I remember go? My hand took on the heat of the drinking glass. How long would it be before I lost all sense of hands and glass?

It's hard now to say that what happened could have been avoided, that it wasn't inevitable, I said. Because I was a source of wonder to all from the time I was born. And because many things of significance happened even further back, before I was born and before my parents were born and their parents.

Light fell squarely on the pages of his notebook, causing the paper to burn bright, but the paper stayed damp and heavy in the humid air. His human hand on paper, writing down my words. I played with the idea of telling him that I remembered when I was born.

They say that a rock dove shat on my head the very moment

I emerged from my mother's womb, which caused my body to grow a coat of armor like an armadillo's.

Tired of standing, the reporter leaned back in an odd way as if being vacuumed into the corner.

Luckily, the rock dove disappeared after a week. There was nothing that as a child I saw or heard of to which my attention was not directed. I could speak the words of other people before they could formulate them on their tongue. And I could foretell events that would happen in the future, even as I could tell the elders about past secrets. Like most, my parents had no money to send me to school, never learned the alphabet. However, the first time I opened a book, I spoke the words.

And I went on like that, naming what no longer existed until my tea had grown cold. In what I didn't say the reporter could find what meant most to me.

Having all he needed over several hours, he slowed his breath, returned his notebook to his pocket, and withdrew himself from the corner. Then he said, So this is still an age of miracles. Thank God.

How could it not be? I smiled and he smiled too.

Now the real work is ahead, he said. Salt, having lost its taste, is useless. You cleared the table. Now they're all afraid, waiting for the next thing to happen, trying to figure out a way to stop it. They've formed commissions, advisory councils, brought in the NGOs, even opened a new ministry, although I can't say that I like the guy they appointed to run it. His eyes are always red, probably from eating too many strawberries. He is out of his depth. Still, he has already put new laws on the books. Here, let me show you.

He showed me. One after another, government statesmen approach an ornamented table, lean over, and sign a document, each man handing off the diamond-tipped fountain pen to the next official. Handshakes and smiles. Libations and toasts. I stood side by side with him, watching.

There you have it, he said. The usual extravaganza. He began to parody the movements and gestures of the politicians, causing his goatee to move in such a way that I thought it might slip off his face. But let's give them the benefit of the doubt. We will know in time.

It was now sundown, the hour when roaches transform into fireflies. He thanked me, drew away from me, and took his leave.

At dawn, the fireflies turned into roaches again. The guards came for me in my cell. By the time we made it into the courtyard, the light was too wide for sight to embrace. They lathered me with accelerants, then tucked me into a pocket of earth prepared in advance. My only regret: the world of the blacks would not burn with me.

Once the fire is lit, I combust and go straight up. I feel fire travel a hard rub along my skin, scrubbing off unnecessary weight, piece by piece, layer by layer. I kick my legs and rise higher, so far up that the capital appears much less a city. I extend my body through all the curves and tunnels of the air right into the sun, right into the sun, a sun that starts to come apart over the sea.

Circle

"Whoever loses their life for my sake will find it."

—Matthew 10:39

The radiologist clips my X-rays into place against the illuminated panel. My lungs glow like two black islands in a white ocean.

Three months with good care, she says. Each word locks into place. Her hair is dyed red and pomaded like an auburn cabbage. Her skin runs a range of brown and tan colors. Some have even made it to six, she says. But that would be at the outside.

My mother gathers in a photograph, a glossy headshot from the days when she acted professionally in underground theaters and low-budget films. (Her lead role in a screen adaptation of *Pussycorners* even made her recognizable to strangers on the street for a time.)

A year ago I received word that she was terminally ill, so I made arrangements and flew across country. At the hospital they asked that I slip on a mask, scrubs, and gloves before I entered her room. The doctors assured me that her disease was not contagious, that they were only trying to protect her compromised body. For them their medicine was that certain. I alone was aware of my mother's body and its dangers. No one knows the mother except the daughter and so no one knows the daughter except the mother.

I found her propped up in bed, her eyes closed, the bones in her face showing hard and high under the skin, and her torso and arms swaddled in bands of gauze in contrast to the colorful bedspread adorned with thin blue petals covering her from the waist down, a bedspread I had stitched by myself and given her for a Christmas present three decades earlier.

I wanted to crawl inside her broken flesh, although when I was a little girl I always felt that she had wanted to crawl inside me when we snuggled up together.

When I took a step closer to her bed, her bones pushed against the gauze.

She opened her eyes and spoke the name that she and my father had given me. She would never call me anything else, although long ago, I gave myself the name of a princess from my favorite book. After all, I was the girl in the fairy tale whom birds buried under leaves in a forest and abandoned until curious dwarves stumbled upon the mound and kissed me awake.

What is the word for the choices we cannot forgive? All things have been committed to me by my mother.

Is that really you behind the mask?

When I acknowledged that it was, she waved me over. She hugged me close and would not let me go.

She doesn't sleep much, one doctor told me. No matter how many sedatives we give her. That's a small matter of concern.

But I found her asleep when I went back into the room. My presence startled her awake. Her words scrambled together.

What was that? And where are we? Fuck was what? But really now, what?

They sponged her body seven times a day. Seven pills every hour. She would open her mouth as wide as she could and take each pill on the tongue as if it were the body of Christ. She seemed to await each bright syringe, time itself injected into her to keep her chronology working.

There is something slow and pleasing about disappearing, she said.

What I remember, one morning a few months after my father left us my mother and I sat down to eat our breakfast at the table, a morning like any other. Then she put down her bowl of porridge and her golden spoon, and we vanished.

We crossed the ocean as illegals and found refuge at Howeth House, a crumbling but spacious building with a hundred flats or more, two hundred flats or more that had been taken over by squatters—crazies, exiles from the former colonies, war refugees, wanderers, the homeless, cripples, addicts, hippies and other dropouts. My mother trusted none of them. She believed that they were spies, foreign operatives, or special agents sent by the church.

Because I live, you will also live, she would tell me. Life is gain, she liked to say. Life is more. We came here for more.

Toward that end, my mother soon decided that she was an actress. She would sit on cushions in the bay window of our flat, sipping then gargling her morning coffee—she preferred instant, tiny brown kernels from a glass jar—her skin drinking in the light. Then she would start rehearsing lines. Her hard work at her craft got her the occasional role here and there but she did most of her acting for the other squatters.

I still have a vision of that alcove in Howeth that she called the library, where she would entertain our family of squatters. A room without windows but with a wide skylight at the top, where I would stare off into the sky. I remember where every object in the room was placed, the red leather sofa and bureau near the bookcase that also had a vase of fresh flowers on top. My mother would select a volume and start fingering through the pages, trying to find a good passage to read, only to lose herself at the mere touch of paper, so easily inspired that she would be moved to thoughts spoken in an intonation that often comes back to me even today, that served as a pretext to expound upon topics about which the other adults held similar opinions. They would do their part and cheer her on.

Because she received few acting parts, she worked odd jobs for minimal pay, rewarding herself upon her return to our flat with a long and deep soak in the claw-foot tub, her entire body buried under a mountain of suds, her arms the only part of her visible, her hands clutching the porcelain sides like someone trying to pull herself out of a pit.

While she prepared her coffee and books and scripts, I would venture with the other children out into the city streets, taking what each day offered us, begging for money, and scrounging or stealing what we could. We might enter someone's yard and climb up a tree to pilfer an apple or pear or plum. More than one of us fell that way and broke an arm or a leg, even a skull once. By nightfall, we would gather up our cloth sacks and satchels and return through cold moonless streets. I am still full of the old fear of coming home, of stopping in the darkness under a bridge to make sure that the way was safe from cops and hoodlums, then continuing on before stopping again under the maples a block away from Howeth. Our entrance into the building did not put an end to danger, so much brick cement and stone, so many halls passageways alcoves and rooms. People would often disappear.

The nurses would bring bags of IV drip like liquid clouds. And my mother would speak to them. Where on earth do you find such bizarre hats?

Her speech was a complete catalog of outmoded forms picked up during her acting days. (I'm sorry. I am somewhat vulgar with my bowels.) Clearly she still maintained the belief that everyday speech is poorer than it is. She had trained me to speak as she spoke.

When she thought I was old enough, she taught me tarot cards, tea leaves, palm reading, cowrie shells, and astrological charts, devices that I could use to ferret out the secrets of gullible people, if I became good enough at it, and by such means earn a living.

Nothing is fair about the world, she would say. We always go in circles no matter how hard we try.

At Howeth, we went about in circles.

One day, she started bleeding in little spurts through the gauze. An alarm sounded, and a team of doctors and nurses rushed into the room, hovering about her, the small talk of instruments and gloved fingers. I stood and waited in the hall while they tried to patch her up.

They allowed me back into the room after an hour or two. Then she coughed and erupted her sutures. I had to wait another hour or two before I finally went back in once again.

Come here, she said. Her skin was slack, exhausted. I have something to give you.

I went to stand beside her. She strained forward, her hand closing around my wrist. She held a small pendant charm in her other hand.

Here, she said. It belonged to the women before me, but it is now yours. Hang it on a chain and wear it around your neck and under your clothing. Take good care of it. Unlike me, it is made to last forever.

I took the pendant. Then I went back and curled into the chair for the long wait. So I sat with her for the night, listening to her body, every vein humming in the dark.

We washed her in icy water until there was nothing left of the old disease. Rubbed her body with honey oil.

I left the hospital under a sky colorless like a greasy bone picked clean of meat.

I made arrangements for her funeral and burial, then went to the house where she had lived her last thirty years to put her papers in order. I searched but I could not find the deed for the house in the bureau drawer where she told me it would be. (It's yours, she'd told me. It's all yours. Everything.) Her bank statements revealed that her accounts were empty. There was plenty to sort through, jewelry boxes filled with trinkets, empty closets with rows of hangers like denuded trees, sun-faded crates and boxes, trunks full of dust and silence, bags of moth-eaten clothing. I left it all and put the pendant in the trash.

Fluid snakes through a tube into a vein in my arm. Three months. Six at the most.

I remember a party my mother threw where she crawled out from under the lid of a grand piano.

The radiologist comes in to check on me. Her hair died platinum blond today, a white cabbage. She asks me a question, and I respond in a barely audible voice, as I learned to do many years ago, a way to force the other person to actually listen, to lean in close, ear near my mouth, to catch every word.

Four Girls

i. Street

"We ain't dead said the children . . .
We just made ourselves invisible"

—Erykah Badu

The little girl lay on her side in the middle of the street, a half circle of blood spreading from her body toward the sidewalk, a red drape drawn down by gravity. Would the blood reach me? I stood fifteen feet away in silent concentration, one of two dozen (more) astonished kids, their voices buzzing around me, half-heard. Taking in the sight. I was ten years old.

A group of adults swooped down on us and tried to get us to move, but we would not go away. Impossible to do anything other than gaze at the girl, watch her body grow where it lay in the tough afternoon sun. One hand positioned above her head, the other near her waist, a dance pose. Her eyes open and hard. Her small braids like the stems of firecrackers. Her dark skin contrasting with her pink dress. Stark against her white bobby socks and black shoes.

I argue with my memory. *Tell me more! Show me more!* But I am thwarted by not knowing how to put it, leaving imagination to build approximations.

My heart beat with such density, something having opened inside me. I write this now feeling my body's weight. Why does the girl weigh nothing? Is it because her blood emptied out onto that street almost four decades ago?

What do the dead owe the living?

My mother turned her face toward me as soon as I stepped through the door. She never missed much. I pretended not to see her.

Why are you crying?

I said nothing.

Hatch? She got up from the plastic-upholstered sofa with a sticky sound and blocked the path to my room. Light moved from one object to another. She repeated her question, waited for me to speak. I didn't. I let the sweat cool on my head and hands. She stood looking at me in the middle of our small living room, her face taking a long time to open out into something more than anger. She reached out to touch me with her hand, which appeared to be fitted inside a long glove of wrinkled skin from her knuckles to her elbow. (The story she'd told me: when she was three years old she tried to remove an egg from a pot of boiling water.) There was a time when I had been afraid for the hand to touch me.

I averted my face, started for my room. It seemed my mother would call after me, but she did not.

I would learn that the girl was the little sister of my classmate, a classmate I never saw again. I would learn that the driver claimed he never knew he'd hit somebody.

I'm telling you that I never saw her, the driver said. I heard a bump, and the truck lifted off the ground a bit, then the next thing I know I hear all these kids shouting at me. For God's sake, this happened in front of the school, right at the corner. How come they didn't have no crossing guard there? Where was the crossing guard? There's always a crossing guard at that corner.

He paused, half turned among a field of cameras and microphones.

I'm going to sue the school. I'm going to sue the principal and the school district. No, I'm going to sue the board of education, and the city and the mayor. Yes, the mayor. So help me God.

My mother refused to let me attend the funeral. And then, a few weeks later, a second girl died. I knew the girl as well as one could. You see Carrie Lavender, my next-door neighbor and my mother's best friend, took in a bit of pocket money babysitting me and the girl and another boy named Daryl in her apartment for a few hours after school each day until our mothers came for us exhausted from work. Just us three. Like kids the world over we had a need to fill time and conquer boredom and somehow managed to do so in Carrie's living room—the rest of the apartment was off-limits—a cramped maze of couches and armchairs, lamps and loveseats, televisions and coffee tables. (Carrie did not mind the fact that her husband felt the need to buy some new item of furniture each time he received his paycheck.)

I'm not sure if Daryl and I liked the girl because she was a few years younger than we were and different. She told us everything, and so many times.

I ain't getting married cause then you got to get divorced, she said.

Daryl and I laughed.

Don't hate on me cause I know what I know. The girl twisted herself excitedly before craning over backward into a series of flips.

Tell us what else you know.

She told us. We liked to hear her talk because she had many funny things to say.

Where yo daddy at?

In another country.

What country?

New York.

Daryl and I snickered.

No wait, she said. He down there in England, man.

Snickered.

I said to the girl, We'll never understand you.

But I speak slow, she said, small teeth in big gums, her braids standing curled up on her head like candy canes.

We found her more amusing than annoying. Because we were older, because we were boys, we could scapegoat her for our wrongs. It never came into my head that she would be anything other than who she was. Neither would we. Mannish behavior was the known world to Daryl and me. Nothing would change. So it was that we'd been happy one day being up to no good when Daryl ventured to say to me:

I'm dead.

What?

I said I'm dead.

Nigger, you ain't dead.

Yeah I am. I got killed dead last night.

I looked at him, at his forward-jutting mouth.

I got stabbed in the head. And the ambulance men came and said I was dead. And they took me to the hospital and the doctor man also said I was dead so I'm dead.

I watched him. If you dead, why ain't you in the ground?

That room in the hospital where they had me was too cold, so I ran away.

I watched him. I was a little taller than he was although we were only a few months apart in age.

But don't worry bout me. I may be dead but I'm that special kind of superhero nigger.

Yeah, soft.

Soft? Nigger, you better recognize.

Recognize what?

Try me.

I tried him. I was taller, stronger, quicker, and always got the better of him although he was scrappy and would put up a good fight. He put up a good fight until I came down on his flailing arms. I felt him brace his body beneath me. We wrestled into a lamp and knocked it over.

I'm telling, the girl said. She was seated cross-legged on the floor before the TV.

You gon tell on yoself? Daryl said.

She pulled a face. Me? I was watching cartoons.

You broke the lamp.

You lyin.

Daryl yelled out Carrie's name, and in no time she entered the room, concerned. She was a big woman so it always surprised me how fast she could move. She saw the broken lamp and stood looking in disbelief, her torso quaking under her housedress, stood shaking her head until she became so upset she had to plonk herself down in her favorite armchair, the great weight of her body settling around her. Somebody better tell me something, she said.

Unlike my mother, she didn't curse. She didn't need to.

Daryl told his story.

Boy, the girl said, why you lyin on me?

Carrie looked at me.

She broke it, I said, confirming the lie.

Carrie looked at the girl, turning her face one way then the other, the girl some strange and rare species demanding close study. I'm gon to talk to yo mother.

I ain't even do nothing, the girl said. They ganging up on me.

You call that nothing?

I ain't break yo lamp.

Heifer, don't backtalk me. I'll snatch you bald-headed.

The girl glared at Carrie, her face pinched as if she were trying to pull her eyes inside her skull.

Thick as thieves, Daryl and I grinned at each other awaiting the mother's arrival, eager for the showdown. Carrie did not disappoint us. The mother was hardly through the door when Carrie faced off with her and gave her a week's notice. She peered at Carrie, startled. Puckered her lips in shock, prompting Carrie to say, I have my limits.

Yes, ma'am, I understand, but, ma'am, things are really tight for me right now.

She was a pretty woman with a natural slimness, well put together in a long black skirt and bright white blouse baring a good deal of bosom. Her sandals made her feet look like birds' feet, the veins standing out, and her toes curling talon-like toward the floor keeping her grounded, upright.

She tried to plead with Carrie but Carrie continued to talk, her voice low, unceasing, and steady, impossible to interrupt, the mother listening with her head tilted to one side, the girl beside her, looking up at Carrie, challenge in her eyes. Carrie's mouth stayed open after she'd had her say, her lips pulled back. The mother stood for a while regarding Carrie in the clarifying silence. I thought I recognized the expression on her face and tried to look at Daryl but he wouldn't look at me. She thanked Carrie, bowed, then told her daughter, We have to get along.

A week or two later, my mother came to collect me from Carrie at the usual time. With something in her voice, Carrie told my mother to watch the evening news. I watched it with her, surprised to see the girl's mother trying her best to answer the reporters' questions about a fire that had claimed the lives of her daughter and her babysitter. Soon there was another funeral my mother would not let me attend.

ii. Fires

"When niggers turn into gods . . ."

—Erykah Badu

Like many others I saw the story on the news. The firefighters leapt back every now and again to avoid flame, the roof spitting fire at them, the sky above the house dense with billowing smoke. The air tight with heat. The helmeted firefighters half men and half beast with their accoutrements, machinery, and serpentine hoses. One fire hose looked like the long neck of a giraffe, the head the nozzle.

I was told that I could find Tonia's parents at a neighbor's house up the street on a block that was as regimented in organization as an ice tray: a neat row of identical structures on either side of the street, each house inside its own plot. I figured out where to go when I saw a front door standing open to the street. The person posted out front recognized me and waved me inside. Mourners stood chatting uneasily in the corners and shadows of the living room, others watching me with suspicion. Then sight surprised, two termite mounds sphering up from the floor at the center of the room. On closer inspection, I saw that it was Tonia's mother and father draped from neck to toe in an old blanket. Mr. Patton sat mute beside his wife while she received a string of well-wishers, lending herself to their comforting hands.

Celeste, I'm so sorry, Celeste.

I filed over to her and pressed my lips against her forehead.

You saw my David, she said. You saw my David when he was alive?

She held me tight. I waited a moment or two then worked awkwardly to free myself. Expected as much when her husband let his head fall forward and he wept.

I felt my skull, a sensation that weakened my entire body but gave me enough time to draw a breath and ease away from them without excusing myself, to cross the room into another where I'd been told I could find Tonia hiding inside a walk-in closet. So I found her, stunned with grief and guilt. At the sight of me she leapt up into the air as if dunking a basketball, banged her head into the ceiling, and came collapsing into my arms, already bursting into talk, apologetic, trying to explain. Candles. Curtains. Someone named James asleep on her bed in her room and her brother David asleep in his room down the hall. I tried to come up with things to say but felt reduced, slow motion, slow thinking. Contained, our voices echoed around us as if we were submerged inside an aquarium.

We struggled out of the closet together, out of the house. I helped Tonia into my car and took her back to my place.

I had made up my mind that I would look after Tonia and get her through the two funerals. She'd been my closest confidant for more than two decades, since that day in third grade when I passed her a note in my best penmanship: *I LOVE YOU. PLEASE GIVE ME SOME PUSSY.* She gave the note to our teacher, Mrs. Clay, who phoned my mother, prompting my mother to give me the worst asswhupping of my life. I couldn't have imagined the affection Tonia would come to feel for me, the small acts of mischief we would carry out from our respective back-row classroom seats that escaped Mrs. Clay's notice.

I made a pallet on the floor in my bedroom and gave Tonia my bed, where she would remain idle for hours on end with her face buried in a pillow like a cat in a bowl of milk or squatting with her back arched over her knees. At times she would stand at length before the bathroom mirror combing out naps and kinks, straightening out her thoughts. And when she was restless I had to put up with her dazed barefoot wanderings through my apartment, her feet so flat they suctioned the floor in a series of rapid farts.

One night she sat down heavily beside me on the floor and shoved her face into my chest. Careful not to pull back, I put an arm around her shoulders, her collarbone, her neck, my fingers feeling in her hair, each kindness a disguise. I had to force my dick down with my elbow and try my best to burn past the feeling.

Astonished at my new existence, I could no longer gauge time and regulate my body the way I could at the firm taking a deposition or trying a case in court. Dawn came with a quiet gaze the day of James's funeral. When we left my place, I was worn out with strain and lack of sleep. The sun high on a miserable afternoon, light striking my skin and fire in my teeth. So this is what the day would bring, light and heat. We shaded our eyes against sheen coming off cars parked rank on rank inside the funeral home's lot and cramped on the street. I kept one arm hooked around Tonia's waist, to keep her from rushing to the body. But we were inside soon enough moving through machine-cooled air saturated with perfume from dozens of wreaths, among circles of clean faces shining under the bright lights and tributaries of mourners pouring down the aisles and converging at the open casket.

I will speak to his family, Tonia said.

If that's what you want, I said.

I need to speak to his family.

We took our place in the line of viewers. Her turn, Tonia lingered before the coffin like someone standing guard over a pot cooking on the stove. Then she started to wail, drawing heads, attention. She tried to muffle the sound by pulling the neck of her dress over her face (a thwarted tortoise), and that was when I stepped into her body, cupped my hand around the back of her neck, and somehow managed to lift her off her feet. Each time I heard her heels scuffing against the floor, I exerted myself and lifted her higher, a moving force weaving around and through bodies until we were outside on the street again.

I eased Tonia back onto her feet, thinking, Now get her into the car. Get her into the car.

But I fumbled my car keys, so much welling up in and around me. Perhaps a walk would help both her and me relax. The lake was not far away. With that thought, my consciousness moved toward water. I embraced Tonia clumsily and started wading with her through the stubborn heat, no easy matter, the air still and thick, slow light breaking everything into glow. Annoyed by the sound of my own breathing, my legs cramping from all the exertion at the funeral home. Tonia was doing much better in the heat than I was. Although her hands and face were bright with sweat, she seemed to have become accustomed to the temperature even in her long-sleeved mourning dress. I removed my jacket but it made no difference, the liquid shapes of cars splashing sun in my face.

We were well on our way to the beach by the time I figured out how to move in step with her. Although my body was heavy, I matched my breath to hers. Once there, we found a spot close to the water, sat down cross-legged on the sand, took our shoes off, and watched waves walk in from the lake, hit some invisible barrier, then break open into a fan of cool spray.

We did not attend her brother's funeral.

I read Tonia's face every evening when I came home from work. Nothing changed. How did she interpret the way I looked at her? Did she know that I felt awake in her presence? We would order takeout and watch horror movies on television until we pressed our faces toward sleep.

One morning, she said to me, I'm not trying to drag this out.

I know.

But that's what you think. Seated on my bed, she eyed me suspiciously. She had made a point of rising earlier than me that morning and was already dressed and groomed, her hair combed into a low neat Afro, the way I'd seen her wear it for close to two decades. (She wasn't much for styling or braids or beauty salons.)

Come on, I said. You know me better than that. What I didn't say, I forced myself not to think about her leaving.

But where am I supposed to go? Before they wanted me out and now they want me back.

Watching me the way she'd done when we were kids, a challenge in her face—those dark pouches beneath her eyes—unlike her body, which seemed relaxed in clothing (a white blouse with puffy tulip-like sleeves and flowered pants) suggesting another ordinary day, same ole same ole, her bare feet crossed, exaggerating her indifference.

But I had become good at getting the slow smile I wanted from her. Indeed, during the many months of her living with me in my sparse apartment that met our simple needs I felt I'd become someone else. So, to put down her challenge, I said what I had to, and she took it up, bringing the pleasure of relief. Things could now go on as they had. And they did.

In the coming days I found it easy to act as if we'd not had that spat. Easy for us to continue on as we had. Then the slave woman appeared.

A smell in her nose, a taste on her tongue, and Tonia would wake in the middle of the night craving crayfish or oxtail or beef tongue, osso buco, apples pears and honey. She would quit bed for the kitchen and chance upon the slave woman seated at the table waiting for her.

Her mother routinely held counsel with the dead, but Tonia—guarded, apprehensive—never took part.

She decided that she would meet with the slave woman on one condition: I had to be there too.

Ghosts leave whenever you're around, she said.

Not a power I claimed; I doubted the validity of ghosts. But the slave woman didn't go away when I sat beside Tonia at the table. Nor did she acknowledge my presence.

I would come to learn that she was a woman of some years, although she'd died after a short illness when she was seven years old.

We were four girls, she said, but I quit breathing, we all did, but I growed til I reached my full years.

Was that how I saw her? What I remember, the way I took in her thick eyebrows moving on her crumpled face when she sat talking with Tonia across the tabletop, the slave woman answering Tonia's thoughts before she could think them.

If it doesn't let you lie quiet, then you should know, she said, you should know. But you never speak to him or come visit.

I noticed some motion trying to awaken in Tonia's body, a quaking, a trembling, but it never fully emerged. Instead, Tonia bent forward, staring into the spiral grain of the table. I did not know if it was my place to speak—what did I want to say in Tonia's defense?—so I continued sitting firm.

I saw and took the child from the fire and brought him here. The slave woman slapped dirt from her dress sleeves onto the table.

Tonia looked up. You could have told me what was going to happen, she said. But you didn't.

Told you and made it worse. The slave woman cleared her throat, sucked her teeth. The world ain't for you. The world is for everything borned.

During these nightly visitations, I could do little more than offer Tonia my usual reassurances. Not that I could easily put aside the slave woman's revelations, a spy in my own home. Perhaps this is why—after a month? two months?—I developed the impulse to serve as an intermediary between Tonia and her parents. (Was I trying to put her into the right again?) I did not let Tonia in on my plan, simply set out one morning to pay them a visit. The smell of smoke reached me in my car before I reached the house. Mr. Patton answered the door in undershirt and pajama bottoms, silent but not particularly surprised. He welcomed me into a house echoing with the vanished voices of firefighters, a burned seashell. We sloshed through a stream of black water from room to room until we reached the kitchen with smoke silhouetted into the walls.

I took a seat at the table, while Mr. Patton slid into the chair where David used to sit cracking jokes on me. (Damn, Hatch, your hairline is running away from your face. I guess you old before your time, huh? Well, you sure are a funny-lookin motherfucker.) I would smile in humiliation, pretending that he wasn't getting under my skin.

You can join me for breakfast, Mr. Patton said.

I'm not really a breakfast person, I said.

But you're in my kitchen.

I thanked him. I didn't expect to be waited on, but he was already portioning grits and eggs onto my plate.

Thank you, sir, but I'm allergic to eggs. And I'm not crazy about grits.

He paused, poised above me, spatula in his big hand. You don't eat grits?

No, sir.

That's why you so puny. His smile was not altogether pleasant. Try putting in some butter and sugar.

He sat down and started eating, looking into his plate, focused, mouth in a hurry, sweat hanging at the edges of his forehead. Clearly something was going on.

I had only started in on my sugary grits and eggs when he stood up from the table, slipped out of his undershirt, and tossed it onto the wet floor, giving me reason not to finish my plate. He turned his back to me—two patches of wing-like hair on his shoulder blades—and I followed him into the backyard. Surrounded by piles of lumber, sacks of plaster, and stacks of insulation, I could no longer remember how I'd hoped this conversation would go. He positioned himself under a tilting load of planks and moved with uneasy strain from backyard to kitchen, then balanced and counterbalanced the wood up the narrow staircase to the upper story of the house, soggy floorboards making spongy noises under his weight.

Load after load, I trailed around in silence behind him. This was who he was and what he wanted me to see. A practical man, lifting planks, putting his legs into the motion, doing what had to be done, the steady rise and fall of his breathing, his back muscles working up and down like wings.

Later that day, I gave Tonia a full report, but she did not let on how she felt about my visit. She remained with me for several more months during which she would awaken at night from the smallest movement or sound, remained until the day she left to move out west to a mortuary college. I never heard from her again, although for years her presence would be so close at times that I could feel her hot breath on my face.

The deposition began to gather itself:

You think I wanted to shoot that nigger? Over a pack of cigarettes? I'm telling you, he was crazy or high or something. He just kept looking at me with his eyes all wild. And I'm standing there with a bead on him but he just started laughing. He be like, Shorty, don't you know who I am? You lucky I'm a good thug or you be dead already. So jus play your cards right so you can go home tonight and give yo nigger some of that good pussy.

My phone rang. My mother. I had to answer.

I put my pen into my pocket and my notepad into my briefcase. Look, I said.

She looked at me.

Try not to worry. I promise I'll get you out of this mess.

Gessie moved soft and quiet about the living room tending to my mother as I watched, showing me that she was on top of things, nothing to worry about. A slender woman, lanky, lean, all legs, so much so that when she walks with her long strides she resembles a jackknife threatening to fold in on itself. She glanced at me and I returned her gaze, looking into her light-complexioned face, the features small as if still developing, growing, under hair styled into knots like black cauliflowers. I could already hear her trying to talk away my panic. We would get through this.

If only I could have her level of faith, optimism. My mother's house had been razed. Upset at the news, I'd circled our block for some time before I settled down enough to park the car and come inside. I had a thousand small feelings for Gessie for all the ways she knew me.

I knew something bad was going to happen, my mother said. Last night, I dreamed that a snake was trying to get into my house.

She was sitting bent forward in the armchair, pitching an ugly strain on the tendons in her neck, her face distorted in a way I'd never seen. Something hurried about her position and her clothing, her wrinkled housedress and the worn-out sheepskin house shoes I'd brought back from Australia (a business trip on behalf of my rapper client DICCC) a few years ago.

She was always finding snake eggs in her garden, eggs she would cook and eat.

Gessie touched her lightly on the shoulders and directed some remark to her.

I ain't never wanted to hurt nobody, my mother said, but I could shoot every one of these no-good niggers from here to Timbuktu.

Maybe they did you a favor, I said.

We looked at each other.

Gessie extended a cup of steaming coffee into my mother's line of sight. My mother accepted it with the scarred hand that had always scared the shit out of me. Then Gessie was gone from the room, leaving me to be alone with my mother.

Did me a favor? The only thing those niggers left me is the clothes on my back.

But, mom, now you can take the insurance money and buy a house in a better neighborhood.

I took the armchair opposite her.

Hatch, sometimes you make me so angry you make my butt want a cup of tea. She had a good look at me.

I'm just trying to see the bright side, I said.

Is that what you call it?

I loosened my tie.

Well, she said, I guess you know what matters. She shook her head. It's a damn shame cause you ain't never had no mother wit. Like when I tried to tell you about that girl.

My mother had developed the habit of calling Tonia "that girl."

Insulted, I stood up, nothing in the room that could keep me there.

Later that night when I went to Gessie, I found her sitting quietly on our bed in her nightdress, the curtains open, the glow of streetlight on her face, a dark weight in the air. I made my way clumsily over to her and slipped into her flesh. Afterward as we lay on our backs, Gessie seemed deep in thought. Had she overheard the conversation with my mother? Had they talked before I came home? Nothing could be worse. My mother knew all my secrets. And now she was living with us.

Gessie tilted her face toward me like a capsized boat. She started to tell me a story from her childhood. One evening, she was sitting quiet and alone eating her usual dinner of starch and beans. Then something told me to look up and I did. And I see this snake slithering through the dirt toward me. He saw I was on to him, and he rushed at me and I kicked him without even thinking about it, and that snake catapulted into the air—she gestured—and was gone.

I studied the moonlight illuminating the narrow definitions of her face. My wife for seven years: on our honeymoon, taking no chances, we imbibed a potion from her village that ensured we would love one another forever.

Don't ever tell your mother that story, she said.

Why not? I said. It's right up her alley. I'd told Gessie the story about the coachwhip that my mother claimed, back home, back in the day, had chased her over into the next county.

I know. She gave a slow blink. But Superman can't go around telling everybody that he's Clark Kent.

In the days that followed, my mother would disappear into the back room once I came home. Because my emotions always flushed near the surface, I kept to the screened-in porch overlooking the garden, reviewing cases and preparing briefs. Our house was large enough that we never had to get in each other's way; still, we had dinner together each night, although she was silent in my presence, withholding her attention, waiting for my anger to burn down. She and Gessie would go out into the garden and carry on conversation and smoke cigarettes, their tobacco sparking among the fireflies, the slow accretion of us becoming three in the same house.

Then the summer reached its peak, cascading casualties, bodies falling amid a tangle of causes at once intended and accidental. Twelve murders in one day: two boys on bicycles, four girls shot on swings in a park, six bystanders in a drive-by. And Mayor Harryette Washington deciding to relocate to the danger zone hoping to put an end to the violence. She vowed not to leave until the violence ended. We watched her standing in the windy radiance of cameras and props, the Redfern Housing Projects behind her like the tallest trees in the world, yellow light wavering down from the sky, converting each building into amber, preserving the residents inside, the clouds barely alive. We saw her Afro expanding in the light like baking bread. Saw her kneel down and kiss the sidewalk, her silver anklet shimmering like a tambourine.

I like her, my mother said. She got a lot of nigger in her. But she won't last a day.

But she's from Redfern, I said. I saw the situation clearly.

That was a different Redfern, a long time ago.

Yeah, Gessie said. Back in Bible days.

The next day, Gessie and I took a drive to access my mother's property. No barrier, the metal fence that once bordered the place coiled around the tree in the front yard. We stood surveying the surviving bricks glistening with sweat in the humidity and giving off dark heat, neither Gessie nor I saying what we both felt. What would we tell my mother?

We started back for the car. Forever on guard, I caught sight of some young blood across the street, his hoodie rising pointed above him like an inflated sail, his high-top sneakers two expansive arks. Then the block vibrating with music from a black sedan—sound I could feel in my teeth—and he took off running. Fire spat from a window again and again, that duration of sound, terribly brief, causing him to slip, lose his footing as he disappeared around the corner, and the sedan speeding away. The screams of other witnesses hanging in the air around us.

We tracked his movements, found he hadn't made it far, only a block or so. He'd collapsed onto the sidewalk, one arm flung against a hedge as if swimming a backstroke. Gessie left my side to go drop down beside him and take his hand into hers, her skirt forming a little hut around her lower body. She put her face close to his and spoke comforting words, this woman my wife who spent most of her time in a laboratory researching ways to modify and embolden breast milk against infection and disease.

Once we were home, my mother's voice pulled us from room to room into the garden. There my mother stood looking down at the ground, shaking her head at what she saw. The dirt churning, turning over and over with worms as big as eels. Moonlight pouring down from above, transforming our garden into a glistening seabed.

Gessie went over to my mother, offered her a cigarette. A match struck and the sound of tobacco fizzing into a slow burn. Together they stood smoking and consulting over what to do. Gessie suggested they fetch hoes from the toolshed. And so they did, returning weapons in hand, hacking the garden to pieces. I thought to take up the third hoe when a sound from inside the house reached me, a familiar voice I could not ignore.

Heads

for David Henderson

"The eye is not satisfied with seeing,
nor the ear filled with hearing."
—Ecclesiastes 1:8

Tangier

All day long the song has kept him thinking, a few clumsy lines scribbled on hotel stationery like black rivers rushing across the page. What imposters his words are. Music pays him to be. Music plays him to be. He sets the pen down on the table and tears off another chunk of hash. Having spent the better part of the day doing just this. See, the beautiful dried hashish in his hand. He puts it in the tall dazzling bong and lights it. Those sharing the table with him inside the café take turns, lips pressed against the long tilted rim of the pipe, then an intake of smoke, causing the bowl to start gurgling. Lazy smoke hovering about the room like gray birds. Four of them sitting at a round table with a mosaic top and heavy iron legs. His skull is filled with feathers, little sleep last night, but he swears that when he finishes this song, this moment will be in it. All of Tangier.

Some time ago he got it into his head that he wanted to get

away from the unpleasantness of London, from the painful atmosphere of his enormous flat, and recover a little for a few weeks, so he had. How long ago was that? No traceable or steady answer, for after weeks or months his life in Tangier has grown firm in his body. Surely were he to ask those sitting with him at the table, one of them would know.

A shout crosses the café. Jimi hears Francis before he sees him, his loud easy laughter. Jimi takes another draw or two on the pipe before he waves Francis over. Francis, a smile gleaming across the air, already a little loaded, a bit unsteady as if his body is being pulled along by the string of his voice like a safety guard guiding a kid through traffic. Francis opens his arms and squeezes Jimi into a hug, then sits down at the sun-dappled table, his elbows propped on the mosaic top, his forearms thick like fleshy pool cues, bowling pins, his hands massive, each finger as fat as an eel. He has thirty years (more) on everyone at the table but doesn't look his age, fits right in. Who can doubt that he's one of them?

No way you're really that old, Francis. How do you do it? Jimi once asked him.

Why, I just make myself young.

It's too hard to speak in French when you're high, Francis says. He puts fingers to forehead as if to keep thoughts from escaping and to push those that have already managed to escape back in. He is wearing slacks and shirt, pants pressed and creased, collar starched, his feet shod in respectable leather shoes, recognizable signs of bourgeois decorum and success. Except one eye is black and swollen. Everyone knows how he spends his nights, and no one has a thing to say about it.

Francis orders a carafe of wine and lets Jimi pour him a glass when it comes. And so they are sitting across from each other again, drinking wine together again, Francis half-turned toward Jimi, Francis a little slumped and clinging to his uneasy chair, talking constantly off the top of his head, easy words on his lips, his thick arms and hands moving the whole while with a certain youth and grace. Jimi thinks about the very first time they met three or four years ago, right here, at this very same café. They were polite and obliging to each other, but the conversation was halting. What did they have to say, to share? He had imagined that Francis, the famous painter, would speak wonders. *I paint heads. That's most of what I do. At least for now.* But mostly he took it upon himself to chastise Jimi in forthright language for being quiet, shy. *Once you reach a certain age it's simply ridiculous to be shy.*

When the menu comes around, Francis orders some of everything and eats all of it, then pushes back from his pile of plates with a self-satisfied look. Long and carefully he wipes his mouth before cleaning each tooth with a fresh paper napkin, which causes Jimi to remember the way his grandmother's yellowed false teeth kept watch on her nightstand, ready to savage anything within reach. He would keep his distance.

The food here is excellent, Francis says. He lowers his face, his chin propped on the table. Through the yellow wine in his glass Francis looks like a bee trapped in amber. But this wine tastes like shit, he says. Like human tears.

That earns a round of laughter.

Try some of this, Jimi says.

Francis sits upright, thinks about it. Why not, he says. I think cannabis is a good idea.

Cannibal? Jimi says, making a joke of it. He breaks off a chunk of hash and prepares it inside the bong for Francis. Soon, Francis is all in, smoke circling above his head, then he starts talking, tells Jimi about his favorite place—restaurant? pub? casino? brothel?—just outside Tangier. A wonderful old building under layers of paint and plaster and abuse and neglect. Frescoes coming off in giant flakes of paint like colorful moths. It's very far away, he says. Takes about a half day to get there, if we travel by—

Don't tell me, Jimi says. He takes a hit on the bong.

Wait, Francis says. Jimi can see some kind of ballooning expansion in the other man's body. Francis struggles to his feet, but then his feet leave the floor. His cranium engorged with oxygen, he is lighter than air, drifts all the way up into thin air until he is nothing more than a black dot in the sky to those viewing him from the ground.

The next evening, they sit outside at the café and look across at the fields and unavoidable sky. Just the two of them. Francis almost never thinks to sit like this, looking out at trees poised in the dusty light, light on every branch, light layered in the leaves. He can see all of the delicate twigs against the blue sky, and each leaf stands out separately on a branch, posing for him. Things in the distance take on more color. The fields end somewhere but he can't see where. Vain, natural life wants form. Some odor blows across the café. Francis coughs into his fist. His neck has been made long by the cannabis, but he is already starting to feel like himself again, only a bit sluggish from lack of sleep, or too much sleep.

Wow, Jimi says. It's good to have you back. Yesterday . . .

Yes, Francis says. Hands are better than wings. He gestures toward Jimi's guitar, which lies flat on the floor near Jimi's bare feet. So isn't that a bit cumbersome?

Jimi lights a cigarette. You never know, he says.

The café owner comes over to Jimi and Francis, urging them to enjoy some special luxury (apricot dumplings), knowing all too well that Jimi will decline his invitation and that Francis will accept it. Waiting for the treat, Francis sits with his chin lifted like someone driving a car, making it impossible for Jimi to tell if he is sober or drunk, not that it matters.

Jimi reaches down and fists his Stratocaster by the neck. He trusts the guitar, the wood and metal it is made from. Plugs it into a little battery-powered amp. Readies his hands, the strings taking up their touch again. Hands moving, strumming a few shimmering chords, raking through some sharp arpeggios, then slaps and snaps of percussive chunks of notes. Tries to put the lyrics to them. Too many meanderings, no holding pattern, in a never-ending song. He chords a four-fingered shape, then bends a string and keeps bending it, waiting to hear the bone snap, every finger broken. He unplugs the guitar from the amp and places it back at his feet, dark strings like the entrails of an X-ray.

But so much of what you played is wonderful, Francis says. Francis being Francis drinks.

If you say so. Jimi lights another cigarette. Or better perhaps to go back to the bong?

Francis likes it when his friends keep secrets, likes the challenge of finding a way to expose what's hidden. I daydream all day long about rooms full of paintings, he says. Tells Jimi about walking through a long narrow hallway lined with doors. Every door is open but a colored curtain keeps whatever is inside hidden from view, each curtain moving a bit in a breeze but never enough for him to peek into any of the rooms.

That's when Jimi sees something astonishing. A long ribbon of light travels from the sky toward Francis, hesitates for a moment, then bends around Francis's body, avoiding his face, his entire torso, landing instead on the objects around him, Francis's body now darker with the shadows, darker than the floor. The light moving here until the ribbon curls up into a ball and plops down on one shoulder, then a second ribbon comes streaming down, curls up into a ball, and plops down on the other shoulder, the unlikely light transformed into two gleaming epaulets.

The afternoon runs out. They leave the café together and walk through the streets of Tangier. Say goodbye inside the garden out in front of the hotel where Jimi is staying. Immediately Francis's breath starts to quicken with the pollen. He calmly wends his way along the road to his hotel, feeling pollen sink to the bottom of his lungs. There is a thing that he forgot to say to Jimi. But what was that? He was almost expecting Jimi to invite him upstairs to his room, but Jimi simply lit another cigarette and waved before Francis went inside.

Once in bed he realizes that his room is layered in heavy blankets of pollen. The heavy fabric of each wheezed breath weaves a shape in the air that hangs in unused stillness. He is soon to die, each heartbeat a concern. He might as well tear open his chest and remove his worthless lungs, prop them like pillows under his head, and wait for Death to take him. So be it. We all have to go. But he knows, his misfortune, that his life will be long.

He tries to picture Jimi in his mind but can't hold the image. Can only see a shadowy figure with cigarette in hand, smoke sketching gestures in the air. Not so easy for an artist to succeed. The difficulty, the object's tireless need to be reimaged by the artist, by paint on canvas. Then sleep loops him in.

He wakes in a clear tangible world. What to do now? Will he look for light in the flawed wine at the café? No. Already London is pulling at him. He decides to sit on the floor and draw. In fact, he draws figures all day, at one point actually reclining on the wooden floor the way the ancients painted inside the caves. The raw back of the wooden floor becomes his back.

London

His studio at Reece Mews still carries the smell of animals. Francis has always preferred to have his studio in a mews. The connection is too obvious, the smell of his father's barn in Ireland traveling through memory. He has been over that afternoon again and again in his mind across the wide span of years, trying to recall all he can of that barn. The neat stalls. The scrambling chickens. Claw feather fur hoof and beak. The floor covered with random tufts of hay sticking up like hairy armpits.

How long did the flogging last? How many lashes did he receive? All he knows is that his father's manservant, mouth sugared with saliva, had sweated through his shirt while his father stood and watched. For the first time in his life he felt someone else's life being lived in his own body, his own head.

The pain should have passed by now, but all the muscles in his body keep their history. He would like to add a gaudy flourish to the memory. But a painting would only betray the simplicity of that moment and magnify its importance. What matters: he is grateful for the lesson his father passed on that day, the only thing his father gave him of any value that has remained part of him.

So it is with painting. Something drops into his mind—he never asks why, nothing purposely planned, he doesn't paint ideas—but the feeling holds for a day, a week, a month, before it is gone. That is the frantic worry hovering over him always. Like now: he is fashioning an image, but why isn't it here the way he saw it before him one hour ago? It's not so easy to bring back the dead. There are many deaths inside him. From time to time in an effort to will something into being, he will drop in on an anatomy class at the university and take in the brown coloring of a cadaver and the tobacco smell of formaldehyde.

He bathes at his studio, leaves pigment in the tub like shed skin, dresses for the night, and leaves, making stately progress through the popping traffic sounds of Soho streets. Little firecrackers of applause greet his entry into the Colony. He's seen them all before, regular patrons, even if their names break up in his mind. They reach out to touch him but their hands pass right through him. Francis taking and giving speech away, full of attention to every detail in the pub. They stand as though standing's what they came here for. And the wobblers, going two ways at once. Words find their feet here in pints and fingers, although the wider net of speech matters more than the speaker. There's always more going on than anyone has the time or wit to notice. (Francis is there, trying to see. Needs to see it all better.) He watches the way a face will change, every word, every gesture, collapse. Almost as if the physical features were shaken like dice in a fist then tossed to random chance.

Comes here because he likes being alive, is in his element, a bottle of claret to move the night along, each and every night. After a hard morning of work, he likes to feel himself in the crowd, holding on to the constant hum of sounds, Francis a sequence of flashes moving across mirrors in the sunken basement. This brightly lit world, a radiance of bulbs, the glow on glow with clinking glasses. After a time, he makes his way to a neighboring restaurant for a leisurely meal. The patrons here make no apparent excitement at seeing him, but the wine is good. Off to another place he frequents, one that shines with pink and red wines. The constant shuttling from pub to pub, this consistency of routine, seems to make the image in his head clearer—at least some aspects of it.

Now someone is shouting at him from across a table. Francis turns at the sound, nods at a boldly oversized gangster dressed in a tailored Savile Row suit. Francis makes his way to the bar, orders the gangster's favorite drink, then turns around and comes upon a brutality. (What else is there?) Watches as the gangster's huge hands nudge a man, watches the man kneel down and lower his lips to the gangster's brilliantly polished shoes.

Your sins are forgiven.

A wave of laughter. Francis laughs too. (Why not? A good clown deserves applause.) Is the gangster doing it all for Francis? People are always looking for a way to get into his paintings. Of course, it is a scene that he could never paint. (Surely the mirror gets tired of telling the truth.)

Soon, Francis settles in. He drinks more bright liquor. Watches people come and go. Holds court.

My eyes are broken, he says. I'm going to give it all up.

And do what?

And do what? Why, I'll be a mother.

Laughter.

Yes, that's what I'll do.

Midnight wine flows from a bottle. The night winds down, the pub empties out. Ah, but he knows another place where smoke waves through every inch of air like gray scarves, handkerchiefs. Nothing to be done but endure it, so Francis holds a serviette up to his face and breathes and drinks through the fabric. Each time he empties his glass, he feels new blood come sloshing through his veins. Spirits the only way to dull the brilliant clarity of existence inside his head. Well, sometimes at least. Spirits can do the trick. Otherwise he will relive the whole day over and over again, and the day before that, and all his days. If he drinks enough, he can hollow himself, force his skull to dump everything.

Francis, don't you think you've had enough?

Enough? Only too much is enough.

But there's nothing left but the dregs.

I love the dregs. The dregs are what I prefer.

Voices knock together like stones, men and women bargaining, arguing, making promises. So it is when he finds himself speaking in that language that he knows something in him has come loose. Now comes the storm of his leaving the pub. When he leaves, everyone feels it, or so he would like to think. The man he takes home to Reece Mews through early morning silence was the last one standing. He longs to be weighed down by his body on the bed, which looks like a long black canvas.

The man stumbles dazed into his skin again and again through the long tangle of the night. After it is all over, the man sounds into sleep but Francis is too warm, too alive. He grabs a fistful of pills and swallows them. How heavy they are, like mercury, pressing his body down onto the sheets and into the mattress.

Up before daybreak. The man (whoever, whatever) takes a piss in the sink then is gone. His fingers have left dark smudges on Francis's skin. Otherwise only a blank headache to prove that he has survived the night.

He pours a glass of morning champagne, takes the chill inside his body. So much is cheerful about this cluttered studio. He makes his way for brushes and canvas, borne up on a stagnant slew of objects covering his studio floor—books, photos, postcards, catalogs, movie tickets, scuffed shoes, rags, paint-encrusted socks, newspapers, maps that have been folded and unfolded many times, crumpled tubes of paint. Walks tracing the dead in every step. Hears or thinks he hears the distant crunching of heavy wagon wheels on a gravel road.

Now, energized with champagne, his hands move. Each separate form, each color, draws him in further. A guessing toward.

More often wrong than right because every movement of the brush on canvas alters the shape and implications of the image. The thought that both informs and deforms what he sees inside his head. Then the thought too is gone, the image blooming at the edge of his reaching.

And then it comes, the new day bountiful, abundant, every object in the studio suddenly brightened and revived. The world hasn't entirely lost its charm. In fact, it shines with defiance. He stands in a room caged in light. The thistles of the paintbrush in his hand are as thick as the hair of the lion he touched many decades ago in Africa. Years stretch in mute kilometers back to the long view of a savanna where he stood in dry heat with his camera, looking at a landscape that was too marvelous. Animals (zebras, elephants, giraffes, rhinoceroses, hippopotamuses) moving through screens of long grass that quickened around him and bowed as if in homage to him, hidden insects humming the landscape into motion. Others in his traveling party were brave enough to move through the hot grass under parasols, each umbrella like a second head that had mushroomed out of the first. Then the guide came and took him and told him that they had found and fed a lion and that he could touch the beast, a moment that would be captured on his camera. The guide led him over to the lion, but he just stood there for quite some time and watched it where it reclined at his feet. Then he kneeled down to touch the mane and pissed himself in fear.

He continues to work through the still bright hours of the morning until the description talks louder than the paint. (The canvas is always so eager to become story.) The picture has become clogged. He will have to start over, start again.

He douses the canvas in turpentine and sets it on fire.

They share a black taxi shaped like a human head. Jimi receives London as a moving cityscape. The light looks different streaking across the small cramped ancient streets, house upon house, corner upon corner, and tree upon tree. People jostling and hurrying about. The noise of these lives. He can hear the trains underground plunging through the tube like liquid through a syringe. He has already had enough of London.

The whole of England has ground to a halt, Francis says. Nobody wants to work, and the pound has gone totally to confetti. It's all falling apart. Won't be much longer now.

Jimi takes a pull on his cigarette but says nothing, the leather seat a startled space between him and Francis. Francis is always bitter and knowing, nothing new there. He thinks Francis wants to know if he's really the kind of person Francis thinks he is, whatever that might be. He takes another pull.

I feel like a homosexual when I'm in London, Jimi says. Smiles. Anything to lighten the mood.

Oh, that's no good, Francis says. Homosexuals are too tragic. We feel too much. Every little scratch is a genocide.

Not to worry. I'm a soldier.

Yes, you are, Francis says. Paratrooping through skies.

They are riding to where? And for what purpose? These few small frames of their existence. They seem to be enclosed in perfect silence until Francis turns to him and starts speaking his rage again in a small storm of his hands. Talking the way someone talks who has kept many things to himself and can't keep them any longer. Jimi figures he should argue back at him—he can put his foot down when he has to—but knows that Francis is stubborn, so he just smokes and smiles through it.

By the time they reach their destination and exit the taxi, Jimi has put another cigarette in his mouth and lit it. Francis moves through the gallery, his whole neck encased in a stiff collar, with his fat face blooming out like a bouquet of flowers. Francis at ease among the photographers and journalists and politicians and important people. He smiles one minute, sidesteps someone the next, frowns and backs off, smiles again, gives a deserving someone the best of his words, then gives someone else a guileless wink. You would expect him to be in a better mood since this is his grandest show yet, dozens of his paintings on display in molded gilt frames inside a gallery large enough to warehouse the world.

It is Francis's birthday and hundreds of well-wishers have sent him flowers at the gallery. Only a matter of time before he starts wheezing.

Do you want some of these? Francis says. I'm not the sort of person who has vases. I would just end up burning them.

Then he and Jimi start to look at the paintings together.

I really like this one, Jimi says. It smells like balls.

Jimi stands at the window of his flat and sees the rim of the sky catching fire, then in the distance the wall of hills catch fire. The smell of the sky and the hills rise from his skin. Something is burning inside him.

> *High crooked mountains receiving the first fruits of the sun.*
> *Brother, listen, he got that devil on the run*

The notes flap up from the strings and fly right through the open window, migrating toward some lost continent. He tells himself, Don't give up on the song. Don't give up on the song. He won't. He will strive for the fitting word, the joining melody. He unstraps the Stratocaster from his body and props it on the floor with the neck on the windowsill so that the guitar looks like some substance that has arrowed into the room.

Monika is already asleep in the bed. He places a hand on her cool forehead before he lies down next to her. He smells smoke in his pillows, feels the mattress suck heat down through his neck, shoulders, back, and thighs.

Head in flames, he swallows nine white sheep and waits for sleep to come.

New York

All along West Eighth Street, trees bent like fingers. All of the little shops and dark knots of people going in and out of them yellow in the streetlight. Traffic changing gear. Metal and chrome shining. Town houses, brownstones, and other small buildings ballooning up in a union of brick and sky. A sky in broken-up pieces above Jimi and Francis, hard and soft, black and blue. Francis, black bruise around his neck, hot in a leather jacket and heavy shirt on a gorgeous early September night. Too much goes whizzing past, surprising flashes of things, but they take the scene on its own terms and stroll right through, seeing and listening (tangled stalks of words) on their way to eat at a little greasy spoon that Jimi knows. Jimi doesn't go unnoticed. It is their right to approach him, singing his praise and touching him as they please in a New York that has grown foreign to the other life (London) that has become who he is, who he must be. Charitable and charming, he never tires of listening to them. Owes them that much. Perhaps that is why he chose to build his recording studio here in the Village.

Once they are at the restaurant, he and Francis place their order, then sit down across from each other in a little booth. Jimi thinks about Monika—things keep getting in between them—then his thoughts slide on. Notices that Francis, eyes flashing, is looking at the cook bibbed in a spattered white apron behind the linoleum counter. The cook holds a knife against a large cone of fatty lamb meat that revolves slowly on a vertical spit. Shaves some curls onto one plate then more curls onto a second plate. That done, he cleans his hands on a small towel hanging behind the counter and prepares their sandwiches. Jimi can't get past the idea that the cone of the meat looks like one of Francis's forearms. The cook brings their plates over, sets them down on the table just so, their modest meal. And they start to eat.

But isn't it dangerous? Francis asks, mouth full of meat.

Jimi smiles. You know, they're very careful about that sort of thing.

All the same I'd watch out if I were you. Never leave something like that in the care of another. He finishes a little glass of Greek wine, then looks out the window at the street with his big quiet eyes.

They listen for a moment to some music hanging in the air.

Jimi thinks about Monika, that thing she does when she sits across from him sharing her thoughts about something, how she will keep her hands on her knees and her face tilted up, looking at some space above her head, then will lower her gaze and look at him in understanding, rubbing her knees a little.

This really is the best, Francis says. He wipes his mouth with a paper napkin. Sees the way Jimi is looking at him. The cat's out of the bag, he says. I'm a just cheap date who will fall for a greasy sandwich.

So now you must buy my silence.

I would only take advantage.

Jimi wants to impress Francis—that's what friends do—so he wastes no time in getting them to Electric Lady, but concern rises up as soon as they step through the glass door. How will Francis handle this confrontation of industrial air and chemical dust? Poor delicate Francis. Days earlier, while Jimi was thick in the preparation for Francis's visit, an idea, a silly one, took hold of him. Why not reproduce Francis's studio here—working from memory and photographs from glossy magazines—a little gag that he was sure Francis would appreciate. Now he has a change of heart, thinks differently about it. Too late since every inch of the hall floor is covered with broken guitars, broken guitar strings and plastic picks, old fuzz boxes and wah-wah pedals and phase shifters and Octavias, and stacks of Marshall amps and Leslie speakers and boxy little speakers. They wade through it all, but none of it seems to make any impression on Francis, perhaps because the studio is still in process, every wall lined with a metal forest of scaffolding and ladders, a growing into being that means so much to Jimi. Soon he'll have to return to London, but overseeing the completion of this studio will give him reason to bounce back stateside every so often and, down the line, for extended stays here in Manhattan to record or oversee the projects of others.

They both take seats in plush leather chairs at the control booth. Lights swim like little colorful jellyfish inside the bulbs on the console, blue and green and white and gold and red and orange and pink and pearl and amber streaked with purple. The room seems awash with sea. Jimi readies a reel—A new crop of work? Francis asks—and plays it for Francis, a song contrived in the correct shape but lacking the right Feel. (Much to do.)

Francis sits perfectly still in the chair listening, his glistening white face reflected on the glass of the recording booth in front of them. (Move, Francis. Snap your fingers, tap your feet.) You're fussy, he says. Precise.

Jimi hears the words, but what do they mean to him? Elsewhere in his thoughts, cut off, contained as if he were sitting inside a hollow tree and listening to wind whistle through it. Which ear must he have and why?

I suppose you're right, Francis says, picking up on a conversation from earlier that night. (Throughout their little dinner, Jimi had wanted to talk more than they had.) These manager types will fight you over something weak, something that they know you can easily defeat. Afford you a small victory to give you a false sense of power, to make it seem that you're the one controlling things.

Yes, Jimi says. I mean that's how it is with some of these old blues cats. They like being sad and lonely and crying. They see power in misery, think that's where the good stuff comes from, but me, I'm like, Hey, cut me some slack. It's a new day.

Strange business, Francis says. Don't lose headway. Fashion says you should be moved by certain things and not by others. But art takes all of that out of you. He smiles. When I was young, I hurt people. Now people hurt me.

With a slide of his hand, Jimi brings the volume of the recording down. Fires up a cigarette. What puzzles him is what his friends find to say, both the friends who come to see him and those who don't. Not that he's keeping track. He has no mental catalog of all the times he and Francis have been together. He reels up another track of the same song, fierce itching dazzle—he can scale back on that, keep it simple, since nothing is as direct as the blues—over a luxuriant foundation of drums. The words make light and shadows of themselves:

You know, baby, you can't treat me like that
And you know, baby, the things you say they ain't true
But guess what, baby, I won't let you treat me like that
Cause you know, baby, all these things I do for you

Hearing something he understands, Francis moves two fat fingers to his thick chin.

So this must be the way he listens.

Jimi imagines Francis standing at his easel, legs apart, squeezing out tubes of oil paint in colors whose names he doesn't know.

I long for people to tell me what to do, Francis says, to tell me where I go wrong. Who looks after you?

Odd question but Jimi doesn't pause. My old lady, he says. Monika. Although there are always plenty of Band-Aids around who pick up the slack. Fill up the boring hours.

There it is. Those Band-Aids must serve some function.

Jimi removes his secondhand Moroccan vest and places it on the floor behind his chair, where it sits stiffly holding his shape or perhaps the shape of the man who wore it before Jimi, someone probably dead. He sits back down in the chair, lights another cigarette, a mask of smoke around his face. Jimi shirtless, his bare brown chest glistening with fire, his ribs all moving with his breath.

For a moment tired recognition gives way to hope. Francis wants to impart some element of himself to Jimi. Jimi's belief burns so bright, although there is still something guarded about him, emerging, resistant like a lightbulb muted behind a lampshade. But what can he give? (So much remembered, so little to say.) I have always wanted to put over things as directly as possible, he says. I think we are alike in that.

Jimi nods, sucks some smoke in, blows it out his nose.

We are in very primitive times again, Francis says. One has only to observe things and know the undercurrents. Perhaps we may all go up in a sheet of flame. Who knows? And you, Jimi, you feel that you must do something, that you must make a difference somehow. But that is the wrong way to think, because you *are* the difference, you and I both.

Jimi's hands are moving on the console, putting this in, taking that out, bringing this up, pulling that down. Fatting and trimming. Fluffing and flattening. This must be that place he believes is his home.

Francis wants to tell Jimi that the good held in common never lasts for long, flourishes, that it can't. That present and past, they boil down to much the same. A thousand years a city, a thousand years a desert. That the old fears still operate, have gone deep. Isn't that what his music is really about? What never changes: War. Brutality. Injustice. Poverty. Famine. One thing living off another. One thing needing another. Death. And so on.

We Old World types know a thing or two about keeping up appearances, he says. Listen, there was this one wretched queen who was long in the tooth, and her courtiers would paint her cheeks then compliment her on her healthy complexion.

Jimi finds that fact amusing, snickering smoke.

But why try to cover up death? It couldn't matter less, Francis says.

Lights flicker on and off on the console, blue and glitter.

I have been to the caves in France. You must go. We must go together. It's nothing like what you see in the picture books, the magazines. When you first step into a cave, you have no idea what you are looking at. Just this crowd of images. He tries to find words to explain it. Every inch of the ceiling and the walls dense with paintings and engravings of horses, bison, deer, felines, ibexes, and aurochs. The experts with their fancy theories and words have much to say about it all, but if I were to listen to them, I would be in continuous irritation. I subscribe to a simple explanation. All you have to do is look and realize that these painters there in the caves many thousands of years ago were trying to best one another. As plain and simple as that, competition.

Sitting cross-legged now in his chair, with his hands in his lap, Jimi seems to be holding Francis's voice like an invisible bird inside an invisible nest.

They certainly outdid everyone else, Francis says, those they had to live among. You see, entering the caves is no simple matter. You have to go on hands and knees through many tight spaces. Few people would have done it. But those bold few who actually went into the depths might have come face-to-face with the something now lost to us, devils and demons perhaps, or other creatures of the netherworld. Who knows. But the important thing is that by going inside the cave, they acquired abilities not possessed by most people. And they began to perceive those new abilities, their new place in the world, even before they left the cave. And then they crawled back out into the world of those lesser others and had to live among them until they died.

Thick light buttered on the wall behind him, Jimi is watching Francis, Jimi's hands still placed in his lap, another cigarette lit, smoke spiraling up from his crotch. Wow, he says. Monsters. Mythical beings. Fantastic creatures. Right up my alley. You know we do have to go there. He takes a drag on the cigarette, tip glowing. Go there and know there.

Now Francis realizes that Jimi has brushed it all aside. The words are a turnoff, or Jimi's head is spinning, too much to take in, too many substances already consumed, or he thinks Francis is too old, too uptight, takes him for a fool. Why should it be any other way?

Sorry for flapping my gums, he says. It's the disease of the old.

Come on, man. Why are you apologizing? We're going to those caves. I'm telling you, we're going to those caves. You make the arrangements.

Jimi places the lit cigarette onto a safe spot on the console, gets out of the chair and fishes something from one pocket of his vest, then returns to his seat at the console.

But what are you painting?

I'm on the edge of doing something good. I've found the way now, although I might need five hundred years to get it right.

It's the material really. I managed to acquire an entire yard of mummy wrap, the real thing.

What? How did you do that? Your secret's safe with me. Here, try some of these.

Jimi's fingers work a vial of some sort.

What is it?

Don't you know? It's just a name.

Yes, why not? I think whatever this is is a very good idea.

You want a glass of wine to chase it?

Yes, but for my thirst.

Jimi produces a bottle—good stuff, a Nero d'Avola—and two glasses.

Mick showed me the one you did of him. Was that mummy wrap?

The pills are warm behind his teeth, flame under his tongue. Mick? Why, I was just being a whore. I would never waste eternity on him.

That gets Jimi to laughing.

Why can't they talk like this forever? Francis feels another kind of duty breaking through. He longs to stay alive for Jimi's careful hands and humor and smoke. But then, before he knows it, his breath is spinning inside a glass bubble. Then he feels someone turn him upside down like an hourglass, all of his being spilling to the other end.

See, Jimi says. There you are. Stone free.

London

He steps through a doorway smell of paint, turpentine, dust, and something else—sheep? goats? cattle?—but the pulsing heat is the thing to withstand. The air is steaming, heat pushing his hair away from his skull. All things grow hot in this place, Francis keeping the furnace on high here, perhaps to kill the London damp that can clog his breathing. They pass by a dresser mirror that is splintered in triangles of glass, then farther on Jimi sees his body reflected from head to foot in a second large mirror.

Mirror, mirror on the wall, he says.

Why you are, Francis says.

Something about the mirror causes him to remember the bottle trees that surrounded his grandmother's house, both front yard and back colored with them, a necessary precaution to protect them. His grandmother believed that the glass would catch and trap any evil spirits that tried to enter her house. He remembers how the soda bottles would stun the senses when sunlight struck them. Remembers the sound of bottles clinking when he threw rocks at them. He could never break one, not a single bottle, but that sound—*ping*—brings back other sounds. He can still hear surging grass and creaking bushes. Metal buckets clattering under pipes. Huge clouds rumbling like semitrailer trucks during a rainstorm. Heavy wash hung out to dry snapping and flapping on clotheslines.

Then things in the studio go crunching underfoot. It's all worse than he imagined, frankly, a bit unkempt, nasty. And too closed in for his liking. But to each his own.

He and Francis sit down at a little table (more like a tall stool) covered with books. A few novels, volumes of verse, art catalogs, studies of Greek mythology, tomes in foreign languages, a thing or two about anthropology, but by and large cookbooks. Jimi picks up one and thumbs through a few pages. (Bread sauce with cloves . . . Grilled scallops with capers, baby carrots, and beach plums on a bed of devil's apron . . . *A man who touches a cabbage is seldom sorry.*) Picks up another. Holds some pages up to the light, as if looking for something inside them. (A sheet of paper is too narrow a space for a song to hide.)

Can I tempt you with a meal? Francis asks.

It depends. I need a hamburger in the worst way.

Francis uncorks a bottle of claret. Pours Jimi a glass then one for himself. Holds his glass aloft. Here's to you, he says.

Jimi raises his glass. The sensation of glass against teeth and wet earth on tongue.

When I'm alone, I never have a drink, although there's tons of stuff here.

We should finish it all then buy some more.

And then do what?

Buy even more.

Slowly the conversation leaks back to fact.

You're not much of a one for writing letters, are you?

No, Jimi says. I'd much rather talk long distance on a public saxophone.

Just so you know, I did try. Although I don't know a thing about any of it. Political causes are always lost on me. But if you say I should give that group money, then I will. Just name the amount.

You're a good man.

Possibly. But that's not why I'm doing it. You see, I trust your judgment.

Is that the only reason?

No, but it's the only one that matters. Besides, I say just burn it all and start over. Why not?

Jimi cannot find his tongue, not that he needs to say anything. Francis heavy upon the eyes with his sculpted hair framing his broad soft face, with his upright collar and black leather jacket.

Drapes cover the few canvases propped against the walls, and the canvases themselves cover holes in the walls but Jimi can still hear air seeping through. Francis sees the way that Jimi, book in hand, is looking, taking it all in.

I can see that you want a peek. Put that book down and come look at this.

Jimi gets up from the table and follows Francis, the wide slope of his black leather shoulders. Little mudslides of debris move under their shoes and run ahead of their shoes. Francis stops before a draped canvas angled on top of an easel, and Jimi stops and stands next to him. Light slants in from the window in the ceiling above them, causing Francis's face to become so radiant that Jimi can barely look at him.

Light on his hands, hands glowing, Francis flings the drape back.

What do you think?

Jimi removes his eyeglasses from the pocket of his hussars jacket, puts them on his face, perfectly round gold-rimmed spectacles, adding up to two glass discs.

Francis looks at him.

Don't tell anybody, Jimi says. Making a joke of it, he puts one finger to his lips to bond their secret. They want me to wear these cause I keep wrecking cars.

There it is, Francis says. So you would do well to look ahead. But first wreck a few more. We must have the freedom to burn.

Jimi can't tell exactly what's in the painting. An animal of some sort. With a fine edge of light gleaming around its body. The animal refracted in shadowy reflections of itself. Indeed, it is caged inside a room full of mirrors, a cage made from bulky white lines, bones instead of bars. And, as a whole, the scale in the painting is so cunningly manipulated.

He flips the glasses off his face, inserts one temple between his teeth, and stands before the painting, biting, wildly watching.

I'm particularly glad you like it, Francis says. Most people have no instinct for images. You have no idea how blind we really are.

Is that the mummy cloth?

You can tell? See the texture? It makes all the difference.

Jimi puts the spectacles back inside his jacket pocket then lights a cigarette. Francis throws the drape back over the canvas the way one might sheet the dead. Passes Jimi a dented tin cup to use for an ashtray. Jimi taps a few ashes inside.

And now I will make you that meal.

He feels in the flesh of his forearms long changing marks on the canvas, letting his impulses settle in so that each movement makes a difference. Francis wet and stinking of his own hours working, his hands strange to him now. Accustomed to thrashing out a solution with his body, huge lengths of movement, all of him stretched unbelievingly out, bones and tendons seeking a new configuration. You never see the pieces all at once. Straight and curvy lines together. Half of something, half of nothing. Then a vague shifting. (What color now?) Transformation, becoming, in the emotion, not the thought.

The furnace trembles heat into hearing, the sound of his own lungs a wordless echo in the studio above the noisy objects swimming under his shoes and the memory of Jimi's voice, low ocean murmur in his mind.

Now in the window above him, the long pink line of dawn, sending new light down. How sweet when something you cherish unexpectedly arrives. A painting that is all of who you are and more.

He starts to remove the canvas from the easel but can't, surprised at how heavy it is, heavy with the weight of history, the bodies of the dead, every painter from the beginning of time buried in thick knots of pigment.

At a party, Jimi gets into an argument with Monika—he believes in free love, she doesn't—and she storms out, causing a scene in front of his friends. Not the first time. He goes after her.

The argument pushes the two of them along. The sky gets into it too and begins to color up, the late sun streaking across London for miles. He follows her for the slow length of a homeward mile until he loses sight of her, a steady vanishing. Summer warmth withdraws from the September evening. How else can it be? A day comes in a month, in a season, and you wish it were some other month, another season. (The days and their different lights.) A car honks twice. At him? His shadow slides along these white houses, a black blur, little houses that always look sad in the falling light of sunset. His shoes hollow up sound from the cobblestones. The cobblestones themselves look like the bald heads of monks. He rounds a corner and the street starts sloping downhill, cobblestones moving under him like an avalanche of skulls. And now the dark comes on, heavy pieces of the settling darkness locking in place.

The weather in the flat and the weather outside the flat are the same. Jimi makes a cold trek through the dark residence to the bedroom. The telephone is ringing. He lets the ringing go on while he searches for a cigarette, rummaging through clothes and closets and cupboards. He hears Monika take the call.

No, not now, he says. Tell them I'm not here.

He resumes his search. Not one damn cigarette anywhere. Imagine that. He'll have to wait until morning.

Monika hands him a glass of wine, kills the lights, and drops onto the edge of the bed, sitting there waiting to see if he will come. Perhaps he should. Then again, why bother? Unspoken things will divide them from now on. He'll pick a fight with her in the morning to push her toward the inevitable. Better that way.

He sits down in a chair facing the window on the other side of the room and sips his wine in the dark. The distance between him and Monika throbs on his back. The bedroom doorknob glows like a lightbulb in the moonlight, and moonlight turns the bed a milky bluish white. Everything is still until the sound of his growling stomach interrupts Monika's breathing.

Her voice releases into the night. Jimi, are you there?

Where else would he be? His stomach growls, something within wanting out. He should eat something, a few nibbles. He is too thin. His bones press against his papery skin. But his mind is on other things. Without trouble or searching, he can see what is inside his head set deep in a puddle of light, the most loved thing, the odd inner peak. He has ten fingers like candles to tell a story and he will, even if the searched-for sound simmers at a low volume, barely audible, barely felt.

He finishes the wine, undresses, and gets into bed, night sealed around him. Folds his fingers behind his head, pressing the weight of his wanting into the pillow. The weightless sound of breathing rises from his chest. Pure darkness holds up a ceiling flecked with light. He feels his lips move, he counts his breaths, but sleep streams away from him. Monika murmurs something and curls closer, her small nude familiar body cradled against his chest and thighs. Soon she is pulled into a blank spell of sleep.

Then he starts to hear the cry of a bird from far away. Another night bird answers, from far way. *Little wing crying. Night bird flying.* Something light in the long blue night. What has summoned them?

He gets out of the bed and goes over to the open window. Sits down on the windowsill facing a line of trees that ends a long way down the cobblestoned street. Studies the street gliding downhill and shining slick as a river. Nosy leaves outside try to look in. Okay, so look. He touches down with his fingers, straps his Stratocaster to his body, and starts to play with no amp, doing all he can do. He starts to feel something and leans into the guitar, solidly on his own. He's got the opening now and makes a mental recording of it, a song cut loose from his body:

Sweet angel so weary and weak in the blink of an eye
The story of life is how often we fail but how hard we try
Still the blood is strong and will abide even when we cry
So keep on pushing keep on pushing till the day we die
Keep on pushing keep on pushing, baby

He unstraps the guitar and props it against the windowsill, moonlit wood throwing broken shadows against the wall. He finds the bottle of wine and fills his glass. Drinks it. Pours another. His fingers are a little stiff so he inserts them into the glass of wine, lets them root in the warm liquid for a period of time, pulls his fingers out of the glass then rubs wine over the strings before drinking what little is left. Pours another. Drinks, swallows, a backward explosion, intake of breath.

Once his fingers feel right, he straps the guitar to his torso, left hand fingering riffs and chords, right hand plucking the strings, as is his fashion. The notes take hold. The white dots on the neck of the fretboard look like seashells buried in sand. Hollow spaces where his fingers can venture. He wants to put it all in the song—the argument with Monika, the way the party got off to a good start and how they were all having a great time until the argument, and before the party the jam back at the club—but that's where his memory runs dry. *Sorry, folks. We're too stoned. We can't make it happen tonight.* Had he really been too high to play and just walked off the stage? No, no, that's not how it happened. He had hit one song, two, maybe even a third before he realized that he was too fuzzy to focus. So then it must have been an actual gig, a concert, not simply a jam. Or is he confusing moments, mixing nights, places and times? So little to hang on. Doesn't remember much except the flashing lights and the noise of sirens and his own voice sounding unreal and the way his fingers trembled when they touched the words of others speaking around him.

But what little he does remember he puts into the song, his hands composedly moving. He watches the song grow, full of wind and sky and dirt and water, coming and going, rising and falling—one heap of sound. He knows what inflections of the blues mean red house, blue rain, midnight lightning. Knows how to worry chords into the black shape of time. Knows how to anchor weight on a string and sink a barbed note into the muddy depths below, then bend that string and yank up a struggling catfish. Knows how to hoist the entire world to his ear, all that he is listening.

He plays until night blurs into dawn, the new sun turning the cool-breathing flat into a box of light. The light is better this way. Ordinary light. And so is Monika, a small white body trembling for balance in the kitchen, where she spoons coffee into a pot without the least thought of him. Maybe they will make it after all.

Fat Time

"Much widened, perhaps winged."

—Walter S. Adams

Stylish, dressed to the nines, Johnson starts up the slanted gangplank toward ship deck one June day followed by a retinue of journalists and well-wishers. His jacket and pants the best cut and cloth, his collar high and tie crossed and buttoned, his shirt bright and shining like a shield, the socks that sleeve his calves and ankles woven from rare African silk, and his feet shod in high-button shoes cobbled from Tuscany leather. He is careful to keep his hands close to his sides, for a man destined to be champion does not need railings to help him ascend to deck. Nor must that man display a serious face. So he smiles under his bowler hat, even if he chooses not to wave goodbye to the crowd assembled on the pier. He knows that the whole world is watching and waiting. *For whom am I fighting if not the world? Burns said. Let's put all money aside, I told him, and fight right here, man to man, chest to chest. And if you whip me I will give you the belt. Gents, do you think this Negro took up my offer? No he did not. For the nigger whether fighter or layman is a peculiar creature. I can't tell you how fast Johnson made for the door. He almost broke his leg running.* So it is that life has stuttered and made it necessary for him to travel to Australia for the second time in less than two years. Early bird after the worm, he plans to reach Sydney before Burns.

His joy does not cease to dominate the ship as it leaves port and reaches open sea, San Francisco a black shimmer on the horizon. Of and not of water, he stands there on deck under morning sun, light reflecting from every wave, dazzling sparkle. His fear sinks and settles at the bottom of the ocean. Alone in his cabin, he recalls the first time he took to sea almost twenty years ago, as a malnourished eleven-year-old stowaway suffering all one could suffer in the airless boiler room of a steamship. Many ships since then. Surely his body is all the better for it. Wrong. As he soon learns, intercontinental travel takes him apart. Three days immobile in bed, all that zealous water out there, all those expectant waves, words like *drown* and *shark* tucked close to his lungs. The world whittled down to what he can see from bed through the cabin window. What can he do with fifty birds moving in the clear sterile sky? (Assuming that there is still air out there. Assuming that the world beyond his cabin still exists.) The smell of ocean may never leave him. But a spell must be broken. He has himself, only himself, as a testimony of his own glory, his own fortitude, and his own reason. Once his strength is restored—a hushed word of thanks to the Most High—he takes to the deck, and the correspondents take to him. Already counting waves before he can answer the first question put to him. His mouth closes around his teeth.

Why, Jack, you look practically white.

That should come as no surprise. He's no different from the rest of his kind, dreaming white.

Dream on, nigger.

Johnson is silent in the face of their taunts and questions. He shouldn't have come out of his cabin.

Ease up, boys. Can't you see that he is not himself?

Johnson goes back down under. The words continue to grind at him. He makes sure that no one catches another glimpse of him until weeks later when the ship docks in Sydney.

He has the hallucinatory impression that he is arriving on the continent for the first time, since so much is a mirror of before.

Tell us, Jack, how was your journey?

I believe I still have two feet, Johnson says. Ocean in his head, salt in his sentences. But I have not traveled alone, for the only true voyage is not for new landscapes and new horizons, but to get the eyes of another to see the world with your eyes, to get a hundred others to see what you see, a thousand.

Would you be meaning your fellow race of Negroes?

Indeed, sir. Indeed.

Mr. Johnson, that is surprising since many of the Negro papers say you are an embarrassment to your people. That you are doing the colored race more harm than good with all of your blatant cavorting around with white women, with your pomp and dandyism, and your other extravagances.

Well, look who's saying it. A little bit of education can mess up a nigger worse than bad alcohol.

The journalists pass laughter from mouth to mouth like a shared cigar.

Gentlemen, know that I am an unbroken chain of purpose stretching back a thousand years or more to the original source, and stretching that source into the future for all eternity to come. Did I answer your question?

But what if you lose?

Now why would I do that? What gives man the greatest pleasure is success.

At town center, he receives a welcome deserving of a man of his considerable fame and position beyond any concerns of race, voices ripping up the winter (July) sky. Johnson's wit, good humor, and all-around fun-loving demeanor inspire respect and affection among his hosts—Jack, what would you like to see?—any place public or private where he breaks meat and bread, Johnson blithe and happy for an entire week at one party after another enjoying the dense textures of the local foods, everything so intensely what it is without garnish, pickling, or spice. Jack drinking it all in. Sydney floating through him, even if he has seen it all before, done it all before.

Once he knows what he needs to know, he sets up camp with his handlers at Botany Bay, where he enjoys a mug of coffee (brewed strong the way he likes it) with condensed milk each morning before he starts training. He does his roadwork bare-chested, letting the Australian winter multiply on his body. Does what he must do day after day on the light and heavy bags then stages stunts for the locals who come to watch him chase jack-rabbits or wrestle razorback pigs and saltwater crocodiles into exhausted submission. Even goes kangaroo hunting—proving that when in Rome he can do like the Romans—mounted high on snorting horseback, four hard hooves and four galloping hounds at his service to pursue and corner prey. Blood on blood, he hits one of the odd creatures with the knob of his riding crop and kills it dead. Just short of refusing, he declines the invitation to skin and cook his kill. (He has gutted many a hog in his time, wrung the heads of chickens.)

At last, he says, smiling, I have found my true métier.

Jack, you're welcome to join us for a hunt anytime.

Truth be told, one kangaroo hunt was enough for me. It's not a sport for an American.

Early one morning, Johnson takes long strides that carry him to a barber who has been recommended. Many customers have passed through already, tufts of hair sprawled across the floor like fish caught in a net. The barber trawls his broom along the floor until it is clean, then asks Johnson to settle into the chair. Carefully guides his razor along the top of Johnson's head, hard-ened skin taking the scrape with a metal resonance that echoes out into the street, causing a slow curiosity, observers drawn to the door of the shop in responsive admiration, dozens of gawk-ing eyes locked in one gaze, although the watchers appear to be afraid to enter the shop. Amused, Johnson flashes his gold tooth at them. But why not take it one step further?

Now that Johnson's head is bald and clean, the barber brings his razor to Johnson's face and sets to work, blade sliding along his long throat in measured increments, and up to his chin, where it ceases to move. The barber tugs once, twice, even a third time, but he can't move the razor.

Good sir, Johnson says, please use all of your force. Do not be afraid of hurting me. I require it of you.

The barber tries to honor Johnson's wish, but the razor will not move.

Behold, Johnson says. He rises up from the chair and stands looking at his admirers, the razor pinned to his chin. He watches their faces change, mouths wide with wonderment at what they are witnessing. Now they know: Johnson is at the magnetic center where every occurrence of significance on the continent for the next six months will both radiate from him and be drawn in motion back to him—nothing random or accidental. Every action, every event, however small and seemingly unimportant, has its purpose and justification in Johnson.

That should be enough, Johnson says. He allows the razor to release from his skin and fall clanging to the floor. His audience emotes in one loud sound, part gurgle, part groan, part murmur, part moan.

Satisfied, Johnson sits back down in the chair and tilts his chin up. The barber thinks for a little while, then he picks the razor up off the floor, cleans the blade with disinfectant, and proceeds. Once done, he touches a hot towel to Johnson's face and lights a small fire on Johnson's skin—Johnson has no words for what hurts—steam rising, his jawline etched in smoke. In years to come, whenever he views his victory over Tommy Burns in his thoughts, he will also feel the steady pain of the hot towel and see Tommy before him in the ring, his spine giving out, his jaw unhinged, Johnson absorbing into his own body every blow and insult that made Tommy ache in the ring as if the other man were forever an outpost of his own skin.

Each night he tries to direct his energy toward sleeping, but he can hear his entire being working, heat building under his skin, more than flesh can hold, steam shooting from every pore. Here in the darkness of this room and in the darkness of many other rooms both from his past and in the future to come, he will be unable to make sense of the silence. For this reason he travels with a music box—any tune will do—to drown out the noise of his body. He can only fall asleep by degrees, in fixed increments, and by this method gets what little sleep he can. A long time sitting upright and naked in bed, with his feet resting on the floor, or half-seated and anxious on the edge of an armchair like someone playing a game of musical chairs. He studies the paintings mounted on the walls. A wide field of uninterrupted grass backed by the horizon. Looking closely, he sees at the very center of the canvas a small book lying open on the grass.

The moon fills the dark with something even darker. He watches it move in slow motion from one corner of his window to the other and back again. His breath blows his eyelids open whenever they try to close, so it is that he goes on seeing in the darkness, dreaming what he must.

The next morning, he sits down to breakfast at the best restaurant in town, the pride of the city. A group of reporters announce their presence, then take up posts at one table after another, watching but allowing him to eat unmolested.

He overhears them while he eats. The waiters serve him the best of what their chefs can offer, food that stains his hands and gives him gas. And now they urge more food on him, but he declines, tries peeling some outlandish fruit, his fingers useless against its rind. Gives up and settles back in his seat with a lit cigar, coffee, and the morning paper. There in its pages, he confronts some parody of his name and character, Coonson, in a bold foretelling of his prizefight with Tommy Burns, christened the Hanover Giant in the story.

The two pugilists break through ink and rise up fully dimensioned on Johnson's table. At the ring of the bell, Coonson and the Hanover Giant step out of their respective corners, Coonson led by the two belts of his lips, his teeth sticking out like fists, and his arms so lengthy that his knuckles drag against the tablecloth. They go at each other in the center of the table. The Hanover Giant finds the challenger easy to hit, landing blow after blow against Coonson's face and head, but the blows have no effect, for his skull is too thick. Soon Coonson is all over the champ with back-hands and rabbit punches and low blows and knees to the stomach and kidneys, gouges to the eyes, elbows to the neck and chin, until he brings the assault to a convincing conclusion by lifting the Giant off his feet then flinging him to the canvas. The Giant lies quite still as the referee starts the count. Will he be counted out? No, for he rouses himself to his feet with only a second to spare, revived by a simple truth, that the man with everything to lose minds it the most.

He stumbles falls rises back to his corner, the whole world plunging down into darkness as he plops into painful exhaustion on his stool. How do you beat a beast that doesn't bleed? He has less than one minute to use his highly civilized brain to intellect a solution. But the rational man is also a spiritual man. He looks to heaven in prayer. Oh muses, oh high genius, help me now.

And so summoned, an angel haloed with stars descends from the chandelier. Making haste, the angel whispers instructions into his ear. So it is that the bell for the second round finds him, energized by his new knowledge, running hard out of his corner and connecting with one hard blow to Coonson's stomach, all it takes to bring his ape-like opponent crumpling and unconscious to the tablecloth.

Johnson sits there, heavy and silent and sick, his body trembling with the force of everything rushing all around him. He takes one deep breath and sucks the entire room into the vacuum of his lungs, and sits there blank and alone, the whole world gone white in sheets of silence for a minute or two until he releases the breath and restores the restaurant and patrons. He tries to speak one sentence that is too long for his tongue, so instead, removes the cigar from his mouth, then stubs the tip out on the newspaper lest his own body turn to ash. For years after he will have cause to remember these burned pages and forget where he is.

A waiter puts his check on the table and goes away, a kind of violence. Johnson orders another pot of coffee. He feels a certain surprise when the waiter returns a few minutes later to tell him that Mr. Hugh McIntosh's servant is outside waiting for him, that he should finish his pot of coffee and come right away. It's all news to him, but Johnson says nothing and does nothing, simply sits and lets the coffee go cold. (The hour before the coffee, the hour after.)

Some time ago, he had been told that promoter Huge Deal McIntosh had left Sydney to meet with investors abroad and would not return for another month or two, but that fact is contradicted when Johnson leaves the restaurant and finds a dark skinny man standing just outside doors of metal and glass. The man stands beautifully correct in a tall black hat and a superior frock coat. He seems unbothered by pigeons pecking at bits of bread around his feet. Cuts a striking figure, almost better dressed than Johnson himself, except that nothing fits as it should. The trousers tattered and a bit too long. The shoes worn down on the outside at the heels. And other neglected particulars. Something exaggerated and base about him, put on, his hair far more candid than his costume, unfurling in soft black waves.

He looks at Johnson for a moment, both timid and bold. Puts out his hand in greeting, trembling when Johnson takes it into his own hand. He is nervous but becomes clear enough. Lately returned from the east coast, Mr. McIntosh has requested his presence at the office. They start to walk away, only to be accosted by correspondents, all talking at once.

Johnson listens and takes in their questions with interest. I can say a true thing or I can say nothing, he says.

The answer does not satisfy them. New questions. He opens his mouth to speak, but they want more than he can give. Lucky for Johnson that the servant takes his assignment to heart. He moves, and Johnson moves to follow behind him along the beautiful road that eventually widens into an immense lawn, the office, as Johnson discovers, a small white house placed at the very center, the single room inside much larger than Johnson expects it to be, as if some trick of perspective, a conjurer's stage set. The ceiling easily thirty feet above the paneled floor, all the more impressive for its fresco (some battle scene), the entire room blocked in flowered chintz wallpaper serving as the background for an extensive collection of quickly recognized paintings after the old masters, all the furniture cheerfully upholstered in bright colors. Hatless, jacketless, his breast pocket stuffed with pencils, Big Deal McIntosh sits with a relaxed attitude behind a huge desk littered with papers. The servant clears his throat and draws McIntosh's eyes to him. He stands up from the desk to shake Johnson's hand, a thin upright man in his sixties, his dark brown hair sprinkled with gray at the temples, accentuating his youthful appearance, his eyes lively and keen. Jack, he says, I am greatly struck. You are everything I thought you would be.

Shaking hands with the promoter, Johnson has no words to say in response, so he simply takes a seat in the chair in front of the desk before Big Deal invites him to do so. Big Deal sits back down.

The servant wheels over a silver cart laden with bottles, decanters, and tall tumblers. Johnson decides on a whiskey that has been flavored with a bit of honey and spice, very much to his liking.

Big Deal waves the servant away. Waits for the man to quit the house before he starts speaking to Johnson. How has he been finding Australia, finding his people, the summation of the human race, to hear them tell it? Surely he is bored. Maybe not. You're on all men's lips, he says, and, what's better, on all women's. He winks at Johnson.

Johnson will not show Big Deal what he is thinking. A certain man like me, he says, has to find himself in the company of a crowd, bump shoulders with other people.

Indeed, Big Deal says. You are for the world. Speak what you like here. I will place no claims on any admission you make within these walls.

I have picked up a fashion or two, but only the amusing ones.

Big Deal breaks into a laugh. You see, that's just what I mean, Jack. Something in me has to go out to you, for your generosity of heart. Few men of your rarity and stature would be willing to carve a portion of your day and suffer the insult of having to put up with the many silly demands of these inferior provincials.

Johnson listens to each hard melodramatic word. Understood, he says, but I've always been like that. I can go about with anyone.

Good that you do. Why, feel free to take up as many invitations as you can stomach. We both know that it's good show. But, Jack, why be a complete prisoner?

Big Deal goes on to say that, in point of fact, Johnson would naturally have a need for action, would want to embark on deeds at variance with the modest local customs and enchantments. He gives Johnson a smile that Johnson returns without hesitation.

So that's just what I will do, Johnson says. I'll keep an eye out for opportunities to be surprisingly better.

Good. I won't point the accusing finger. He pours Johnson another whiskey and one for himself. And please count on me for whatever you need.

Johnson holds the whiskey in his mouth so that he can feel his teeth, each and every one.

But you know, first you must come down and spend a few days in my house. Big Deal goes on to describe it as a getting-away place. And believe me, he says. That is no small matter in a barbaric land like this one. You are in the wrong republic if the wallaby recognizes you.

Johnson studies Big Deal's smile. The white man seems to relish challenging Johnson with questions he knows Johnson doesn't want to answer. How kind that would be, he says. But I ask that we put off my visit until after the fight. As you know, I follow a daily hygiene.

Of course you must. I am wrong to invite you. What was I thinking? Hope is good for business. They think Tommy can win, so let them go thinking that. Jack, Big Deal smiles, I ask only one thing of you. Once you get little Tommy in the ring, please make a good show of it for those motion picture cameras.

You can count on me for that, Johnson says.

Once he's outside, the correspondents stare at him for a moment before starting in with their questions.

Of course I'm happy to see you all, Johnson says. You newspapermen shed a rosy glow over life.

To a man, they hold their hands over their eyes to better see Johnson in the bright field.

Another question.

I have no opinion about that. It's better not to understand too much sometimes.

But Jack, Tommy has quite a punch. How do you plan to stay out of its way?

That, gentlemen, is the whole tragedy.

Jack, will you give a concert while you are here in Australia?

Johnson makes out the servant moving in the gaps of the crowd, now here, now there. Gentlemen, he says, I'm here to fight. I'm here to fight. Music accords us beauty, but sports make life.

The following week, the well-dressed servant shows up at Johnson's camp with a missive from Big Deal. He has started a campaign encouraging officials to decorate Johnson with an honor. As well, he is seeking the good offices of influential friends for the same purpose. Any excuse for a celebration.

Hungry for contact with his own kind, Johnson starts to frequent saloons, pool halls, bordellos, and clubs when he is not training, Johnson relaxing for a few hours in the wonderment of good company, playing cards and dominoes in rooms lit with smoke and booze and dirty words, men and women alike putting on dog and pulling to pieces, smiling right into his eyes and speaking all at once on a wide range of subjects, issuing challenges—Smell my finger—with exaggerated ease when Johnson slips down at a piano in song, leaning so low over the instrument that his face seems about to drop onto the keyboard. He has found people such as these every single place where he has traveled.

He leaves the establishment of choice with a light head, that upward swing of emotion, which indicates that he is feeling his life fully, the smell of tobacco, whiskey, suckling pig, fatback and jerky, perfume, and picked-up phrases on the breath.

One night, Johnson steps out of a bar and finds the fashionable servant waiting for him. No word passes between them. The servant turns and starts to walk, and Johnson follows him, a bit dim and unsteady, going on for some time, thirty minutes or an hour, not that he is counting, the servant starting now up a steep path overgrown with weeds, the darkness thick with the smell of putrefaction, the servant moving quick and agile up that difficult incline with the ground dropping away beneath them.

Soon they arrive at the top of a hill, the night high and clear with an endless sprawl of stars stretching above a great crowd that has gathered in wait for Johnson, men and only men, dozens of them, all completely naked, no boundary in that red light between him and them. One by one, they introduce themselves to him, old names that they have somehow held on to, that they refuse to bury. He is touched.

Then he feels motion under his feet, a slight tug, dark pressing in and rooting him down, a blank obscuring where objects in the distance lose their edges, one shape merging into another. White jacket, white shirt, white bow tie, white pants, white patent leather shoes, straw hat, he's looking down for any hint of ground beneath them. He floats above the world, afraid but unwilling to suffer the damaging consequences of his failure to regain himself and speak to this needy audience of natives who demand words from him:

My brethren, I am no more than a simple and conventional spokesman, who has but a few sentences to say to you. The Promised Land might be here. The man who cannot set himself down on the crest of the moment, forgetting everything from the past and about the past, that man will never know what happiness is. Even worse, he will never do anything to make other men happy. The first quality of a man is the elevation of his style, the purity of his speech, and his selective discipline. I stand here before you now. Let my example be vivid to you. Now, gentlemen, shall we have at a few rounds?

In November, the Burns camp convenes a press conference in Big Deal's splendid office, with all the pomp one might expect, Burns himself noticeably absent almost six months after the signing of contracts, Johnson, covered in sweat from a day of training, marinating in doubt, moody, curt, irascible, his discontent larger than the distance between this continent and Burns. The fight will never happen, he tells himself. Tommy will never show. Damn you, Tommy. Damn your bitch heart.

Then Big Deal starts to talk to all of the men assembled there. By means of a special carrier, the champion has sent a magnetic recording for them all to listen to. Big Deal places the mahogany cabinet on his desk, turns a crank, and soon Tommy's voice comes rising up out of the black box.

Many of you have asked why I would sink so low as to engage in a contest with a representative of one of the inferior races.

In first consideration, it is important to remember that I have already defeated each and every white man who was deserving of a challenge to my title.

So who is there left to fight?

Give me a white man and I will fight him.

What Johnson hears in the silence between one word and the next.

With good reason the white man imposes restrictions on the lowly black, brown, and yellow races. Even so, I do not draw the color line, although I would be the first to confess that the sight of a black man displeases me. However, fate conspires that I fight this animation of African stock, Jack Johnson. What choice do I have? That said, it seems to me that the larger public concern has been one of fairness.

In short, some of my accusers feel that I only seek to inflict cruelty on this Negroid beast, like a man kicking a lowly dog. Of course, nigger boxers are indeed of a limited caliber and lack science and skill, so there is no escaping the laws of probability. This nigger Johnson will be defeated, but hopefully without serious injury. In addition, I promise not to punish him simply because his motives are purely financial. A nigger has to eat too.

Johnson hearing it all, tucked into his chair. Sentences circling him, he continues to sit before Big Deal's desk and listen courteously to the magnetic recording as the afternoon goes on and the light grows long, thankful for this light that straps him in place in this chair restraining his violence until the recording comes to an end.

Did you hear that, Jack? The champion says that you're only doing it for money.

He's right. I want money and plenty of it. How much can a penny buy?

Why, Jack, you should be happy. The champion is granting you a fight. Only a real stand-up guy would do that.

That's right, Jack. Cheer up. Why, you never know. Your chances are good. In fact, I'm putting my money on you. The correspondent winks at him.

So we've all heard plenty from Tommy Burns, Big Deal says from behind his desk, his speech a little thick, his hands locked behind his head. What Tommy thinks is what he thinks. It's none of my business, but—write this down—I for one stand against many of his assumptions, for I am my own man, and as such, I am no racialist.

I'll write that down, Big Deal.

Please hear me out. Thank you. And so it is that I am certain that Mr. Johnson welcomes this opportunity to get Tommy into the ring and test these racial claims and show them to be the untruths that they undoubtedly are. Big Deal talking, comfortable and cool. Then he looks at Johnson. What do you say, Jack?

Johnson is careful to look Big Deal in the face before he starts to speak to the reporters. I say that I'm nothing yet. Indeed, I'm the lesser man of many of you here. He gestures with his hand. Coming to Australia has taught me that. I'm fortunate beyond measure for the lesson, because when I visit your museums and see the numerous specimens of prehistoric man's art, your boomerangs of many varieties, your stone axes from various states, the many implementations of musical instruments and cookware and utensils, and the many other examples of Paleolithic and Neolithic man's skill in art and craft and construction, why when I see all of that I simply envy you all. Your natives must have been men of genius to turn out such fine products.

The motion picture camera captures Johnson's entry into the ring, his flesh (under the light, in natural light) a single unbroken tone that resonates darkly against the pure white dominance of the ropes and the flat blank surface of the canvas. Six feet of man, muscled up perfect, game to the heart. Then on the other side of the frame, Burns ducks under the top rope. The two men face off in the center of the ring, Burns's trunks noticeably lighter in color than Johnson's.

Wow, Burns says. Just look at you. Aren't you a sight.

Yeah, Johnson says. A nigger through and through.

They strike a series of aggressive poses while the camera operator cranks the handle in timed circles, the camera shaking and groaning, the entire machine lit with noise. Big Deal has each man stand on a farm scale to record his weight, then with the greatest aplomb and care uses seamstress tape to take other bodily measurements—height, muscle size, the length of the arms.

My Dearest Hattie,

I want you to receive on Christmas Day, you and all the family, my warmest and most affectionate wishes, together with all my love. Remember me to all our friends. I bless each and every one of you and send my fond wishes. For my part, I am fairly well, adequately and solicitously looked after. Nothing is urgent, although of course, I will make you all proud. So raise a glass and say a toast. The thought of you doing so fills me with longing. I see you in every window, I hear you in every song. Be that as it may, I guess I must make do and suffer your absence since the very thought of you fills me more than another's presence ever could. I should stop there lest the yearning kill me.

Yours truly,

Jack

Johnson's gaze becomes lost in the intricate tangle of bodies puzzled into patterns as far as he can see. The sight sends him into a state of growing excitement. He hurries to his dressing room and slips out of his clothes and into his trunks. Limbers up, snapping punches into silent space until his arms and legs and chest and back are warm with his own sweat, his thoughts racing ahead to the blow that will put Burns on the canvas for the count, a moment that blooms in a bright flash inside his skull.

Johnson's voice crackles up in black circling motion: I hit him at will, whenever I wished, but I never exerted my whole power on him. At no time did Burns have a show with me. His corner did all they could to resurrect him after each round, pouring cold champagne over his head and massaging his muscles with boiled cognac, doing their best to force the air out of his bones, and calm his wheezing. What are you scared of, little boy? I asked him. Don't forget we're playing a man's game. Find that yellow streak that you talk so much about. Tommy, look at these arms, these feet, they do not wear out. One time I told him, Let me see what I can do to make your face look better. Then for the rest of the round I socked him in both eyes and on the chin.

See Burns in the shocked light. He refuses to look into the glass face of the motion picture camera. Johnson a camera himself between rounds, scanning the crowd to pick out unusual faces. He spots a colored man sitting on a fence and from there watching the fight with set eyes and open mouth. His glance returns to the man again and again. The man becomes a sort of landmark for Johnson. Mentally, he fights harder than Johnson does. Whenever Johnson unlimbers a blow, he also shoots one into the air against an invisible antagonist. When Johnson sways to avert a blow, the fighter also sways on the fence in the same direction and at a similar angle. When Johnson ducks, he ducks. But his simulated battle comes to an inglorious end when he tries to mimic one of Johnson's movements and falls off the fence.

Burns loses all sense of this way or that, fast or slow, up and down, and for what will be the final time this afternoon, goes clattering to the canvas. The footage stops just as the police enter the ring.

Jack—

Mr. Johnson to you.

My apologies. Mr. Johnson, I'm trying to wrap my head around this conflict between you and the champion, Mr. Louis.

Don't worry your brain on that one. He is one kind of man, and I am another. That's all there is to say.

Johnson stands looking at the Jim Crow diner that has refused him service. Longs to set fire to it. Maybe he should. Now he goes moving away from the establishment unwanted and wild through the dark and the light, bends and stoops himself inside his Aston Martin. The road winds through a succession of curves, all around him a sad countryside of black trees. Then he catches an angle of far-off glitter, something red in the distance that impresses itself on his sight and attention. The road starts to ripple under him before erupting into the sky.

Johnson leaves behind a storm of mourners swaying and rocking and moaning in a minor key inside a church where heat pours in through the open windows in rolling carpets of steam, and where light itself congeals into heat, cleaving to the benches and floors, and to the clothes and skin of all of those assembled, who sing as is their wont, song forming white shapes that hover and hold in the air. With paper fans the mourners wave the shapes into motion.

Later at the cemetery, the pallbearers lower the waterproof casket modeled in the form of a boxing glove down into the earth on lengths of silken rope. The pastor clears his throat, looks directly into the motion picture camera, and begins the eulogy. Listening to the body, the mourners know the pattern, the responses and the breaks, seed sense and memory into an image that flowers into a full cinematic frame, the wide golden grin through which all time wants to escape.

PART 2

Water Will Carry Us Back

Pinocchio

"Please give my reflection a break from the face it's seeing now."

—Rihanna

My sister is trying to get me to put my grandnephew in my band.

I tell her, I already got a guitarist.

Yeah, she says, but it ain't him.

And it ain't gon be him. Ain't he sick?

Sugar. Just sugar.

Sugar? I'm thinking, First I heard about it. Shit, I was talking about his crutches. The nigger walks on crutches. Didn't even know about the sugar. Cannonball had sugar. Dolphy had sugar. Plenty of niggers dead from sugar. But I don't tell her that.

Yeah, sugar. Just hear him play.

Cicely keeps giving me advice where it's not wanted. I'm open to her words as long as they don't involve the music, my music.

Hearsay, she says. People calling him out of his name.

Is it? I say.

Problem is, I don't know what to believe. Got to keep an open mind. Rumor is just that. In this world full of haters and the self-righteous, evil tongues will say anything.

Cicely says she don't want to hear all that who-did-what, that who-shot-John. So what if Herbie likes men? Why do you care? He's your pianist. You ain't got to fuck him.

I look at her sideways. You got some lip on you, I say.

You should have thought about that before we got married.

I wasn't thinking about it then and I ain't thinking about it now.

So go ahead and fire him, she says.

Now you telling me who to fire?

The air in the room moves from the corners.

No, she says. I'm just trying to help you tell yourself, seeing that this is such a cause of concern. What will the world think if it turns out you got a—

You got a lot to say today.

The room listens. She hums back into resolution. As it should be. She should know by now, you're either for me or against me. No in between. Like music. Only two kinds. Good or bad. No in between. We are stable: me, Cicely, the furniture and other objects, stability everywhere on the earth.

You want to hear a joke? she says.

Shoot.

How many New Yorkers does it take to change a lightbulb?

What?

It's a knock-knock joke. Knock knock.

What?

How many New Yorkers does it take to change a lightbulb?

How many?

What the fuck do you care?

Wait for the right moment. Then catch into it with everything you have. One bar may hide another bar in the same way that one complaint usually holds another. (Why an argument once it gets started can never end.) Be in there somewhere. When you think too much you get something you don't mean.

Begin with yourself underfoot. The beat is laid on your shoulders. Get up on the one.

The point between here and there is where you are your best. In coming to find a note you may find another. The call, the response. The sweet science of improvisation.

I came naked out of the mother. My daddy, a dentist, bought me the best garments for my body. (Got that from him, the clothing bug.) I never had to elbow my way up.

Music? I took if from where it came from.

As for anything good, you play it for me and I'll listen to it.

Music recalls its steps. Ahead. And that feeling of coming after, late, behind the beat. When you're soloing, when you come to a passage, breathe and be patient so you can hear all that is there.

Let it lift and steady you.

Get up on the one. Get up as high as you can get.

The elevator opens. It's full of white people, ofays. I don't step on. Too white for me, I say. The doors close.

Unknown dust near me. Darkness in the trees. The white buildings leaning into the ground. The sky spread out. My ears penetrated by the noise of frogs and crickets. My body. And mosquitoes flying about. The grass wrapped in clouds of red and white. The streetlamp casts tiny globes of light, little planets. The curb kneels so I may cross. Breathing on all sides. All things on all sides in motion. Darkness running on all fours.

I am the Prince of Darkness. My shadow lengthens at night. Night extends me.

Cicely, I have lost you. Have I lost you? How could I let that happen? You left me. I forced you to leave me.

You're still in my heart. I can feel you go through there. Jigsaw fragments. Returning always.

Take this as it settles, then: why should we mean nothing to each other when we're really nothing?

I'm making no gestures. You're two years older than me. The

wiser one. More experienced. More mature. You are always the wiser.

Other troubles I can stand. Money. Ofays. Family. Music. But my woman?

My form takes up with you best.

Who took the message? Who lost the keys? Who left the door unlatched? Who forgot the dry cleaning? I left the sprinkler on? The heart going out over everything.

Out walking. Trying to clear my head. Thawed afternoon. Dust in the shallow air, green notes. Fog rising from my mouth. The light breeze can't sway the branches. Black buildings thicken around me. Instead of going home, I walk some more, walk until I can't walk anymore and just stay put, remain standing, my shadow growing inch by inch, a giant.

There is a certainty that makes us love each other. So how then did this separation come about?

Shaped by whatever breath I draw, whatever I finger. Lungs and hands. Valves and stops. The trumpet convinces the hand, the mouth that what you have you hold to practice with to play with to pose with. Backbreaking leisure. The stalled tightening of a run. The buzzing in the beehive of the mute. A language takes hold. What calls me is that sound that announces, insists at each moment that I am individual. Dark dazzle. Blowing fresh.

The music teacher lends me some sheet music ("St. Louis Blues"). He asks me to let him hold my clarinet (my second instrument, something to cut my musical teeth on). Weeks pass but he never returns my reed. I ask for it back.

Sure, Miles. After you return my sheet music.

I gave that back to you weeks ago.

He looks at me. Young man, let me tell you one thing. I have a PhD in niggerology. Don't try to run games on me.

I gave it back to you.

When you come clean, you can have your clarinet.

I thought about it. Where do you keep your sheet music?

He pointed to the place.

Motherfucker, go look.

Death, get all the way away. I will concede to anything stronger than I am. Give up. But even Death the butcher can't cut me down. Only memory dies. When I was a kid I saw a little girl get hit by a truck. She lay in the middle of the street. The blood was thick like one big red note dropping from her body, the sound all the other notes wrap themselves around. Over the years I have lost so much of the day, how the recollections thin and disappear. I am no more certain than you are of the details. In her bright colorful dress she resembled a pink silhouette against the black tarmac. One foot propped behind her. This apparent precision of gesture. The shoe off. The layers clear now in the slant light of remembrance.

I ran home, the world tilting this way and that.

For days after, for weeks, for months, perhaps for years, I was spooked. Something would startle me, a voice in a room I thought was empty, pushing a door open and catching sight of a blurred shape fleeing from the room, an echo in a room that shouldn't be there, my body making an extra shadow. Some slight fear of the dark even now. Spooked.

My grandnephew Tony wears his hair slicked back, a wing over each shoulder. He's chilling with his knucklehead friend, some nigger whose name I didn't catch, whose name ain't worth remembering.

A week later I hear his crutches thump rubber feet against the floor. No easy matter to both walk on crutches and carry an instrument. He carries his axe the right way, like a fragile mummy.

He sees me and breaks out into a great grin. Uncle Miles.

Hobbles into the room, his right leg bent back away from the floor flamingo-like. He's got his own style, dressed in vintage clothes, ruffled sleeves, checkered pants, all of him sunk into a motorcycle boot on his left foot.

He looks at the bowl of blow sitting on my counter, his big gaze opening by the minute. What has he gotten himself into?

Nigger, I say, that ain't popcorn.

I point to a chair, and like a construction worker making his way down from a scaffold, he maneuvers his crutches then flops down into the chair.

I hold him in a long gaze, but he doesn't seem to be intimidated. Only perks up his ears to take in what I'm listening to. He grabs one crutch and uses his ringed finger to tap out a little polyrhythm, Philly Joe Jones, then laughs out loud, taken with himself.

He's handsome, a pretty boy, smooth skin, Roman features, smiling an animated smile, but balding prematurely (thirty-three years old), his receding hairline like a body of water at low tide. Our chairs closely approaching, he rushes into talk, a mouthful, selling himself. How good he is. How he's ambidextrous. And how he owns both left-handed and right-handed axes. How he has perfect pitch. How he can read. How he knows all my songs and thousands more à la Sonny Rollins. Everything he will bring to my band.

I'm thinking, A damaged boy with an instrument.

I ask him about his leg. He rolls up his pants leg, unwraps the brown bandage, shows me his calf black with the missing flesh as if bitten by a dirty-toothed shark, the whole muscle eaten away.

How did that happen?

Two years ago.

Two years ago?

Yeah, he says. At the end of the semester during final exams. I took my last exam, knew I had aced it. I was so happy, so proud, so relieved after all the stress. So I found me an empty classroom, took a seat over by the radiator and figured I'd take a nap. I touched the radiator. It was cold to the touch, the heat off, the room nice and cool, so I propped my legs up on the radiator to get comfortable. Fell asleep. When I woke up I smelled a funny smell. This is the leg that was actually touching the radiator.

Your leg was burning and you couldn't feel that shit?

No. I guess because of the diabetes.

I shake my head. Ain't that a bitch.

Yeah. Surgeries and skin grafts and more surgeries. Antibiotics. All because of one nap. The doctors don't think it will heal and want to amputate. Fuck that shit.

I keep looking at him. Let them take your leg. If they cut off my dick I'd find a way to get it back. As long as I have my mind.

He just looks at me.

Anyway, fuck all the talking, motherfucker. Just play something.

He picks up his axe and plays me something, blows my mind. Sounds like Jimi.

I see myself rising to give him a spoonful of cocaine.

At least once a week someone rings my bell thinking my house is still a place of worship. I open the door and find a living breathing person on my doorstep. I only let in the ones I know I can fuck. (The evil of living.) The pretense of amazement when I open the door—How did you find me? You've come to the right place. God must have sent you to me—letting sunlight and a body into the granite airy space. The basilica remains untouched: confessionals—a priest's haunted face behind the grille of one booth for all eternity—side altars, baptismal fountains, stained glass windows, the holy pictures and crucifixes, oval prints and paintings of ordained faces, and the reliquary housing the flesh from a saint (lips, I'm told).

Through my body I see, feel all the other bodies I have had.

They come. And I await them. Summoned. In the depths of one face I can see all the faces I've had.

I'll take them into me, the ones that come here, my house, this old basilica, a listening post.

A perfect set. The band takes bows. I look at Al Foster. Played his ass off tonight. Solid shifts of drumming charged with invented changes. Fat time. I go over and kiss him on the mouth. Fat Time.

It took a black cat to make two white cats play their asses off. Jimi.

The sense that she was trying too hard. The flowers perfectly arranged. Lemon-scented soap. A gondola. In the middle of her fucking living room. Framed watercolors of every variety (storms, landscapes, still lifes, portraits) cheapen the sight of a Steinway with lid raised up. Chimes out on the balcony, banking in and out of view. The view of the city in the windows muted through the glass. Pastel walls. Painted birds. Light seems to come from everywhere. Her crib more like a supposition than the real. *Suppose I place this here.*

I had accepted her invitation. Is this what I'd been waiting all week for? Too eager to visit, now too eager to leave. Not the first or last time a rich white person will invite me to their home because I'm Miles Davis.

She enters the room with a bulky mobile phone pushed to her ear, her appearance a mixture of formal and casual. Wearing flip-flops. (That crunch sound like a shoe pressing into snow.) Her face makeup-less, shining with power. (What difference does it make how you look close-up?) A long tangle of fat pearls. A silk scarf. Rich white bitch.

She wipes back her dark hair and greets me joyfully. It doesn't feel good to touch her hand.

She's edging in, bringing me a cup of tea. The charms on her bracelet jingle. I take a few sips then set the cup back onto the silver serving tray.

The curtains sway softly.

She asks me some question about my music. What can I say?

I say what's on the tip of my tongue. Too late in the day to think anything through.

I find myself in her garden. The hedges have grown past the height of the windows like stacks of children's blocks. Several grasses grow raggedly together. A branch bends burdened with six-winged birds spying on our conversation. She speaks very little, sensing that I have things on my mind. We go a little way into the greenish, almost submarine grotto of a cluster of tall trees, where we hear wind lashing and rain splashing on the top branches. Sunshine in the rain.

The sound of the afternoon starting to part. About us the environment crumbles in red light, bits of darkness gathering around us, the darkness that appears as patches of black gauze, banners.

Stained with sunset, she moves through the dark garden, her heavy funnel of skirt bearing her down like a bell, an anchor.

She says I should learn to ride horses. The talking authority of she who knows, passed on with a look of hard-ass wisdom. I could tell her that my daddy was rich, a dentist, and owned his own farm where I learned to ride horses.

Fireflies spark on and off around us.

Okay, I say. But only if you'll teach me.

Saying these words because we should play white people, play them for what we can get, even if we don't need what they give, gift. Listen, don't get on the elevator with them. Instead, wait for them to invite you into their home. Then take them for everything you can.

A train hurtling through lonely night. Finding my way home.

The look I see on my father's face. For days I walk my father's farm sick, living on the nerve. Pulsing at the cold borders of a world borne down by smack like a black iceberg frozen in place. Heart high sorrowful, burning forehead, parched tongue. Heat making me. The wind making my body ruffle. The wind pummels a tree, and the branches rise and fall like a conductor's baton, thick leaves spilling to the ground. That same wind rolls the earth over, waves.

I rotate inside the black silo of my body, burrowing into the tunnel of the past. The hours given and taken in school. The scuffles in the coatrooms, the arguments with my mother and pissing contests with my father (strong-willed and stubborn like me; he gets it from me, Father of Darkness). The scrapples in the Apple, the time sat beside the sick and dying holding their hands, feeling their last days, the light going out in the body, the cells going dark. (I will never die.) And the cats like Navarro, Clifford, Cannonball, Dolphy (bean eater), Chambers, Bird (grimy motherfucker), Trane, Jimi (horny motherfucker), and Rhoads who died before their time like leaves that drop from trees too early.

I hurry back up the river of time until I splash into the sea where present past and future exist all at once. Fat time. My brain passes me pictures of the future. See myself. Older now. So much still inside me. Prowling the streets in the shook heart of New York. Full of energy. Saddled. A horse. Looking to fuck, get high. The city dragging strays about it. Down and out in New York City. Sirens reddening the air. What can be remembered and can never be forgotten. (What is the word for a future foretold and remembered?)

Memory stops. So much still beyond the reach of my eyes.

The sun sinks toward the darkening hills. Dark bodies pass by far out at the horizon, a countryside of black plants. Gobble up. Strong horse circling for me alone. I circle with it until I can catch up, hop on, ride. Raking my fingers through the horse's mane. Blood galloping inside my body. Thousands of years go by. Wheezes of air. Past the gatepost stained with goat's blood. Along the edge of the woods that echo a rustling junction. Through the cemetery, the gravestones rising and falling in sleep. Following riding/walking trails through bent grasses that go over long fields, including a stubble field with water standing in it. Small in the passed-through air, I dismount. Move through that swinging soil. Drink water with my hands, my cupped fingers ladling silt.

On the damp steps of the Mississippi River I lose my footing. A half me of water, a half me of air.

I must fall no further. Breathe in rectangular solitude. Listen. Uncontested spasms. Listen. All the way back into life. My ear in each stone. Hearing everything the world has made this day.

Flocks of birds moving in their great element, turn their eyes down and see me, turn back in the air. Fuck you too, motherfuckers.

The house is winding its way across the fields.

Trembling. Particles of skin flaking away. Coughing bits of flesh. I use pipe cleaners to poke the sludge clogging my veins but no luck at getting them open, clear. I move along the ground near the fallen twigs.

The sun stands out in black on a reddish background like a funeral chariot on a piece of terra-cotta. The doctor arrives, rattling with green bottles full with the light of the sky. He speaks to me in even tones. Brain-ready, he plans to inject me, thinks I will let him. No. Only one way beyond this pain, addiction. Cold turkey.

He can't believe what he's hearing. Starting to humor me.

Listening upward, two shapes inside me rise and move away. I say, Leave, motherfucker. Carry your doctoring ass off this farm.

He does.

I hear far in and far out from me.

I rise and walk. Going to show the bats and the birds and the rockets and satellites that I can fly too. Prince of Darkness. Rise above the high trees surrounding the house, far into the piney tops. Beaming distances. Idling in space. The moon rolls on in shadow. At this elevation, I feel deprived of weight. How uncommon the light when clouds clear. I lean back from the glow of the moon. I can always come back to earth.

Frances the dancer: her slim legs like a tuning fork. Wife number one.

We were the same height, the same size. I make an accidental discovery. I can fit into her clothes, into her shoes. Wearing her around the house becomes habit. Like an extension of myself, another me, Miles plus.

Betty: wife number two.

Everyone wants to know: will Jimi and I record? I want to. Then I catch them together, Betty and Jimi, tangled in six strings.

I can't stand a pianist with busy hands. All that thumping around. Making all the right motions but one. So I tell him, Play like you don't know how to play piano.

Play a little more of that.

Set list: E.S.P. Spring. Cicely. Paraphernalia. Dolores. Masqualero. Ice Nine. Freedom Jazz Dance. Riot. Hand Jive. Nefertiti. Prince of Darkness.

What is it like to be a musician? I hear music all the time, even now. I heard my father's deep voice rumbling from the body of his layers of tailored clothing. I hear the cry of small animals in the furs I wear. Fuck them.

The world tells me what it wants to tell me. Can't turn it off. Tell me, freight train. Tell me in the voice of the sea, deep structured roar, or in the light chirping of a bird. Train. Whistle. Trumpet.

Now and then I wish I had the option of taking my chances with silence.

You're supposed to like your "listeners," be grateful for these ordinary motherfuckers because they buy your records and come to your shows. Fans. Fan clubs. No, I wish I could club all these motherfuckers. Clobber them. They take up all the space in the world, suck up all the air, crowd you into corners. No, motherfucker, I don't care if you like my music. No, I don't want to meet your girlfriend or your wife. Take that bitch and get out of my face. Give me some room. Some quiet time to myself.

Can't you see I'm here drinking at the bar. I don't want to see no fucking body.

The one good thing about being on stage, the chance to be alone with motherfuckers you want to spend time with. That's why I turn my back to those ordinary motherfuckers sitting out there looking at me, admiring me, wishing they could be me.

Give me your money. I don't owe you shit. You should be eating crumbs out of my hand.

Motherfucker, you want to do something for me? Here's what you can do. Cut off your arm. Cut off your leg. Better yet, just slice your throat from ear to ear and die. Give me some room to breathe.

Before I can reach her, Cicely senses me like an owl, flies up to the ceiling, wings spread, claws out, beak at the ready. I leave the herd of four-legged furniture, three-legged stools, and one-legged lamps for the garden. Cicadas cover the ground like carpet bombs dropped from a fleet of war planes. They don't relent. I think about Cicely, her features glazed. Color and velocity.

I sit down on a low two-armed swing and study the garden sexual with ferns, butterflies, banana trees, flaring branches, twittering birds, droning bees.

Cicely, why are you still with me? Don't you know by now who I am?

Miles, she would say, I know where you been and who with. She would reel off facts: name, place, positions, the number of strokes it took for me to come.

Still, she doesn't know me.

I've said all I have to say. If the thing hasn't been said this way, then the Devil can't say it.

She keeps a compact inside her antelope purse. She fills the sink with water, removes the compact, stares into her reflection. Puts her mirror at the bottom. Every day her face becomes clearer. Can't she see me there? Mirror mirror on the wall, who's the meanest son of a bitch of them all? Me, the Prince of Darkness.

Darkness feeds me, sustains me, provides longevity, eternity. I cannot die. Be that as it may, Cicely saved me, more than once. Like the time I snorted the longest line of blow ever, around the four corners of a room inside the apartment of an abandoned building, snorted from one corner to the next then out the door, into the hallway, along the floor to the next corner, then around the corner, through the door, and onto the stoop where Cicely waited.

Motherfuckers think they want religion. They don't want no religion. Every angel is terrifying, not just me. Religion is a bitch.

Dazzling with drink, Jimi glides forward to take the joint.

I dig Jimi. So much is not spoken. We compare notes. Which bitches are fuckin and which bitches are not. Who among our friends believes in free love—I fucking don't—and who does not. The best characteristics of Band-Aids.

I toss off the wine. Jimi tips the last drops of the bottle onto his tongue.

My fingers crack. Hands. I paint my daybreak. Folded in faint light. The snot and blow clotted inside my nostrils. Trudge. No words as well. The skin touches glow. I smell the odor emanating from the canvas. A few random straws from the brush sticking to the trapped canvas like whiskers or trapped rays of sunlight. I breathe. The air getting raw between me and the canvas. Blue and red squares. Fragile yellows, rich greens. White nailed there. What these colors are growing through. I extend my figures, laying out in circles. The thing itself before it is made into anything.

In the looking glass it's you I see, time after time. Wobbly with dimensions.

The phone rings.

Why the fuck you calling me?

Your nephew here in the studio.

I said why the fuck you calling me? What's my nephew got to do with me?

He's here at the studio.

Nigger, I ain't deaf. I heard. He's there and I'm here. I'm painting today.

. . .

Is there anything else?

He really thought you was going to be here since you told him to come.

Did I say I was going to be there?

. . .

Just let him play his part. I'll listen over the phone. And then pay him.

I don't think he needs the money. His father—

I don't give a fuck who his father is or was or what he did or how much money he got. I already told you. I'm painting today.

I take out my phone to show my nephew and his friend a holograph of me when I was young, just starting out like them.

How old are you?

How old do I look?

Hard to tell.

Uncle Miles, you been around forever.

Longevity, I say.

Forever.

Since Bible days.

You got jokes. I can still open a can of whoop ass.

Damn, bruh. The OGs always come quick with the violence. I thought you was a professional man, whatever profession they had back in biblical times.

They got a good laugh.

The window with the measure of its own light. Light seeps under the door, through the walls.

Sound of suitcases snapping shut. Time is a canvas. Said she was leaving. So go ahead and leave. I bought her some boxes.

Her shades on the table. Nothing but air where she had been moments before.

Three wives. I'll never get married again. At least to a woman.

The trance of driving. I steer my whip up a light beam to the stars. And I return to earth just as fast, a drop of sweat falling from a chin.

The cop signals me over.

I pull over but don't kill the engine. The doors lift like two wings and I step out of the whip. Exposed. Like a turtle out of its shell. How do I look? My hair brushed back, shellacked in a windblown manner like the speed of my whip. The day is all sun. I don't remove my shades. They blaze with darkness. My whip idling in its nest of smoke.

You want to remove the sunglasses.

I would prefer not to.

Remove the sunglasses.

. . .

Whose car is this?

Nigger, it's your mamma's car.

I stand wobble-rooted. Human faces swim through the fog inside my head. I remember the way the cop's face popped on, glowing with anger.

They stagger me with their lights, their questions, the room pitching and rolling. I have to hold on to Frances.

How many times did the cop hit you?

Do you think I was counting?

Did you say something smart to him?

I am smart. I always say something smart.

Will you sue them? The police department? The city?

I'm going to do more than that.

What can we do to help?

I take off my red-stained blazer and flip it to the reporter. Here, take that to the dry cleaners and see if they can get the blood out.

You're either for me or against me.

I tell everyone that.

Don't try to change me.

I told her, Cicely, you can't change me. Just help me get clean.

I can't get rid of myself enough to just be with one woman.

Cicely, you are my sunshine. Raying in and out of my body. My sunshine.

I'm listening.

I attended the awards ceremony in an outfit of my own design, studded with creatures.

The shape of sound. The shape of light. The shape of sense. The shape of years. The shape of dreams. The shape of the blues. The shape of listening.

The microphone buzzed at first, more common than you might think. I stand under the overhead lights, at the edges of the darkness.

I raise my trumpet up vertical in front of me, antennae pulling a million sounds through the air, all the frequencies. My consciousness hovers like a cloud above my head.

I fly into the lines. Shoots of joy.

Sound winds into the ear, far back into the head. The mud brightens under my feet. I can feel the music through all distances and time. The notes fall off the sheet like rotting worms.

I change my body into time. Fat time. Incredible to myself, music all up in my body.

The producer touches a button on his computer. He touches another button. Everything seems purposeful. I'm not about to set the time right, get up on the one. His beat. His groove. So be it. Wait and make the sound surrounding "No."

Now a soft option, a few light thumps. Some sound comes jangling along. Jimi. Sampled. And Herbie too. Sampled. I play my riff. Quotations start to rise.

Now a slow plunge and lift. I play my riff although I don't feel equal to the track. I'm already sensing a new shift, the anticipation for what is to come already giving way to some other feeling I cannot name.

It comes. A new sound. Me. Sampled. Musical hand-me-downs. Another Miles.

I play my riff, the day with its usual tangle. Wait for the loop to come back around. What will I find when I return?

Swirling sentences. So many words for the dead.

All of us stand round in silence looking at the casket. The pull of six strings of grief toward the grave.

Throat-sick, I can utter no words about Jimi.

Jimi. How shall I mark his departure? In the grave he will not rot. Maybe he will bring himself back alive. What is the hardest part about coming back alive?

The host asks the rapper about his religious beliefs.

Speaking in a southern twang—did they say he's from New Orleans? Houston? Atlanta?—he gives a rambling monologue filled with long passages of obscenity (he has a fixation on shit), oaths, aphorisms, curses, and his Five Percenter beliefs—he keeps calling the host God—that makes the air buzz violently around his head bee-like, a beehive of thoughts about his head.

Then the question is put to me.

I say, The question is too hard to answer.

During the commercial break, I whisper, We should record together.

Old-timer, he says, I would like nothing more. This time, speech bubbles pop up above his head.

The hosts ask him about his significant other and his children.

He turns the rage of his monologue against himself, saying he wishes he was a better husband and a better father, but he's nothing more than a pimp player hustler pussy-harasser.

The question is put to me.

I never talk publicly about my wives and kids. No family shit.

Back to the rapper: and what about his influences?

He speaks another block paragraph, reciting his pride in all he knows, going all the way back to the origins of hip-hop, an archive.

My answer to the question: Everything.

The host asks still another question.

The rapper thinks hard. The thought has completely exhausted me, he says.

I say, Such youth, such gaiety, such free and easy ways.

The rapper responds in a spill of syllables.

Do you like touring?

I bend my frown into the camera's light. Say, Who can prove one place more than another? The man who finds his homeland sweet is a tender beginner. He to whom every soil is as his native one is already strong; but he is perfect to whom the entire world is as a foreign land. Let the place talk.

What makes you such a good bandleader decade after decade?

Since they rely on me, the judgment I form is important. They are stronger with me than against me. Reach the heights together. The rise of any bird is larger the larger the bird is. A leader. Not some ordinary motherfucker like 95 percent of the world. What it means to be a leader. Support and surpass.

The hosts asks me, How do you keep young? You don't seem to grow old. You have outlived all your peers. You're almost one hundred years old and still going strong. What's the secret?

I can't tell him that I owe my longevity to darkness. Instead, I answer him with questions of my own. Why must I never repeat myself? Why do I grow into something new, invent new styles?

Where will I go? Who will I meet? What will I do? What am I after?

I look at the score, hand-steadying brightness. That note is not saying what you think.

When I step out my door, the trees go motionless, holding their leaves back. Darkness massing behind me.

Like Dracula, I come in and out of being with a ghostly drift of wings. Silence and slow time. Release blackness onto whiteness.

I move unevenly across the room, hitting joyfully against objects in the dark. I starfish onto the floor, into the pool, onto the bed.

My nightmares rise and fall. Now crossing the body, in and out and around. Now under the body, up and down.

Nothing for the mouth.

I dream. I play a note and my trumpet grows an inch. Another note another inch. And so on, notes and inches. By the time I awaken, my trumpet stretches from coast to coast.

Traveled too much. Screwed too much. Drank too much. Spent too much. Scored too much. Too much love. All the postcards sent. The gifts bought. The places I never got to.

Where haven't I been? What haven't I done? Who is there left to meet? Just one life. The old cliché. Life is short, so they say.

It all hangs together. What they call a career. The designs of time. What they call a body of work, your oeuvre. You made it. *You made it.* And you changed music five times. How many people can say that? Fifty years of fingers, of mouth. Five times. Move among stars. Keep the ground turning with the earth. Set the heavens moving around us. Five times. I know. And I ain't dead yet.

One day my doctor says, Miles, eventually the wheels will fall off.

Thanks, motherfucker.

He says, Once you turn fifty the warranty runs out on everything.

He wants to replace my hip with metal from a newly discovered planet. Why not? I had three trumpets made from the material. Good shit.

Other things also need to be replaced. All my body bolted together with rare metal.

Filled with fluid, his body is wide as a tree trunk. His right arm is swollen the size of a tree, too heavy for him to lift. He's lying on his right side, his right arm extended, his defeated body like a black horizon along the white bed.

He tries to lift his head to greet me. Uncle Miles, I'm sorry you have to see me this way.

I grab a chair and pull it in full view of the bed and sit where he can see me without straining himself. You're all fucked up, I say. A sight for sore eyes. Just try to get well.

He mumbles a response.

I want to touch him but I can't. I'm sure he now regrets not letting them amputate his blackened leg, infection coursing all through his body.

I sit with him for as long as I can, sit until I can no longer tolerate the smell of sickness, of death.

I say, Call me if you need anything.

Taking the last look. I watch him, alone in my body, alone in my sweat.

Just wait, Uncle Miles, he says. The next time you see me I'll be up out of this bed and walking around the room.

The Lucky Ones

"You know how when something really touches you . . ."

—Leonora Carrington

Here I feel welcome. A room of my own, spacious compared to where I lived, the compound cluttered with too many families and the two-room house too small for me and my kids. Here a bare expanse of walls and floor. And machines clocking my bodily functions and forcing the life spilling out back in. Not bad, all things considered.

Up until recently our biggest concern had been the drought. For years running the reservoir levels decreasing throughout the country from lack of rain and encroaching desert, forcing each person to take on the burden of rationing water even here in the city.

But we managed. I managed. The most important thing, I had a job and could provide for my family. I had not much else. The type of poverty one can manage. Even be proud of.

I was given to spending time with the Leather Lady every evening after work. We had long been firm friends, from the day my husband and I as newlyweds took up residence in the compound more than a decade earlier. Turning away from the compound, we would take a slow spin around the neighborhood, passing by many spots that were hot, dangerous. But we were safe since gangsters never do their dirt at home. Then too she dressed in a way that could not escape notice and that identified her to every beholder, always some combination of brown leather—pants and a top, or jumper, a skirt, and sandals that encircled her calves and shins with straps, even an ankle-length leather dress. Topped by a leather cowboy hat with small birds perched along the brim.

I was always surprised by the ease and swiftness of her movement. Life had thickened her and slowed her down, but she still maintained a plurality of youthful features. Her face entirely made up. Acrylic nails attached to her fingers like colorful beetles.

In the course of our walks she might smoke a cigarette or two, and she would speak to me about her day. (Now she made whatever she could from babysitting, cooking, sewing, running errands, and other odds and ends.) She never permitted her past to come up in conversation, and she wasn't the type of older woman to know-it-all you, to advise and chastise. Rather, when you wanted her advice or her opinion, she was quick to say, "Oh, I don't know. What do you think?"

The only time I ever heard her speak her mind was when the quarantine was announced. We started out on our nightly walk, masks fitted over our mouths. I asked her what I should do. She offered me a cigarette. Taking no chances, I declined. She accepted the risk. Took a few puffs. She was insistent that I remain at home during the quarantine. Once back at my house, we sat down on the stoop. The stars were out above us, light pasted to night. She was sweating, so removed her hat and used it to fan herself. For the first time I caught a glimpse of her hair, microbraids patterned into small squares, each braid drawn tightly to connect it to another.

We decided it would be best for me to spend the twenty-one days of the quarantine at the studio. Would eat, bathe, and sleep there. And while some would starve, I would continue to earn a wage, and be safe doing so. Of course, I would miss my children. That would be the worst of it. Still, all things considered . . . so, when the time came, I kissed them in turn then entrusted them into the Leather Lady's care.

The job never stretched my faculties or talents, but having any job was no small thing in our country when work was drying up along with the water, leaving a desert of unemployment and a few sparse oases of hand-to-mouth hustling. I was one of the lucky ones.

Up until the time that my husband found out about my job, we were the happiest couple in the compound. To this day I'm not sure how he found out, but the night he confronted me I did not lie.

I'm not giving up my job, I said.

No? You'll just continue to let the whole world see? he said.

I'm not giving up my job.

He let the subject drop. Conducting himself according to the laws of his making as a man, he stopped speaking to me. Affected disdain whenever I tried to talk to him about the subject and make peace. When his voice finally returned after a few weeks, he had packed up his few belongings and was threatening to leave.

Do it all on your own, he said, since you like your job that much.

But it required only a few words for the Leather Lady to coax him out of the house that night, to have him rather than me accompany her on her nightly walk. What would come of it? Much. When he returned to the house, I could tell he was restored to his old self, even if his pride remained hurt.

A few weeks later, just as things were getting back to normal, he got killed on the job while making a delivery. His coworker was behind the wheel. My husband was always a careful driver so I still wonder if that change might have made a difference. I'm left with the knowledge that he and his coworker had to be pulled from under seven other vehicles piled up on top of theirs. Authorities said they'd never seen anything like it. Like magnets stuck together. Nothing good came out of it. (What could?) At least the policy provided enough money to give him a proper sending off, and enough food and drink for everyone who knew him to celebrate his memory.

My boss was astonished that I showed up for work the day after his funeral. But I am a practical woman. Without his paycheck, there could be no days off and there would be many double shifts.

I fitted the mask onto my face and snapped rubber gloves onto my hands, then left the compound, made my way to the long queue of dollar vans, ducked inside the one with the fewest people and paid my fare, then took a seat at the back, trying to make myself small, doing what I could to maintain distance from the other passengers. By then this habit of conducting myself like a leper had stuck, but soon there were too many bodies inside. Against regulations, the driver insisted on the van being full before he took off.

The ride took an hour. Once I exited the minivan, I started the long trek up the hill. Before I knew really what was happening, they came up strong behind me, two men. They wanted my purse, but I refused to relinquish it. They shoved and pushed me, and I punched and kicked. I would not make it easy for them. We tussled, fell to the ground, and started to roll down the hill, drawn down by gravity and the weighted anchor of my purse. Once again, I found myself prone on the ground where I'd exited the van. One gangster was quick to produce a knife even before he regained his feet. He slashed the straps of my purse, allowing his partner to snatch it from my hands.

Not the first time. And probably not the last. Gangsters are always looking for a jackpot. I could have lost my head completely. Instead, I fitted my mask back into place without a thought and continued back up the hill to the studio. The moment I stepped through the door, the other women (of comparable fortune, poor like myself, survivors, lucky to be working) saw the state I was in and came and stood excited around me. Set about setting me right. Washed away the dirt, cleaned my nicks and cuts, put some salve on my bruises. Someone even kneaded a quick massage. Helped. Considerably. I stretched a bit, trying to limber up, still sore, but this would have to do.

As soon as I logged on, a client punched in his request. I complied, performed a ring dance around the bed, my limbs moving without thinking. Trying to stretch the session out as long as I could. Then the first cough made my jaw drop like a cartoon character.

I couldn't keep up with all the doctors were saying to me. Too much at once. Breathing like spacemen while an intern took notes, writing backward with her left hand, writing forward with her right.

The nurses flipped through the door with plenty of warm words. Blue-skinned, they swim about my room like dolphins, leaping above me to insert an IV or inject medicine. Then swim away.

My skin dry and ashy although pumped full of fluid, the memories pumped back in so they can circulate, my arms and legs filled, bloated. My chest rises like a parachute catching air then deflates, rises again.

The priest asked me if I had anything to get off my chest. And when I did not answer he pried my mouth open and put slips of paper on my tongue.

Once, I woke up in the middle of the night and still half-asleep called out for the Leather Lady. The stars outside my window answered back, rattling like tambourines. There would be no visitors.

And that was when I heard something pop, felt fluid spilling out of me and splashing through the floor, enough to replenish this land.

March 11, 2020
Johannesburg, South Africa

Big Ugly Baby

"If you had a twin, I would still choose you . . ."

—Drake

Two Lamonts

When I was living out there in Colorado, Mr. Hines said, I had this big house with a deck and a huge yard, and I had this tall fence surrounding my property. Must have been a good twenty feet high. No, higher than that. Thirty feet. Thirty-five. I liked to sit out there on my deck and just enjoy the clear air and the view, snowy peaks and all that. The fence was so high that it looked like the sky was sitting down right on top of it.

Lamont nudged Hatch and whispered, Yo, what is this nigger talking about? Curly hair atop his head like a pet, he was seated at the desk next to Hatch, his wide and muscular chest moving with deep breaths under his T-shirt, face and torso loud with snuffing sounds and noisy breathing like somebody snoring while wide awake.

You tell me, my nigger.

So one day I'm just sitting there drinking a glass of sherry and watching my two dogs scampering around the yard. I had two big Dobermans, male and female, full grown. I'm just sitting there, and the next thing I know, I see this mountain lion up on top of the fence, big son of a bitch, just sitting there looking at my dogs. And those Dobermans saw that mountain lion, and they got real still and quiet. Then that mountain lion jumped off the fence, scooped up the male Doberman in his mouth, and jumped right back over the fence with him.

Story done, Mr. Hines looked out at the class, his face composed, no emotion, the meaning of his anecdote unclear. Would he explain? No. He stood up from his chair, came around his desk, and sat down majestically straight on the hard desktop, his attention hovering over the class, looking at them with interrogatory watchfulness, his short dreads intertwined like the tentacles of an octopus atop his head. Each day he wore a loopy length of platinum chain around his collared neck instead of a tie. He continued his surveillance of the class, filling the room with the scent of some new and exotic cologne or body oil or aftershave, nothing like anything Hatch had ever smelled.

He started to hold forth on a new topic, providing blunt facts about a tribe in the South Pacific who believe that men have limited life force (sperm), making necessary a practice where young men suck off older men to inherit it.

Smiley said loud enough for everyone to hear, Lamont, come over here and drink some of my life force.

The class flashed up in laughter.

Mr. Hines gave Smiley a sudden seizing glance. Mr. Buttersworth, only grown men have life force, so I think that leaves you out.

Laughter now directed at Smiley, who had no comeback. His whole body and face seemed dislocated from the insult, but he seemed to be laughing at himself since he could not relax the muscles around his mouth that caused the permanent smile that had given him his nickname.

Smiley silenced, Mr. Hines started a new monologue. No escaping it. All the windows in the classroom were closed, shutting the world out and keeping his voice in, words flying around the classroom like trapped birds against walls painted sky blue.

Much of the monologue lapped without distinction around Hatch. Mr. Hines punctuated his speech with nods and smiles, taking pleasure in himself, that self-assurance that came from knowing that he was on a mission to save these at-risk youth. Even if he could not save them—unlike Hatch, most of them would not go to college next year—he would forever remain a role model for them. (The school sought every opportunity to celebrate the fact that he'd been nominated for an Image Award, twice.)

They claim that they have minds of winter, but we are a warm people, thoughtful people. That's why in all Yoruba sculpture the head is always out of proportion to the body.

Okay, but why they make her ass so big?

Laughter.

I'm just saying.

Mr. Hines gave Lamont a quick up-and-down inspection. Mr. Harris, don't shame yourself.

Lamont allowed himself to look at Mr. Hines. Mr. Hines looked back at the class, formed his lips (little birds' nests), and shaped more words.

So, it seems Harriet Tubman will get her holiday. A precisely imposed pause. Mr. Dodd, what do you think about that? That's what I thought. Ask me, a holiday is too little too late. If they want to honor her, why don't they name that new planet after her? Mr. Hines said this with blunt wonder.

Somebody said, Cause they already named that planet.

Did Mr. Hines hear?

Choose your heroes carefully. Now they are people calling for Seancé to get a holiday. Does that sound right to you? Let's look at the facts. Here's what I know: this woman made fifty million dollars off of a project inspired by HBCUs but when all was said and done, she only donated one hundred grand to one HBCU. Now does that sound right to you?

Somebody said, It's her money. But Mr. Hines continued on with his monologue.

She gives private concerts for kings, queens, and dictators, but she is now touted as the most famous and "influential"—Mr. Hines used his fingers to put the word in quotes—feminist in the world. Young people, don't be duped. You know, her husband, this Knigga Tha Nuckle, that "nigger"—fingering quotation marks—is even worse.

Many voices crossed back and forth coming to Knigga Tha Nuckle's defense.

Everybody gets all excited just because he drops a few rhymes about black folks' problems. I already know about my problems. Now why would I want to listen to some music and be reminded about it?

Nawl, Mr. Hines, Hatch said. You don't understand.

Well, explain it to me.

A sudden silence in the classroom settled around Hatch.

Hatch started a faltering response but thought better of it. He would only make things worse for himself, a battle he couldn't win. Punishment sure to come. Bullshit homework. Detention. Mr. Hines started to speak but his voice caught when the bell rang. Throngs of bodies scrambled out of seats and left the room, Hatch with his crew, a quartet with Lamont, Smiley, and Dodd. The four bogarted the hallway, walking side by side, scarcely room for anyone else to pass. Out the building and into the light of the world. Hatch walked where they walked, turned where they turned, from corner to corner and block to block. Dodd kicked off the argument.

Yo, Mr. Hines is always talking some yang.

Yeah. Tryin to diss Knigga Tha Nuckle.

Man, fuck Knigga Tha Nuckle, Smiley said. That nigga gay.

What?

Yo, they pumped ten pounds of cum out of that nigga's stomach. He must have been smokin mad dick.

Sperm, my nigga. Not semen.

You mean life force.

What the fuck difference does it make? That nigga is straight up gump.

Hatch was carried into the conversation, his voice crossing against and raising with the others.

Nigger, you need to learn some biology.

Nawl. You jus mad cause I'm speaking truth.

Yo yo. You talkin about Knigga Tha Nuckle. The greatest lyricist of all time.

Yeah, my nigga. He been crowned.

That nigga is fake. He probably don't even perform his own rhymes. He just a showpiece, a face. Have you ever heard a gump flow? It's an impossibility.

Nigga, you way wrong. Come on, he a billionaire. Think about that, my nigger. Have you ever heard of a fag who's a billionaire?

Hey, I don't give a fuck about all that. All I know is that nigger is a gump and like to suck mad dick.

Youse a stupid motherfucker.

Straight up hater.

Yo. Yo. Knigga Tha Nuckle. Think about what you sayin.

Word. Trust me, I know a gump and Knigga Tha Nuckle ain't no gump.

That's what I'm saying.

Yawl niggers is just in denial. Don't you know, some of these niggers is bitches too. Straight up mangina, fish. What you need to do is stop listening to his music before you turn gay too.

The wind took up their voices, carried them.

After exchanging a series of handclasps-chest-bumps-hugs-pats-on-the-back, Dodd and Smiley went in separate directions, the quartet dwindling down to a duo, Hatch and Lamont, who continued on together, their talk burrowing into the late afternoon, Lamont's face constantly changing with enjoyment, curiosity, flashes of disagreement or fellow feeling in response to Hatch's thoughts and ideas. The landscape they moved through familiar territory, the neighborhood where they'd grown up, their square of the world with clusters of three-story brick courtyard buildings looming over diminutive range houses.

Yo, my nigga, you better stay up out of those projects.

Nobody knows my name, Lamont said.

Nigger, that ain't no reason to be hanging out in the projects.

How else I'm gon pull that bitch?

Fuck a bitch.

Man, I ain't studyin them project niggers. They got to catch me first.

Catch you? You ain't hear about what they did to that one nigger from Kenwood? Hatch started to tell the story, until his account was interrupted by two gunshots from somewhere in the distance. They hurried on to Lamont's front yard.

Man, these niggers be trippin.

Every day.

Crazy.

Lamont stood with his back pushed up against the chain-link fence surrounding the small range house where he lived, a fuzz of weeds growing against the ground's will and yard trees exploding toward the sidewalk. Their range house was one of three on the block, all exactly the same in size and construction. Hatch thought that with its rectangular shape and picture frame window the house looked like a microwave oven. Inside Death was slow-cooking Lamont's mom. A thousand conflicting rumors in the neighborhood about the specific nature of her affliction. His understanding that she had come down with some kind of rare bone cancer that made her body swell up in pain and that also caused her to grow six inches each month. When she died six months later, she would be the tallest person on record.

The sun grew tired of looking down on them and took a seat on the rooftop of a building, causing the sky to bruise over like fruit and draw colors out of the ground.

Lamont kept shifting his feet as if the grass were a surfboard rising and falling beneath him. He looked in Hatch's direction without meeting his gaze. Yo, your name is all up in people's mouths. With some reluctance, he explained that everybody was saying that Hatch and the other Lamont were roaming around everywhere together, day and night.

Everybody? Who is everybody?

You know, everybody.

For a moment, Hatch said nothing, only stood, absorbing the smell of evening light like fresh-cut grass. Damn, he said. Niggers sure like to talk.

So why you giving them something to talk about? Guilty by association, my nigga. Lamont eyed Hatch coldly and knowingly.

Hatch stiffened with surprise. Damn, niggers really know how to twist shit. It ain't even all that serious. We jus like the same music.

Really? Since when? Lamont seemingly aloft in a surge of light above the grass.

Why you all up in my business?

Lamont watched him, jaw jutted forward in a frown. I'm jus trying to look out for you, my nigger.

Pushed up against the chain-link fence, Lamont was bathed in light so intense that it seemed to radiate from his whole body and dark clothing. He held his arms crossed in front of him, his head tilted sideways.

No need to invent an excuse. No reassurance to be given. Still, Hatch said. Anyway, that was all last summer. I ain't seen Lamont in a minute.

He felt no particular concern—true?—about last summer, he and Lamont together each day, each day as alike and unlike the next. Summer long gone/over, he and Lamont already a thing of the past.

That ain't what they saying.

You think I give a fuck? I don't care what people think. Do I look like I'm trying to win some sort of popularity contest? I'm just trying to be me.

Lamont shook his head. Man, you playing with fire.

Lamont stood still for a moment with his ear against the door. He grasped the handle and with a quick movement tried to open it. Hatch gave the weighted door a few quick yanks with his skinny arms and it came completely free of the hinges, releasing a gush of dark cool air into the bright summer afternoon.

Damn. You broke it.

I'm stronger than I look, Hatch said.

They stepped inside and Hatch fixed the door back into place as best he could, closing off all the light, complete darkness. They stepped down the few stairs into the basement heat. Hatch heard Lamont's sneakers on the floor, heard the noises he made in his throat. Heard him fingering into the low ceiling above them. A bulb flashed on. Lamont gave a small metal cord another tug and the single bulb hanging from the ceiling snapped brighter. Hatch and Lamont both made themselves comfortable against a standing pipe. Inside now, Hatch could feel the space around them, so much concrete and cement and pipe metal radiating the day's heat. Lamont had said that this would be a safe place to smoke. Good choice.

Hatch pulled his stash from his pocket, unrolled and opened the plastic bag, and held it up to Lamont for him to smell.

What is it?

Bo.

Bo?

Bo.

Lamont looked at him with quick ready eyes.

You don't know nothing about this. Just wait.

Lamont watched him while he rolled a joint, excitement in his flat light-skinned face, the cheekbones high and well fleshed out, a bit of stubble above his lips, the makings of a mustache, and the small ears that appeared stamped into the sides of his head like the tabs inside soda pop cans. People often assumed Hatch and Lamont were brothers because they shared the same last name, while people often confused the two Lamonts because they shared the same first name. But even if they had been twins, Hatch would have been able to distinguish the two because one smoked lovely and the other didn't. Smoking required cunning, flexibility, daring, and determination. Humor and excitement in knowing that Lamont's mother and siblings were none the wiser in an apartment somewhere above them.

A match struck and their session began. Lamont took the first hit. Liked it so much he hit it again before passing the joint to Hatch. They stood together seeing the smoke.

Lamont took the joint from his fingers and took a hit from it, another, three, four, then passed it back to Hatch.

Thinking back, he can see the smoke now, as if it never dissipated those many years ago in that muggy basement. Reasons why that day is coming back to him now, not that any of it could ever be forgotten. The memory swells. He can touch it under his skin.

He spoke words past the joint before sticking the wet end into his mouth. Turn that off. Nodded at the lightbulb. What was he thinking? The tip of the joint glowing in the heavy deep darkness.

Man, I can't believe you tryin to holler at Deidre. You must like them raunchy bitches.

Hatch heard that Lamont's mouth was full of smoke.

Why you say that?

The other day I saw her in the bushes with Marlon and Mitchell. They was taking turns. Then they double-teamed her. It was disgusting.

Word?

I kid you not, my nigga.

Hatch only half believed Lamont's story but decided he had to smooth away any doubts. It ain't like I want her to be my wifey, he said. I just wouldn't mind hittin it, that's all.

I wouldn't go up in that. The most I would do is mack out with her.

Hatch stood against the post, eyes closed, listening, focusing on the joint glowing in the dark. Accepted the joint. Heard a crack, Lamont twisting the cap off a forty ounce.

He took a swig. The malt liquor felt both warm and cold sliding down his throat. He felt it climb his legs before spreading through every part of his body, solidifying something inside him.

They knocked back most of the bottle.

You want the last sip?

Nawl. Go ahead. You kill that.

Hatch killed and tossed the empty bottle onto the floor, aware of his own breathing in the darkness, taking in the damp, pipe smell, and oil. The floor beneath him rose and sank away. There was something he wanted to ask Lamont, but he couldn't remember what. Hold out your hand, he said.

He heard Lamont move, then he made some calculations about his body in proximity to Lamont. That done, he slapped his dick into Lamont's hand. Lamont snickered. Joke made, Hatch pulled away from Lamont unsteadily, doing all he could to maintain his balance.

Why you scared? Lamont said.

Hatch found himself turning toward Lamont, drawn by a strange half sense of panic. Lamont touched Hatch's dick as if weighing it. Then began to stroke the skin like a glove he was trying to fit onto his hand. Silence uncoiled around them like smoke. Stretched up to the ceiling in the darkness. No sound came from within the basement or from outside it. Somebody was standing in the middle of Hatch moving, feeling, and speaking for him.

I think you should do that with your mouth.

He felt Lamont's mouth enclose him, wet and warm, and breathed in, inhaled as he buried his fingers inside Lamont's hair, the other's head bobbing up and down buoy-like on his dick. Heard Lamont's mouth working in the dark and felt exhalation escape onto his thigh. Then his dick slipped out of Lamont's mouth, and he registered the difference in temperature, a localized chill, the other's arm wrapped around the back of his knee, now his thigh, resting to catch his breath, a second wind, panting (almost) loud and hard, short intakes of oxygen. He guided his dick back inside Lamont's mouth, the only part of the other that existed.

Some time later, Hatch followed Lamont into an apartment with a low ceiling and a floor that creaked, the wood worn gray like dry skin. He took a seat on the couch in the living room, weary of light after the basement dark. Stale night air lifted old body odor from the couch's faded fabric. Lamont flopped down in the one armchair across from him, seeming almost to disappear into the overstuffed cushions under a tall floor lamp shining its halo around him. The cone of dissipated light bringing back to Hatch the memory of weed smoke. Was Lamont still high? Was he? How to tell? The room a bit fuzzy, but was that the place or him? Furniture and objects did not seem to be arranged for comfort or beauty or convenience of movement. They just were. A dozen or more sun-faded photographs on the walls in cheap ill-fitting frames. Raggedy-ass plants straining away from the must and funk toward the open window. In one corner an aquarium full of black water seemed to be suspended in air like some magician's trick. Hatch couldn't see any stand mounted underneath it. Perhaps the black water held in its depths some sort of record, history. Who knew all that this apartment had witnessed?

He tried hard not to throw his mind backward to the basement, a new territory of experience that had been opened up to him. So now what? Plenty of time to think about it later. Lamont's mother called out from somewhere in the apartment, snapping Lamont out of his lethargy. He noticed a wet spot on his light-colored T-shirt and took up the bottom fold of the shirt and wiped his forehead, hiding the evidence of Hatch's semen. He smiled at Hatch, and Hatch smiled back, thick as thieves.

The mother's voice rang out again, angry and impatient, summoning Lamont. Lamont signaled that Hatch should follow him into the kitchen, and so he did, crossing the squeaking floorboards past an open doorway with Lamont's younger siblings wreaking havoc inside a bedroom. Hatch knew them more by sight than by name. A hodgepodge, every shade of nigger, a real rainbow coalition. Lamont's mother stood in the kitchen at the metal sink under a long tube of fluorescent light, trying to wash dishes, the reluctant tap coughing out water.

Lamont tilted back a metal chair, pulled it scraping against the floor away from the table, and sat down. Hatch took a seat next to him. She turned off the faucet, dried her hands on a dish towel then, turned toward them. Looked at Hatch but did not acknowledge him. She looked nothing like Lamont, short, fat on top of fat, one ring of blubber stacked on top of another like a baby's toy. Her tight dress constricted around her knees. Her hair was cut too short, showing the barrenness of neglect and defeat, and the tendons in her neck strained under the weight of her face like tent poles about to collapse. It hurt Hatch to look at her, knowing that she hurt. But also hurt for him to feel anything for her.

So you come and go as you please?

Lamont said nothing, only waited for her to continue.

I'm gon be late for work. Ronda ain't back yet so you gon have to fry your brothers some chicken.

How come you ain't cook?

Because I got you, heifer.

She pulled open the kitchen door. Come here. Let me talk to you for a minute.

Lamont went to her. She engaged him in an awkward undertone conversation, mostly her talking and Lamont listening and nodding understanding. She did not leave soon enough for Hatch.

Yo, your moms be trippin. Why you let her talk to you that way?

Lamont crossed his arms. What am I supposed do?

Hatch stood up from the question and returned to the living room couch, rumpled among the old cushions. Soon he could smell hot vegetable oil and hear greasy chicken protesting in a frying pan. The consumption was just as raucous. He rolled a joint and listened while Lamont put his siblings to bed and waited until they fell asleep. Came back quietly to the armchair without looking at Hatch.

In one hand he held out the joint and lighter in offering. Lamont drew his hands from between his thighs and strained forward in the chair, reaching to accept. He stopped, looked to see if Hatch was making fun of him. At last he took the bo with a strange expression of effort around his mouth.

Soon they were deep into another session, smoke filling the

room. Could they resume the normal flow of the evening, just like that?

I knew I had you. Lamont smiled to himself. He sat with his legs pulled up to his chin and his chin on his knees.

Hatch hit the pinched joint and sucked in the words, hearing Lamont's laughter hang in the air, return.

But look, don't feel bad. Yo, I got all of them niggers. Michael. Snoop. Omar. T. Man. Raymond. Moogy. Shaquille. Alfonso. Darius. Bruce. Daryl. Tim. Big L.

Big L?

Yeah. That nigga got some good pussy. In fact, we was together for a minute. But I had to break up with him because he wanted us to be exclusive. I'm like, Nigger, I ain't trying to hear that shit. I am Legion. Too many niggers and bitches out here to fuck. Maybe when I'm fifty. Maybe when I'm old.

Hatch handed off the joint. Smoke sucked in then blown out. Words came from Lamont in the same way.

But I could fuck that nigger today if I really wanted to. The last time ain't never the last time.

Hot air hovered undisturbed, something both seen and felt, Hatch feeling this habitation around him. He felt everything shift. Lamont seemed to be a man who knew his own mind.

And your boy too.

My boy?

Lamont.

Lamont?

Yeah. I got him a long time ago. But I can't fuck with that nigger. He's an earthling, boring as a motherfucker. Nothing like you.

Hatch thought about it. His moms is sick.

What's that got to do with anything? If you boring you boring. Lamont scrunched up his face, causing his throat to grow big as if he were about to throw up.

Then Ronda entered the apartment, changing the look of everything. She grinned when she saw Hatch. Rather than greet him, she delivered an understanding nod, causing his stomach to tighten and his dick to get hard.

Lamont looked up at her. He put his feet back onto the floor and sat up straight. About time, he said.

She paid her brother no mind. Hatch figured that she and Lamont shared the same father since they shared the same skin complexion, but at age nineteen she was the eldest, older than him by two years. He watched her jounce across the floor, slim but voluptuous in a top that left her midriff exposed, frame for a diamond-pierced bellybutton, and short shorts, her thighs thick like rising bread. Her hair combed back from her face in such a way as to put her smooth skin and sharp features in relief. All of her a unity, the finest woman he had ever seen.

Let me hit that. She reached out and took the small illumination pinched between his fingers and brought it to her lips.

Once home, he put himself before a mirror, completely naked. Examined the parts of his body to be sure they were all there.

The next afternoon, he followed Lamont up three flights of stairs and three funky landings to reach the apartment where Lamont's grandmother lived alone. Lamont opened the door—she always kept it unlocked—then ushered Hatch inside into the intense brightness of the living room, every badly shaded lamp switched on. His grandmother sat on a shiny metal folding chair at a small card table and peered out at Lamont and Hatch past a red plastic cup tilted at her mouth. A cigarette burned up from a plastic ashtray on the table, a crumpled pack of Kools next to it. She had on an old red cardigan over a plain housedress, her wide feet pushed into fuzzy slippers, her wig her one fashionable adornment, modern, stylish, and fly. It fit her head tight like a protective covering and tricked the eyes, drawing attention away from her face lined and baggy with age, the skin losing its dark coloring.

She set the cup on the table. A sight for sore eyes, she said.

Lamont went over and kissed her on one cheek, Hatch on the other. Then they took positions on metal chairs at the table. She put the cigarette into her mouth, smoking burning past her face, causing her to frown. Hatch's gaze went around the few items in the apartment. Several fish were thawing tail up in the sink like springboard divers. A boxy television muttered sound and flickered images. The lack of furnishings made the combined kitchen–living space appear larger than it was.

Hands free, she pawed the deck of cards. Don't worry, she said. I'm gon take it easy on you two. I don't like to hear nobody cryin in my house.

I see you already talkin shit, Lamont said.

She quick-fingered the cards, fancy shuffling, cards snapping in place. Spread the deck face down across the table before them. Now cut, she said.

Lamont cut. She dealt the hand, starting with Hatch on her right. They studied their cards, played without talking. Breathing through open lips, she won the first two hands.

Damn, Lamont said. That's why I don't like to play cards wit you. You always cheatin.

Boy, you think I got to cheat to beat you? Them years. Wisdom.

Like hell.

Talk to me when you half my age.

You still be cheatin then. Beneath the table Lamont's hand discovered his.

Hatch dealt but she won again. Whatever was in her cup had a strong smell. She drank with a speed that must have burned her tongue and by now she had finished her drink and was gently shaking the ice cubes at the bottom of her cup. With all of her funny habits, she was an easy person to mock.

Can we get some of that? Lamont said.

Nawl, you can't get none of this, she said. What I look like givin you liquor? I don't even drink but them doctors rather me drink for my pressure than take pills. Both bad for the liver but them pills is worse.

Yeah right.

I'm telling you the truth. Boy, you ain't got a bit of sense. Are you sure you my grandbaby?

Whatever. Just deal the cards.

She went through her ritual of fancy shuffling.

Where Ronda? How come she don't never come see me? I ain't but a hop, skip, and a jump away.

Hatch released Lamont and picked up his cards.

Why don't you ask her?

I'm asking you. She took a pull on her cigarette. You tell her what I said.

You got a phone. Why don't you call and tell her?

Ain't she there in the house with you?

Lamont studied his cards.

Or she run them streets?

Look, grandma, I ain't tryin to keep up with Ronda.

They played the hand. She won again. Hatch felt good about it.

Next time you bring somebody to my house, make sure they know how to play cards. He worse than you. She took in Hatch.

Lamont cast a pained look at Hatch. Yo, don't pay her no mind. She's all talk.

She placed the deck before Lamont for him to deal. Hatch and Lamont shot furtive uneasy glances at each other.

Grandma, we need to take a break.

You gon need more than a break to beat him.

Maybe so. Lamont rubbed his palms against his thighs. Look, we be right back. We gon smoke in the bathroom.

Smoke?

He showed her a twisted joint like a worm in his hand.

Why you got to show me your reefer like I'm stupid or something? You people today act like yall the first ones to puff. People been smoking forever. Gon and smoke. That's your business. But you can't get none of this. She took a sip from her cup.

Lamont looked at Hatch and nodded in the direction of the bathroom. Once they were alone, Lamont brought his face up toward Hatch and laid his mouth over Hatch's. So this is what it was like to kiss. Thinking while feeling the stubble of the other's face. He felt Lamont hard against him, making him hard in return. Soon they were grinding belly to belly.

Hey! Her voice came loud from outside the door. Run to the sto and get me a pack of Kools.

Lamont slipped his tongue free. Damn, grandma. We just got in here.

I know but I need my pack of Kools.

Why you trippin? Can we finish smokin first?

I need you to run to the sto and get my cigarettes.

Five minutes.

No, now. Run to the sto then yall can smoke.

Yo, schoolboy, what up?

Oh snap. My nigga.

They touched each other in the way that black men do.

How long you been back?

For a minute. But who said I was gone? Huggy Bear talked loud like someone on stage. Tall skinny lanky nigger as if his body was made from pipe cleaners. He was decked out in chains and bracelets made from the new metal that astronauts had discovered. Every few seconds the jewelry changed colors, shifted into some new shape, hummed some sound.

Some months back on the day Lamont turned eighteen, he and Hatch caught a bus down to Pontiac to visit Huggy Bear in the state pen. The three sat around a circular stainless-steel table, where visitation rules dictated that the inmate's hands needed to remain visible at all times. They touched hands in greeting, Hatch quick to slip Huggy Bear three twenty-dollar bills rolled cigarette tight. The latter accepted the money into his palm using his thumb as a grip, a disappearing act.

For the next two hours Hatch and Lamont listened to Huggy Bear pontificate and complain, his breathing noisy as if he carried surf in his lungs, and did their best to engage him in light conversation—

You seen Marcus?

They said they had not.

Damn, I miss that nigger. He was my relief up in this bitch.

Hatch pondered the statement—while spending all their cash and coin on food from the vending machines, a one-man feast. Candy bars, hard candies, wax chews, sea salted potato chips, flavored nachos, spicy pork skins, peppered almonds, chocolate eggs, squares of cheese, pop, cupcakes, canned coffee and canned tea, edible toothpicks, and microwavable filet mignon.

Damn, I can't stop eating. Like I got the munchies or some shit. Cain't wait to get up out of this bitch. I am going to cel-e-brate. You know how I do. Huggy Bear made theatrical gestures. Smoke me some hydro, drink some syrup, maybe tap a little blow. And lay up with a honey or two.

Then it was time to leave. To his astonishment, Hatch observed that both of Huggy Bear's hands were free of contraband, realized that at some point during the visit he had thought ahead and taken steps to pass the post-visitation inspection, had inserted the bills into his asshole.

Yo, Lamont. Tell your sister to holler at me.

Lamont made a face like he needed to spit. You tell her.

You look good.

You know how we do. I'm all bout the clothes, bankrolls, and hoes. He copped a pose, holding what remained of a hoagie behind him like a discus. Then he took Hatch roughly by the shoulder, hoagie upright in his other hand, the wax paper wet with grease. He held out the hoagie.

I'm good, Hatch said.

He stuffed the last of the hoagie into his mouth, cheeks ballooning, and wiped his hands on the paper bag before crumpling it up and tossing it onto the ground. Hatch picked up the bag and tossed it into a nearby trash can. Huggy Bear gave him a look he couldn't read.

You mean you out and you couldn't holler at a nigga.

Man, my p.o. jus lookin for a reason to violate me, so I been workin like a bitch, jus some bullshit gig. A yard a week. Two if

I'm lucky. I jus spend that shit. He flashed his jewelry. But my boy, he sposed to hook me up wit this other gig. And once I get that I'm gon save up then invest a few grand in the trap and jus lay back and let my money work for me.

I heard that.

But damn, all that workin got me stressed like a motherfucker. I really need to bust. Huggy Bear fisted his crotch and shook it up and down a few times, Hatch aware of curious or traitorous or bored eyes spying down upon them through apartment windows above.

Good luck with that, he said. I need to bounce.

Where you off to?

Fin to knock off a piece of ass.

My nigga. Yo, put in a few strokes for me.

Moving with her usual sprightliness, Ronda went into the bathroom and closed the door behind her, only to open it again a minute later. She came out butt-naked from the waist up, clutching her folded-up T-shirt over her breasts, a strip of purple thong taut between her butt cheeks. Disappeared into another room of the apartment, came back. She had removed her bra and was holding it over her breasts, her bare brown elbows titled upward in such a way that Hatch could spy the sides of her titties. Back into the bathroom without giving any indication that she was aware of his presence. He remained seated on the couch as if he were not alone in the room. When she emerged from the bathroom, she was fully clothed.

She dropped down on the couch next to him. Started running her hands up and down the length of her legs. Moved her hair away from her face as if to give him a better look. She had squeezed her body into a sundress, a sleeveless lime-green cotton covered with big yellow flowers. Hatch made aware of her beauty and the way she assumed it. She caught him looking at her.

Are you okay? She unleashed a brilliant smile.

Hatch said nothing.

I started to wear my green dress, she said. But I knew you couldn't take it.

From some other room the voices of Lamont and his mother came, elastic, springing up and snapping back.

Hatch wondered what he could possibly say to Ronda that might be interesting to her. Ended up saying, Yo, guess who I just saw?

Who?

Huggy Bear.

Really? Ronda said, I ain't seen that nigger in a minute.

I know, right? I guess he just got out.

From where?

He did a two-year bid.

Is that what he told you? That nigger is lying. Only prison he been in is his mother's womb. I'm going to tell you what happened. That nigga got some bitch pregnant then got the fuck out of Dodge before she could get papers on him.

He started to correct her when Rhonda and Lamont's mother made a tentative entry into the room, took one look at Hatch, and backpedaled. Bitch, didn't I tell you you can't have no company?

We going to his house, Lamont said.

You ain't going nowhere til you finish all yo chores.

Ronda smiled at Hatch through this exchange. He kept his head turned from her. Heard Lamont shuffling from room to room. Music in his movements. Objects were picked up, put away. Other things were put down.

Bitch, didn't I tell you to take out the garbage before I got home?

Okay. I'm taking it now.

And when you finish that, scrub these floors. You know what, heifer. You tryin my patience. Can't you see how this house look?

Why I'm the only one who have to clean?

Bitch, you sassin me?

I ain't sassin you. I'm jus sayin I got to do everything. Ronda don't do nothing up in here.

Ronda knows what he has to do. She the oldest. Worry about what you have to do.

Damn.

You cursing up in my house?

I ain't even curse.

You cursing at me?

But I ain't even curse.

Bitch, don't sass me. I'm holding down two jobs to put food on the table and to put clothes on your back and shoes on your feet.

Silence.

And you better fix yo face.

A short time later, naked and hard, he installed Lamont on his bed.

I want to fuck.

Lamont lowered his gaze. I don't know if I can handle all of that, Lamont said. Still, he removed his clothes and positioned himself on the bed.

Do I need to use something?

Yeah, Lamont said. Yourself.

He had difficulty entering Lamont, but Lamont coached him, the delay extending desire, giving him longer to enjoy the moment. Lamont quick to respond to the first motions. He would never be able to describe the feeling properly to anyone. Excitement only the body knew. How not to forget? He kept his eyes open, determined that nothing in the room would distract him, determined to store each sensation in memory, each as tangible as the two layers of window curtains, one sheer, the other silky.

Lamont made a noise, a hollow groan. Then another. Chanting under his weight. He had to concentrate to keep from laughing.

It's good for me, Lamont said. Is it good for you?

Hatch didn't know if it was good. So he said nothing and continued to push into Lamont, pressing this other into the mattress as if he were not really there, mere matter beneath him. Lamont's voice rising, as if the want of it all wouldn't allow him to take another breath.

As soon as he came, he pulled out of Lamont and rolled to the far side of the bed away from his friend's body. He lay there suspended between alertness and astonishment, trying to settle back into his own body. The in and out of breath. Had it really happened?

Overwhelmed by a feeling of weary disgust, he was the first to rise and rush into the bathroom and into his clothes. In no hurry, Lamont came and stood naked before him, looking into his face.

Don't you think you should clean yourself? he said.

Lamont gave a little snigger. He yanked off a few squares of toilet paper, shaped them into a flower, and attended to himself. Then he threw the soiled flower into the toilet and flushed it.

He made every effort to smile. Lamont had been entered and filled, used, but it was time for him to go. How to put that fact into kind words? Sorry, he said, but my moms will be back soon.

Lamont came up awkwardly, touched his elbows, and tried to kiss him. Hatch moved his face free. Still, Lamont wiped excess saliva from his mouth as if Hatch's mouth had been there. He watched Hatch, no indication of what he was feeling, although Hatch's reticence did not seem to upset him.

Don't be too hard on yourself, he said. A man is still a man.

Another hot afternoon, the air above raw with the squall of wings, birds circling the sky as if stirring the heat. Heat drawn to him. And there was Ronda, bright afternoon light behind her, her hair loose like the light. Feet showing in flat leather sandals with flowers painted on the toe straps. He saw the outline of her pubis in white skinny jeans. She called over her shoulder.

Why do I keep running into you? You stalkin me?

Nawl.

You sure? She caught his hand. She had the air of someone who was never undecided.

The words his mind made.

That's right: you scared of me. She gave her playful encouraging grin. You look like yourself, she said.

What to say to that?

I'll catch you later, okay? She squeezed his fingers and moved away at the same time, their hands remaining linked until they dropped apart.

Things got going quickly that afternoon, and for the second time, he entered Lamont, his whole weight pressing into the other's body. Lamont made a complaining noise that he ignored. He could not contain himself and came quickly.

Sorry, he said. You're so tight.

No biggie, Lamont said. That's good for now.

He continued to lie on top of Lamont, wanting to pull out but unable to, surprised that it was over already. Kissed the back of the other's shoulders and neck, offering this bit of affection as compensation.

Lamont spoke muffled from under him. It's okay. Let me get you hard again.

Leaned sideways, Ronda rocked her baby brother on her hip, trying to quiet him. Lamont ain't here. You want to come in and wait for him? She held the door wide for Hatch to enter, her fingernails adorned with tips like so many colorful postal stamps.

The baby gave a bouncing jerk against Ronda then went still.

What time he tell you to come through?

He was supposed to meet me at my crib. Never showed up. And his phone keep going to voice mail.

Hatch could feel the biggest vein in his dick pulsing.

Don't you know by now, my brother is trifling. He has a bunch of errands to run. He should have told you. He might be a minute. Ronda studied him. Don't just stand there. Have a seat.

He took a seat on the funky couch.

I'll be back. Ronda left the room with the baby, who was now asleep.

He sat waiting, his body held stiff as if driven in place, his hands shuddering in his lap.

Sorry about that.

She had changed into something new, her outfit suggesting ease in his company. He would be careful not to be caught unaware by her gaze.

Here, I brought you something to drink. She unscrewed the cap on a bottle of cognac.

No. I'm good.

You don't like Henny? She smiled.

I do. But I'm good.

Good? You don't look like you good. You look like somebody who need a drink.

Just some water.

Water? She studied him. Look, Lamont gon be a minute. And I'm trying to be nice and offer you a drink. She spoke using the bottle and glass as extensions of her words. I know you drink. So what's the problem? Ain't nobody here but me and you.

I plan to drink later, he said.

She looked at him for a moment, offended. Shook her head in wonderment. Okay, don't ever say I ain't try to give you nothing. Wait. Hold on. She bent at the waist and set the bottle of Henny down on the floor with the glass and left the room only to return a few seconds later bearing over to him a whiskey tumbler filled with water and ice. Half-smiling, she set the glass quietly down on his knee.

I see you got jokes. He picked up the tumbler, drew a noisy sip, then returned it to his knee clutched in one hand.

She sat down on the couch next to him and poured herself a glass of cognac, then placed the bottle on the floor between her splayed feet. You sure you don't want none? She shook the brown liquid in her glass in slow circles. This that good shit.

I'm sure.

Okay then. Cheers.

Cheers.

They touched glasses.

She shook hair from her eyes and drank looking directly at him, but he did not turn away, only sipped his cold water with unease, trying to drink in regular swallows and make as little noise as possible.

Glass in one hand, she lounged back against the cushions, light swimming like fish inside the brown liquid.

Something thumped against the window and he jumped. Perhaps a rock or a bird had hit the glass. Or nothing at all. He saw the water trembling on his knee. What must she be thinking about him? He saw, as he continued to remain on exhibit before her, that his having a drink would free her of her doubts about him.

Perhaps he and Lamont did not know how to stay away from each other. Perhaps Lamont mistook Hatch's lust for something else, affection, warmth between them, connection. Hatch the beneficiary of these untruths. And okay with that. Nothing between his skin and the skin of this other, Lamont a body calling him from the light into the dark of his own sweat.

But then, on what would have been the third occasion, Lamont refused to let Hatch enter him.

I'm not turned on, he said. He hugged Hatch around the waist and pulled Hatch against him. That was how they fucked from then on, standing face to face, dick against dick, grinding against each other, Hatch always the first to nut on Lamont's belly.

Lamont told Hatch to wait for him on the landing outside the apartment. Hold up a minute, I'm coming.

The ashy door clapped shut. Hatch listened to voices on the other side.

You better get out of my face.

And what you gon do if I don't? You fuckin faggot.

Bitch, I got yo faggot.

Whose dick did you suck today?

Why you so worried about it? You jus mad because you on the rag.

Nawl, bitch. You the one on the rag.

More than sibling rivalry, brother and sister talking shit. What had he intruded upon? The door slanted open granting a quick angle of vision of Ronda before Lamont stepped out.

Damn, Hatch said. What was that all about?

Lamont pretended as if he didn't hear Hatch. They continued on in silence until they reached the corner store, where they chanced upon Huggy Bear and his crew out front passing a forty-ounce bottle.

There go that nigger right there. One of them pointed at Lamont.

Hey, Lamont. Let me holler at you.

Lamont ignored him. Huggy Bear stepped in front of him, blocking his entry to the store.

Yo, Lamont said, you better get outa my face with that.

Nigger, I'm in yo face.

Lamont was not as tall as Huggy Bear so Huggy Bear could look down on him.

So what, I'm sposed to be scared of you?

What you need to do is stop runnin yo fuckin mouth.

I don't know what you talkin about so what you need to do is get out of my face.

Why you spreadin rumors and shit?

Nigger, Lamont said, I already told you I don't know what you talkin about.

So now you don't know. Okay. Bet. But let me tell you this one thing. Huggy Bear's face screwed toward Lamont. You better keep my name out yo motherfuckin mouth.

And what if I don't? What you gon do? Who the fuck is you? I bet you wasn't talkin all that shit in jail.

Yo, H. You gon let that young nigga talk to you like that? Yo.

Snuff that nigger.

Yo.

Go ahead, Lamont said. I'm right here. I ain't into all that mouth-fighting.

You done fucked with the wrong nigger today, Huggy Bear said. I'm gon show you how the Peter-Roll gang is.

Huggy Bear took off his T-shirt, now naked to the waist. Prison-skinny, all muscle, his chest and arms crisscrossed with a map of veins.

Hold my shirt.

One dude accepted his shirt.

He took off his necklace and handed it to someone, then the watch and bracelets encircling his wrists. Fists at his sides, he stood looking at Lamont.

Am I supposed to be impressed? Lamont smiled. Is that how you took your clothes off in jail?

Huggy Bear punched Lamont's bright smile and Lamont went down. Then his crew pushed forward in a flurry of fists and feet, Lamont quick to ball himself tight, knees to chin, hands covering his head. Careful to roll from one side to the other like a chicken roasting on a spit, bucking and bolting from blows and kicks. This went on for a minute or two—the sight filled Hatch, one mind to leave, one mind to stay; one mind to intervene and share the beatdown, another mind to run away—until Huggy Bear nodded his head and brought the assault to an end. Nothing more to be had from Lamont. The crew shook out their limbs and checked their knuckles and hands for cuts and their sneakers for tears and scuff marks.

A face in the crew wheeled toward Hatch. You want some too?

Forget that nigger. Let's bounce.

They bounced, Hatch keeping out of their way. His quick attention took in Lamont. Helped him to his feet, Lamont's body jammed against his, shoulder to shoulder, the buildings sagging and bulging around them. He could feel Lamont's blood speeding through his veins.

Yo, why didn't you just squash that shit? You know that nigger Huggy Bear fight dirty.

Man, fuck that nigger and his bitch-ass crew. They can't even punch. How I look?

Lamont's eyes moved quickly. Hatch pretended innocence staring at Lamont's face, little damage from what he could see, little but enough. Then the intimacy of a movement directed to Hatch.

Every night I pray that these niggers just leave me alone.

The next afternoon, he found himself once again waiting for Lamont on the landing outside the apartment. He sat down on the stairs, marking the time sipping pop, feeling the aluminum can cold against his fingers and tasting the fizzing cold grape soda on his tongue, and listening beyond the border of the shut door.

You pay rent up in here? Well, you sho act like it the way you come in and out of this motherfucker at all hours of the day and night.

Silence. One. Two. Three.

You better look at me when I'm talking to you.

I am looking at you.

And I ain't in the mood for all your backtalk today.

I ain't talkin back.

One. Two. Three.

Now you want to give me the evil eye?

What?

You better fix yo face.

Hatch sat there, listening to the burn of each word.

I swear if I come home again after I been working myself ragged and find this house lookin like a pigsty, I'm gon beat the shit out of you. They gon have to come up in here and pull me off you and carry me to jail.

The door shook open. Lamont stepped out, but his mother was still yelling at him from inside the apartment.

And you better be back here before your curfew.

Lamont looked at Hatch then looked away. What did Hatch witness in his friend's face before he started clambering down the stairs, Hatch in pursuit, the sound of a thousand feet, a migratory herd?

Damn, yo moms got you on a curfew now.

No loss of breath.

Man, I ain't studyin that bitch. For some reason, Lamont looked back over his shoulder, and there was his mother twenty feet behind him. The whole of her could be seen clearly, shouldering a broom like a baseball bat and coming at Lamont fast in house shoes at a speed beyond her capacity, her hips wiggling under the thin fabric of her faded housedress. Lamont turned and faced her. She swung the broom, but Lamont was quick enough to take two steps back, causing her feet to cross up, one going this way, the other that. She lost her balance and went down hard against the sidewalk, all flailing arms and broken straw.

They played it off and starting walking away.

Bitch, don't bring yo ass back up in my house. I mean that. You know what, come back. I got something for ya.

Her voice faded away with distance.

Damn, bro. I ain't never seen nothing like that. Hatch shook his head.

Fuck her and her house, Lamont said. She don't run me. Shit, she did me a favor. I been needing to get up out of there. He paused, thinking. Can I crash at your crib, I mean just for a few days?

Hatch heard this appeal, aware that he was privately present to Lamont, although his sympathy and concern made it no easier for him to come up with the right reply. Instead, he gristled out the words, Can't you stay with your grandmother? Right away he saw and felt something slip between them. Lamont moved his head just so, smoothing into silence anything else Hatch might say. With that, the summer came to an end, the sidewalk buckling in the heat, a burning world, trees and grass aflame.

Damn, Smiley said. Did you see that? The parentheses of his smile. His voice secret and low. He nodded his head as if he and Hatch were in on a private joke.

What?

Here. Smiley thrust his fist across the desk where Lamont usually sat, empty today, a space of mourning, Hatch having received word the night before that Lamont's mother had died, knowledge he had not shared with anyone.

Hatch reached his hand across the desk to accept Smiley's offering, but Smiley opened his hand too soon and let what he was holding drop to the floor: a used condom.

Up at the blackboard, chalk in hand, Mr. Hines stopped in the middle of a sentence and turned toward Hatch. He was superbly turned out in a designer shirt with a row of gold safety pins inserted into fabric on the upper chest areas.

So you like to hear yourself talk, he said.

But I wasn't even—

Shut up, you big ugly baby.

The room erupted into laughter, one loud boom. Some doubled up in their seats, others fell against one another, hands grabbing in all directions, still others tumbled out of their seats onto the floor.

Took a while for their energy to recede, a wave of relaxation, although floor and walls remained thick with echoing laughter. For Hatch, he was alone in the room, the mass of his feeling occupying it.

Smiley looked at him, trying not to laugh.

Mr. Hines resumed his lesson at the chalkboard. The more he talked, the more Hatch retreated into the invisible shell enclosing his desk-chair.

The bell rang ending the period, but no one made to leave. They were waiting for Hatch. He stood up, legs stiff and bizarrely spread. Mr. Hines eyed him with cold detachment. Hatch stood there afraid to cross the space between his desk and the door. Then he awakened to the action of his own muscles and moved through the large sunlit classroom, Mr. Hines's insult clinging to him, stretched elastic-like behind him. He almost collided with a posse of arm-locked females strutting up the main hall. Each in turn blew him a kiss. Continued on, laughter and chatter trailing behind.

The large double doors flung wide open, expelling him into a low sun in streaked sky. He felt his way slowly along a row of trees that lined one side of the street. A few wrecking machines, a few cranes, chalked lines and chain-link fencing, scaffolding and wooden horses. Partly demolished, antiquated buildings were coming down to make way for new buildings going up, although in the future he will not be able to remember if they were ever completed.

Joe College

He's holding in his mind the picture of sitting with her at a table inside the Chinese restaurant, the air ventilating rich aromas of food and spices. The table by a window overlooking the street where he could see their reflections moving on the glass.

I'm sure I heard him call me a nigger, Hatch said.

No, Tonia said. It's a Chinese word.

You speak Chinese?

I studied it in high school.

After this first date, they would come to frequent this restaurant for the two years they remained together, trying out a new table each time, each featuring a small vase of fresh flowers centered on bright white cloth. But he is thinking of the woman she was that day, of her high cheekbones, dark raccoon eyes, and short hair. The smile that lingered on her face. The blouse and jeans she wore. (He would come to learn that she never wore dresses or skirts. Once, he would see her rock a power suit to a job interview.) And her manner of eating with slow bites.

While she ate, she told him about her mother who was a seer and made a living blessing houses, which primarily involved spitting in the corners and spitting on the owner's shoes. Told him about her father and her older brother, how they both worked two full-time jobs, her father teaching during the day and driving a bus at night, her brother a graphic designer by day and a train conductor by night. She too would work two jobs after she finished college. Why not? For now a desk-intake job at the university hospital's ER paid the bills. The crazy shit you saw. Like the guy with a showerhead stuck in the back of his neck.

He expected her to ask him about his plans, but she didn't, almost as if she knew that he didn't want to talk about himself. He did not say much. Said what he could, words hard to form. Whenever she directed her gaze at him, he would look elsewhere. Feeling himself trembling throughout it all. What she could perhaps sense if not see outright.

Then she brought her bright-colored tropical cocktail to her lips—he was surprised that her small wrists could hold the heavy bowl-sized glass—looked at him with enthusiasm across the thick liquid, and he had the feeling that he'd made a discovery. She presented the considering face of one who respects learning and intelligence. Encouraged by what he saw. (Up until that point in his life, how much of the world had gone unnoticed by him? Wonders about it now, thinking, remembering.) No longer afraid to reveal that he was bookish, a quality she might appreciate, even vibe.

Between sips of his own cocktail he told her what he could about himself, making conversation.

Wow, she said. That's so cool. How did you get into that?

Back in high school. He shifted uncomfortably for a moment in his seat.

He could not tell if she was serious. Did she really find him interesting? He sipped his cocktail.

Isn't that a girl's drink? she asked. I'm just saying.

I don't buy all that stuff, he said, you know, girl's drink, boy's drink. Who came up with that?

Wow. Mr. Serious.

She told him that strong liquor in moderation rid the body of worms, parasites, toxins, and carcinogens. He did not challenge her facts.

She said she knew a drink he might like. Ordered it. He sampled the substance with a long thoughtful sip and supposed it was all right, although today he still can't describe the flavors.

At another table a couple bent toward each other in a kiss. He saw that she saw. They observed together then resumed their meal, mostly in silence.

Soon the waiter came and collected their used glasses, plates, and utensils and brushed away crumbs from the white tablecloth, his checked shirt smelling of starch and fresh ironing. Their meal was done. He did not wonder what to say to her. Perhaps he did not need to say anything.

Why don't you get the check?

He paid the bill to the exact penny. Then he pushed his chair away from the table, the wooden legs making little scuff marks across the floor, and took to his feet.

The waiter flashed them an annoyed look against the light. Don't I get something? he asked.

He took the words full in the face. Startled, embarrassed, he counted out a bill or two and some random coins for a tip, more coins than he had to. How far could his money go tonight? How far might she expect it to go?

Despite the glowing reviews, the movie was nothing special, the usual shootouts, car chases, explosions, and the obligatory scene where the token Black character in Jesus mode sacrifices himself to save his white counterparts. At some point, she reached for his arm and placed it around her. And so they sat until the credits.

Afterward she threaded her arm through his and they walked slowly along Rush Street, lines of people forty and fifty deep waiting to gain entry to clubs. Other people stood about or sat on steps, curbs, and fire hydrants, smoking, drinking, and talking, thrilled voices that rose through night air. At one establishment the doors were open, music spilling out.

We could go inside, Tonia said. But before he could answer, she added, But it's got to be pretty crowded, right? Imagine how it must smell up in there? She wobbled a little with laughter as if she knew that he didn't really want to go in.

They continued on along the lake, forcing the still air into motion. In the harbor the boats sat still on the lead-colored water, not the slightest stirring, angled sails sticking up like the dorsal fins of underwater sea monsters. One vessel seemed to accompany them, step by step. From a distance the water looked muscular, denser than the ground beneath their feet, which was almost invisible in the dark. Closer up, he was surprised to discover that the water was shallow. He saw his image tangled up with rushes and seaweed and a swarm of shadowed fish under the surface. It was as if the moonlight were dissolving everything into one substance, the borders of lake and land, air and ground unclear.

We should go over to the Japanese pond, he said. The idea coming like a clear reflection off of the water.

We could, she said, but I'm fine here.

They continued, letting the bobbing boats take what talk might be between them, along the curving lakefront, other couples sauntering by holding hands. He was three people at once, nothinking, thinking, and overthinking. Floating his own dreams on the water.

They reached Grant Park. Stopped and stood long enough for a breeze to rise and die in the grass at their feet. They sat in the quiet of the tall dark trees. He stopped noticing things and watched her. He seemed to say something, a couple of thick syllables, only to reach over, take her by the shoulders, and draw her toward him. The impulse took him by surprise. Amazed that lips can meet soundless.

Wow, she said. I finally got a kiss. She made some movement to adjust her blouse. Cupped one breast. Wait, she said. I can't take that out here. Smiled.

He would have liked to give the perfect response.

They took the long way through the park for the building where he lived in a seventh-floor apartment. Once in proximity, they looked across the even darkness to see every light shining on in his building and the one next to it and the one after that. Everything seemed to be in place. On this nice night people idled near open windows, on stoops, and lingered on corners.

Nothing remarkable about his small studio apartment with a single sleeper-sofa couch, a round glass dining table that fit halfway in the kitchen and halfway in the other room next to his small library of books arranged inside a built-in case.

You don't have central air?

No.

She opened the one window as high as it would go, letting in a breeze mixed with street sounds and human noise. Went over to have a look at his books.

He asked, You like to read?

Yes.

What?

Anything. She kicked off her shoes onto the kitchen linoleum—bare feet—then sat down on the couch. Looked at him, chin lifted, eyes trusting.

He took his place next to her.

Oh, she said, as if she'd just remembered something. There's a tattoo I want to show you. She removed her top. Removed her bra. And some experience missing to him was no longer. Both breasts before him, jiggling a little, a first sighting, a woman. More than enough for him. Little interest in the praying hands inked into her dark skin above her right titty.

Why do you have on so many clothes? she said. Aren't you hot? She started undoing his shirt buttons. He stretched and pulled free of his shirt. She stood and stepped out of her shorts. Naked, she came to help him out of the last of his clothes. His sense was not clear, then he witnessed her face break with vivid excitement. At last he understood. Another kiss. Touching her, aware of her body, careful, his caresses calculated not to exceed.

She pushed her fingers into his hair, eased his head back, and encased him in one motion. The pleasures of bearing her weight.

So this is what it was like. A new perception. Now within what his body knew.

They flipped positions.

Afterward, she curled against him, the outlines of her body disappearing beneath the sheets, and he closed his eyes and lay in her sounds and her smell. They lay in silence for a time. He spoke, and the night air returned his voice to him causing him to recognize by the change in her breathing that she had fallen asleep, her hand under her cheek, time moving over her face. He breathed in her hair, a chemical smell mixed with ginger, mango, cinnamon, olive oil, and other scents.

When he closed his eyes his body was forgotten, only the comfort of his own skin under the black weight of breathing. Sleeping dreamless beside her.

At some point during the night he felt her hand on him, and he waited until it moved on.

Day broke with him standing in the small kitchen where she could observe him from the sleeper-sofa. A morning truck grated by. A rush hour bus hissed its doors open. Horns blared. The voices of schoolchildren hung in the air.

You hear everything here huh? Tonia said, blinking away sleep.

Pretty much.

Light handed her to him. Waited for her to take shape under his touch. Unconcerned about morning breath, she drew her mouth toward his, fingers pressing into his shoulders. He made her a simple breakfast of oatmeal and biscuits. Strange that she was actually here. No way to know that in time everything would be cast into question.

At nightfall, they made their way to the Japanese pond, at whose suggestion, he no longer remembers. The cherry trees ignited in color against the dark. They plunged into a copse, coexisting with the grass. She straddled his body, a candle waxed above him, her head the flickering flame. She leaned forward offering a titty for his mouth, her breathing against his neck. They fucked for some time. When she separated from him, he remained stretched out on the ground, unable to move. She used the time to remove dirt and pebbles embedded in her knees. Then they went again.

A sound. She gave a stir. Someone easing among the bushes. A flashlight split the skin from the darkness, and he pulled out of her, tugged up his jeans, snatched up his zipper, and caught his dick in metal teeth.

In the time it took his dick to heal, he became well studied in her habits and movements about his tiny apartment, the pleasure of hearing her near him, his life distilling into a small radius around her, one day touching the next, no sense of hours passing. She liked to sleep with the window open, even in the winter, cold wind on his forehead, on his neck. He needed her upright in the bed beside him with a textbook, comforter, blankets, and sheets raised like a sail. Her past was transparent, every word she spoke weighing so much in his ear. *I just wanted to see what it would be like to sleep with a white guy . . . It didn't hurt as much as I thought it would . . . I just wanted to sleep with an Indian guy . . . They say it's best with an older man because he has to work hard to keep you. I guess that's true . . . I guess he flew me to the base in Alaska to see how many times he could get hard each night for the two weeks I was there. Then he broke up with me . . . I liked the veins in his neck . . . I liked the shape of his head . . . Gray hair is sexy . . . He acted like it was a big deal, but it was just a hand job. We were sitting there on the park bench, and I thought, Why not. I was never going to give him any. I cleaned his cum onto his shirt to make him look stupid . . . But I was first. I had that one thing on them. I did that for him before his girlfriend could. That's something they can never take away from me no matter how many years they stay together.*

He fell in the habit of making up experiences and secrets to tell her, a trick to ease himself into responding readily to her daily string of revelations.

Like every couple they tried new things. Once they smoked

some unicorn. Laughter, jubilation, delight. For three whole days. In fact, the drug caused chronology to move in the reverse, the hours to go backward, giving them three days to relive, the secret to time travel. He remembers hearing her say at some point, Nothing ever dies. Whatever you imagine in this dimension becomes reality in another dimension. No thought ever dies. He chickened out when she suggested they drop some mermaid.

She seemed firmly confident in her feelings toward him and was quick to point out his shortcomings. Each day she made an effort to shape him, suggesting changes to his grooming—You could put some waves in your hair; Why don't you grow a beard?—and asking him to improve the way he dressed.

Do you have to wear jeans all the time? Don't you think you should change up a bit? People might start to think you're sloppy.

Forever talking, especially after fucking. Should he have been offended? He offered utterances of his own—That's not really me, my style. That's just a trend. I don't want to look like everyone else. I don't care what people think—but most times, speech could not find its way out of the darkness. Still, he was mostly content. Easy enough to please through small acts of kindness.

Then one day he prepared a special meal for her. Showed her the transparent backbone of a squid. He knew that she was impressed.

After the meal was over, she stood before the bathroom mirror for quite some time, comb and brush in hand, trying to fix her short hair into a style.

What do you think?

It was her way of asking many things.

He said, I think you're going bald.

She looked at him. What? That's a stupid thing to say.

He crooked his mouth into a line, surprised by his own words.

He was willing to forgive any wrong she might inflict on him. She wasn't willing to do the same.

The hurt that followed opened a hidden channel inside him. How could she have left anything in him for the women who would come after? He would see something of her face in every one of their faces like a rosary of shrunken heads that he carried everywhere reminding him.

A year after the breakup, he needed more than just the memories and set out to make a pilgrimage to the Chinese restaurant and the Japanese pond. Lingered for a time inside the copse willing himself to believe that he had once been there with her. He started crossing a little footbridge that stretched like a zipper over the pond and saw Lamont crossing from the other end. Could it be?

Stopped and met at the middle of the bridge, Lamont looking at him with disbelief.

They both spoke at once.

Lamont became animated, his face showing acceptance that it was indeed Hatch before him. For his part, Hatch remained steady and calm when he spoke—What did he say?—given that he'd never been one for dramatics, had a need to be plain.

They did not touch one another.

What about Lamont had changed? He can no longer say since all Lamont's physical characteristics run together into one in memory.

They should keep in touch. With that in mind, he fingered and tapped his contact information into Lamont's phone. Could it have been otherwise? Although he was not a religious person—he did not believe in God—he saw in their chance meeting on this bridge the workings of some higher power, what was meant to be.

So it was that Lamont came to be standing in his apartment a week later. He can well recall all the walls reflecting light on a spring evening advancing toward night.

You got a nice place, Lamont said. He drifted aimlessly around the room, looking at this, picking up that. I see you still like to read, you all up in those books.

You know me.

He saw Lamont eyeing him up and down. (What comes unexpectedly into vision.) In the kitchen, he poured wine into two glasses and came back. Lamont was already seated at the dining table. He sat down across from him and held out one glass. Lamont reached only to draw back.

What is that? Lips parted, he lifted his mouth, challenging.

Elba.

What?

Some fancy wine. Somebody gave me a few bottles. It's all I have.

Lamont gave him a disbelieving look. Is it cold? Well, is it strong? Okay, then I'll try some.

Without thinking, he started to place the glass on Lamont's knee, caught himself, settled the glass into Lamont's hand.

Lamont took a taste. Not bad. It could use some ice.

Knowing better, he did not honor Lamont's need for ice.

Lamont tipped his head back and kept his glass held high in his hand, swirling the dark liquid. You ever see any of the dudes from the hood?

No. Not really. I don't go back. No reason to.

He tasted the wine thick and gritty on his tongue.

I know what you mean. I don't go back. Man, I got so tired of fightin them niggers every day. Lamont squinted his eyes half-closed, savoring the wine.

Yeah, you had it rough.

Did you hear what happened to Dodd?

No. What?

Yo, that nigger doing twenty.

Word?

Yeah. He broke into that computer store over on Touhy. He left his tools up on the roof. They found his fingerprints. And his DNA on a bag of pork skins.

Really? Had he heard this all before, a twice-told tale? Perhaps. And was it true? That doesn't surprise me. He was always kind of stupid.

Who you telling. Lamont held out his empty glass. Hatch retrieved the bottle, poured Lamont full, and placed the bottle on the table.

What about Huggy Bear?

Dude, that nigger dead.

What happened?

Don't know. Don't care. I ain't into all that Who-shot-John.

I hear that. He took a sip of wine. He wondered vaguely about Ronda, what had come of her? A husband? Kids? No way he could ask. So what you been up to?

Not too much. I mostly stay to myself. I got me a piece of job. Looking for something better. Trying to get up out of where I been living and find me a new place.

He waited for Lamont to finish.

But hey, I see you doing your thing. Mr. College Boy.

Lamont was back on his feet again in the thickening shadows, marveling at his collection of books. Have you read all of these? He held out his empty glass. Hatch retrieved a second bottle, returned to Lamont, and popped the cork, filling the room with the aroma of wine. He passed Lamont a fresh glass, opened the window to let in some night air, returned.

Without spilling wine, Lamont bent forward and pushed his face into the case, nose almost pushed up against the books. He ran his finger along the spines. Took a volume off the shelf, studied the cover, spoke both the title and the author's name, flipped through a few pages, only to return it. Then a second volume.

Can I borrow one?

Hatch said that he could.

Which one should I read? He waited for Hatch to answer.

What do you like?

Lamont thought about it. Which one is your favorite?

Hatch tilted the book off the shelf and handed it to him. As before, Lamont studied the cover, spoke title and author out loud, and opened it. To Hatch's surprise, he read the entire first page in silence.

Looks interesting.

Their eyes met for a few seconds and then Lamont carried on. Read another page. Reading done, he shut the book and set it carefully down on the table, finished his glass of wine, was poured another, resumed his survey of the case. He flipped one book over and studied the author's jacket photo.

He looks like a racist. Took a drink of wine.

Hatch did not disagree.

Lamont returned the book to the case. I guess you must date women who like to read? He put out a brisk hand and took another title.

Trying to pick apart Lamont in his mind, Hatch did not answer the question. What about you?

Me? His face paused at Hatch. I don't mess with too many guys, he said.

It seemed an odd thing to say.

Don't get me wrong, I still like men and everything. Lamont turned back to Hatch's collection.

His strong awareness of Lamont at his bookcase brought to him the realization that maybe he had it wrong: looking through his books, Lamont was picking him apart. Lamont looked from one book to the next as if thumbing through the years of Hatch's life, turning Hatch's life backward page by page to parts of his life he thought long forgotten.

At some point, he and Lamont came to be seated on the couch together. Hatch no longer recalls how or when, but the longer Lamont sat there, the more room he seemed to take up. Growing and spreading. Speaking in low sentences. Filling up the room with words. How long did they sit cramped together on the couch before Lamont asked him, So how do you like it?

What he's needing to remember: Lamont slumped on the couch in repose and relaxation, his left hand on the armrest, his legs stretched out before him, and face staring up at the ceiling.

Cocooned in his own thoughts, Hatch did not know where to begin. University was giving him a language for pinning down the world. What he wanted to say, should have said, but some other impulse came faltering through him.

Man, I thought nothing could be worse than high school. This is infinitely worse. Nothing but a bunch of phonies, posers, and wannabes. Ass kissers and apple polishers. Liberals smiling all up in your face and inviting you to parties. Gatekeepers. Pseudo-intellectuals. Flossers. Fake-ass revolutionaries. Bougie niggas talking about how woke they are.

These words overlaid by many others now lost to memory. Put together without thinking. (Where were they coming from?) Each word working him over in a way he had not planned.

He looked at his friend for any sign of understanding and saw that Lamont was no longer staring at the ceiling but at him, his eyes drawn as if against glare and his features heavy as if he were sinking into the floorboards under the weight of Hatch's diatribe. Whatever had flared up inside Hatch faded away in embarrassment.

Lamont said nothing for a moment. Then, You're lucky. It's nice to have a worldview. His eyes came to an assuring focus.

He liked what Lamont had said well enough.

Lamont said, It might take you a minute to figure out where you fit in. Don't sweat that. Look at what I had to go through.

Well, I actually joined this group that I like. Feeling a confirmation of the experience running within him, he started telling Lamont about the organization.

Sounds good, Lamont said. Maybe I can go with you to a meeting sometime.

We'd love to have you, he said. Such practical matters were now open between them.

Who made the decision to move away from the couch? At some point, Lamont resumed his survey of the books. At some point Hatch needed to walk to the other side of the apartment to flick on the lights. (Lamont would not have attempted to read in the dark.) And more wine was poured. (Was he surprised that Lamont was still intact despite all the drinking? For his part, he couldn't keep up, hadn't tried.) Did Lamont imbibe without being aware of the exchange of his empty glass for a full one? Hatch wishes he could see it all clearly in his mind. Needs to remember. Needs to slip from the present and return. Easy enough to rifle through the stacked deck of years and pluck out some random recollection. Harder the full assembly in sequence. He recalls seeing through the open window the world wavering from the distortion of darkness and distance. And Lamont making elliptical gestures at the shelves, muttering under his breath, disappearing into his own thoughts. In the disorder of books pulled from the case and pushed back into the case their bodies touched. His leg brushed Lamont's leg. Or Lamont's arm brushed his. The grainy flow of that moment. Whichever way it happened he apologized.

Don't worry about it, Lamont said. Face moving with all the wine he'd drunk.

You want more?

More.

Here, hold out your hand.

January 12, 2020
Harare, Zimbabwe

Orbits

The fumes from the super limousine dirtied the snow. The vehicle stretched a full block. She could see her father's kufi hat duck under the roof as he got inside where ninety-nine other members of his delegation sat looking like packaged food waiting to be microwaved.

The limo drove off in a cloud of white smoke, dragging winter behind it. It came to a stop three blocks later before turning the corner and curving out of her vision. What could she do but watch? What was he leaving behind for her other than his shoe prints smeared black mush against the snow?

She felt snowflakes touch her cheeks and melt. Her bones rattling in the cold. Now that her father and his contingent had left for their mission on the moon, winter birds again acquainted themselves with leaves. (One bird deserves another.)

A voice said something in her ear. Spoke her name along with other words. Miss Shabazz. Security protocol. Having spoken, West waited for her to about-face and go back inside the mansion, him trailing protection behind her. Rising as she came in, the other three guards—East, North, and South—greeted her mildly then left for their respective posts. Despite the plush white carpeting, she heard their footsteps echoing almost as if the house were talking, apologizing to her, ashamed of its barrenness. The cold had taken up residence inside her. What to do with herself now that her father was gone? She wanted to believe that he had secrets to be discovered. She set off to explore the mansion. Went breathing through the warm darkness of the halls. What might her father be hiding? Any locked chambers or compartments? Dungeons or attics? In this house space tended to hide from itself, dark empty rooms. Portraits of her father everywhere as if it was his gaze that held up the walls.

She installed herself inside her airy room, as spacious as a museum gallery, and situated on the second floor at the front of the house, comfortable and convenient with downy sofas, two full-length couches, a full workstation, and a home theater. What to do now? This: she rang for the moon woman and had a fire lit in the raised brick fireplace, a cascade of red flame. Task done, the moon woman communicated with her telepathically to see if she needed anything else. She could feel the question arc like a basketball from the four-foot-tall moon woman's brain and fall into her own brain. No, she did not need anything else. Alone now. Oddly quiet, the hearth crackling in silence and flashing gold light.

She turned on the television and settled into a historical drama set in ancient Greece, all the actors speaking in British accents. Two armies engaged in battle. Shuffling of many feet, cursing, neighing horses, clinking of harnesses, of stirrups against the sheath, creaking of wooden chariot wheels, rattling of steel armor, leather, a thicket of spears, a forest of arrows, helmets shining. The clangor, the smashing and crashing, the gore, beheadings, bodies crushed, torn apart. She thought about her father's words, *The survival of our race is at stake.* Hence, the need for her father and the other men to journey to the moon only a few days before her sixteenth birthday.

Put herself before the bay windows. Evening came on, casting red bands of light against the snow. Shadows closed on the colors of the street, robbed it of width and dimension. She gazed through the window into a dusky otherworld. The Champ's estate took up the full block across the street, the house a thousand feet away faintly luminous, stiff and white as if covered in starch. How were they passing the evening? If only she could communicate telepathically like the moon people. *Save me!* The dreaded Hawk rose off Lake Michigan from the east and flew talons first into the windowpane, rattling the glass. What she saw. What she heard.

She heard some commotion downstairs, voices and movement, and went to have a look. A dash of suits and bow ties: the night security detail had arrived, Ground Floor, Upstairs, West Wing, Right Wing. North, South, East, and West faded from her presence. The new men were wordless and busy with security concerns, grim and determined. Their task the same every evening: sleep this night with their ears to the ground. Four men who bore the assignment of guarding the mansion of the Nation's leader, the Honorable Isaiah Shabazz. In their excitement they glanced in her direction and their apprehensions became alloyed with care. Each man in turn nodded courteously toward her.

Upstairs was the only one of the four men she'd made conversation with. He'd walked in freezing weather all the way from another neighborhood. He had been recruited in prison. (As Brother Malcolm said, *America is our prison.*) This security detail was a step up.

He came cautiously up to stand in front of her and said, Miss Shabazz, let me know if you need anything. Spoken in a voice grown hoarse from smoking and hawking the Nation's newspapers on street corners. His hair was so close-cropped that from a distance he looked bald. She averted her eyes and went back upstairs.

The moon woman crossed her field of vision, two curved tortoiseshell combs in her hair. She—all the moon people—usually wore no adornments, just a plain black jumpsuit and black Nike sneakers. Somehow, they managed the earth's atmosphere without any special equipment that she was aware of. Day and night in the big house she heard their labored breathing rising and falling as they went about tidying with a machine that resembled a Phillips-head screwdriver. The machine spasmed, sparkled, groaned, whistled. The moon people worked in silence.

The fire was now a shapeshifting animal, her room cozy with heat. She felt her face ripple beneath her fingers as if she were transforming. Some craving within. Painted images of her father in her white memory fields. *The survival of our race.* She had full confidence in his abilities, this soft-spoken man followed by, worshipped by millions worldwide.

Surrounded by high trees, the Champ's mansion stood glacial white in the moonlight. Straining, she thought she could dimly see the Champ out behind the house dancing and shadowboxing, lightning-fast punches. He still had his fast hands. (May Allah bless her with such a fine and talented man for a husband.) Something beautiful and alive in his movements. Be that as it may, she had an intimation of true foreboding. At year's end after a two-year hiatus from the ring, he was scheduled to fight the current champion Holmes for a five-million-dollar purse. Everyone knew that he needed the money. Could he win?

She breathed out noisily as if breathing for the Champ, hoping he would catch a second wind. He did not, only went into his house, making it possible for her to lie in bed. Falling asleep she heard from a distance birds out on the street, Your father is gone! Oh, your father is gone! Whetting their beaks, passing a verdict, mocking her, *Your father is gone but you're such a Goody Two Shoes. Goody Two Shoes. Goody Two Shoes.* What was she meant to be doing?

She slept badly in her huge bed and felt like some beetle or other strange creature until darkness lifted, spreading dawn, and she could rise and decide what to do with her Saturday.

Then, before breakfast was served, her uncle Daoud arrived under a coat of frost. Instinctively, she knew why he had come. He was there to manage things, meaning her, while her father was away on the mission. He would be around day and night, night and day, until her father returned.

Her long eyelashes (false) fluttering, the moon woman took his skullcap, coat, and scarf.

One hand on the banister, he began a prayerful journey up the thirty-three steps to the top of the landing. Laila looked down at him as he climbed, but he never looked up at her. He was sturdy but short with perfect little sideburns like shoe-boots. His cravat plump like a baby's diaper. Lathered against his scalp, his black hair (dyed) rose to a peak on one side (left) like a wave splashing up against a boulder. At the top of the landing he looked up at her—she was slightly taller than him—smiled, just the slightest bit. Unlike her father's lined face, her uncle's face showed complete mastery over age, not a single wrinkle. The floor-length oval mirror held him and doubled his features. One uncle was more than enough for her to bear.

Sorry I couldn't come last night, he said. There was an emergency at the clinic.

In the manner of his own telling he explained how he had performed a routine amputation, cut off the tail of a white devil in her fifties. What was not so routine was that he could not stop the bleeding. Such thin veins and such thick arteries. The woman almost died.

He asked, Do you know what color these devils turn when they die? Green. He spoke the words half in anger.

What was she to say to that? He looked into her face expectant.

Who's minding the store now? she asked.

He took her hand, My dear niece, don't worry about that.

She held on to his blank hand while he questioned her about school. As she began to speak, he let go her hand, seemed disappointed. Why? Her grades were stellar. She asked him about his practice.

One must not sleep, he said.

Indeed, despite his smooth skin, he looked old and tired, in need of a rest.

We must remain diligent, he said.

Her uncle made a killing off these white devils who for some reason wanted to be separated from their birthright and have their tails amputated. And now he was making a killing on the amputated appendages, sewing them onto brothers and sisters who felt lacking, who wanted a pink and functioning tail, one they could move from side to side and up and down, one they could twerk, drop low to the floor. Her father condoned the procedure since it boosted the self-esteem of their fallen race that was badly in need of uplift.

Her uncle owned a car but preferred public transportation, buses, and the El, places where he could solicit potential clients firsthand, even offer them free procedures.

We know what we are, her uncle said, but not what we may be. Like this woman last night. Again his distaste showed, ill disguised.

She smelled cologne and aftershave coming off his skin and clothes. Thought about her father slapping aftershave lotion on his face like shoveled dirt flung on a coffin.

She tried to tease out information about the mission. Her uncle laughed, his hands trembling as if from electric shock.

He said, On the moon much of the old way still goes on.

She knew that there was something he wasn't telling her.

I know you miss your father, but he has to fulfill this important undertaking. The Honorable Isaiah Shabazz sees everything as it was in the beginning.

She studied his masculine jawbone. He's your brother.

Again he laughed, body gone jelly. She felt his warm hand on her shoulder. Yes, my brother.

He needed to collect some blood samples. Might she accompany him? Stumbling, wheezing in sorrow and weariness, he made his way through the mansion and into the remote wing that housed the hog pen. She fell in beside him. Before they entered they slipped on gas masks and snapped on surgical gloves. A moon man worked in silence, performing his chores. He greeted them with a Black Power salute. Her uncle returned the salute, but she did not, only nodded. Hog noise echoed in the morning light, no sound stealing past the squawking and squealing. Her uncle climbed over the railing setting off a stampede, each shape and form becoming vague. He produced a collection kit from a blazer pocket. She wanted to turn away and hurry off. He was one among a team of Nation medical professionals and scientists working on a process to reverse the effects of eating pork, the porcine curse that had, centuries ago, turned some black people into pigs. Could he undo what had been done? Her uncle told her that her father's contingent would be bringing back volumes of a special elixir from the moon, which they hoped would be the cure.

After he was done, her uncle slipped the test tubes into the side pocket of his blazer then climbed back over the railing. They thoroughly cleaned and sanitized their hands before they sat down to breakfast in the main dining room. The moon woman had prepared pancakes, scrambled eggs, and turkey sausages. The moon people had mouths and ears like humans but communicated only by telekinesis. The woman's utterances popped up in Laila's brain like cartoon bubbles. She could actually see each question inside her skull, had to take time to read it, every word opalescent: Is the maple syrup warm enough? Care for some more milk? Care for another flapjack? The moon people looked human but for the strange greenish tint to their skin that made them appear to be made from terra-cotta.

Snow fell, blotting out the sky. They spent the remainder of the morning in the game room playing chess—You got me again! his small sharp teeth shining in the light—sat down to lunch, then returned to the game room to play cards (tunk, hearts, and gin rummy). She won every hand easily. A hollow enactment of family time since she could tell that her uncle didn't like losing. He suggested they enjoy late-afternoon tea squared off at Monopoly (the Sopranos edition). She seated herself half-heartedly at the board. Long before her fingers touched her token she had lost interest in her uncle and the game. Still, she won.

It serves me right, he said. That's what I get for pitting my wits against yours, dear niece.

She spent a few minutes reviewing strategy with him. That seemed to comfort him.

How will we occupy ourselves until dinner?

She had no answer.

Well, perhaps something will come to mind. He excused himself for the lab where he would run some tests on the blood samples.

From the chair her uncle's scent lingered, a sticky fog that kept her pinned in place. His presence had embittered her. All his talk about labs and pigs. His constantly quoting her father's teachings—*The Honorable Isaiah Shabazz teaches that we have been robbed of our name, robbed of our religion, our culture, our God. And many of us, by the way we act, we have even lost our minds*—words she'd heard a thousand times. How would she endure him for a week or more? Rousing herself, she went up to her room, sat down before a window. The late-afternoon snow gleamed. She had made up her mind: she would not leave her room again today. She contemplated an excuse she could make for dinner when a text pinged on her phone: *Come over.* The Champ.

Word was delivered to her uncle not to expect her. (The Champ could not be denied.) She did not waste time putting on a hat. Upstairs accompanied her across the street, making small talk. Winter wind riffled through her hair. Once inside the mansion, she saw the Champ sitting at his dining room table busy with a portion of smoked turkey much too big for any man or two men, his fork clinking against the china. Looking casual and relaxed in dress slacks and a short-sleeve shirt. (Apparently, the cold weather did not bother him.) His body gone a bit round now, his rectangular muscles swimming inside a layer of baby fat. Gray stubble salted his chin. Life after the ring.

He was more than twice her age, old for a boxer. More so since the white devils took away his belt and barred him from the ring for almost four years because he refused to sign up for Selective

Service and possible military deployment. Her father and the Nation had kept the Champ from starving by giving him a home and allotting him a monthly stipend. Then the Supreme Court ruled in his favor and he made a comeback, recaptured his title with an eighth-round knockout in the Congo. He'd had a few more fights, all tough, brutal, then gone into retirement. She wouldn't understand until later that his best years were behind him. He will lose the fight against Holmes in December, unable to answer the bell for the eleventh round, never having thrown a single punch but showing the world once again his ability to take one, absorb punishment. Six months after that he will have his final fight and lose. He will continue to live high on the hog for a few years, until his money runs out, then her father and the Nation will once again have to intervene and put him on their dole. By then he and Belinda will have gone their separate ways.

Both she and Upstairs walked across the gleaming parquet floor to stand by the Champ. The Champ finished his food and pushed his plates aside. He turned his attention to Upstairs. Took a deck of cards from his shirt pocket and passed it to the other man.

Shuffle the cards. Cut the deck. Deal yourself a hand. Now place the cards against your forehead. Yes, like that.

The Champ placed his hands before his torso like a squirrel holding a nut, peering down into the hollow created by his palms. One by one he guessed each card.

After a stunned pause, Upstairs asked, Champ, how do you do it?

The Champ stood up, took a bow, rejoicing in his spectacle, the Greatest of All Time, for good measure firing off two quick punches at Upstairs's face. The other man had no time to react. He put his hand on Upstairs's back. A person can be made to believe things, he said. Then again, all matter is insubstantial around me. He winked.

Upstairs turned to look over his shoulder as if not really believing the Champ's hand was there.

The Champ asked, Have you ever seen a match burn twice?

No.

Next time. You're done here. The Champ gave Upstairs two light taps on the back and guided the bodyguard toward the door. Soon he was back with Laila at the table. Laila alone in the commanding presence of this tall handsome man who had taught her how to jump rope as a little girl. Bending, he kissed her on the forehead. Despite a nagging awareness of disloyalty to her uncle, she felt a measure of excitement.

He explained that he needed her to babysit tonight. Apologies for the short notice.

He did not sound sorry.

Laila felt deflated. Not sure what she was expecting from the Champ after he had summoned her. Not sure but not this, babysitting.

At once the Champ's wife, Belinda, was in the room already thanking her and passing on instructions. It was as if Laila's future self had manifested, who she would be as a fully grown woman: Belinda. (Her Christian name had been Mable.) Pretty skin, freckles, reddish Afro, firm bosom, thick thighs, and big butt. Belinda went quickly about the house with last-minute tasks—alarm disarmed, emergency phone numbers, car keys, bedtime snack for the toddlers—beauty spinning from her body. And then they were gone.

Liberated from their parents, the two chubby toddlers worked out an impromptu itinerary for Laila that included Hide 'n' Seek, Giggles, Llama, Getting Light, and squealing like pigs. She floored them with her impression of Patrick Star. Chasing was the best part since they knew they were quicker than her.

Come on, Aunt Laila. Run faster.

They even afforded her a head start.

What activity might tire them out? She stripped them down to their disposable diapers, getting them relaxed, comfortable, to better tire them into exhaustion, but they would not be stymied.

Affection seemed to help, tickling and huggy kissy poo. Energy ebbed, she managed to put them to bed at nine.

The Champ and Belinda returned after midnight. The flick had been so-so. Belinda did not care for CGI, which she deemed phony, while the Champ thought the movie was cool. The zombies killed and ate people almost at will. But the filmmakers introduced a plot twist. The ghouls were hunted down and eaten in return.

How were they? Belinda asked.

Laila threw up her hands in silence.

The savage mind, the Champ said.

Belinda gave him a love tap. Those are our children. She tilted her mouth up toward his. After the kiss she left her husband and Laila alone. The Champ rubbed his stomach through his summer dress shirt, indicating how hungry he was. It seemed to him that he had not stopped being hungry since the first zombie was boiled with rutabagas. Laila offered to warm up some leftovers. No, she'd done enough. He would walk her home.

You know, only a fool does something for free, the Champ said. I've been thinking about how to repay you. A word stalled on his tongue. It sounded like *farty*. She had seen it in him before, the blur while thinking. Wait, he said.

With evident excitement, he retrieved his top hat from the coatrack, pulled his retractable magician's rod from the side pocket of his cashmere great coat and extended it like a blind man's cane. Then, employing grand stylized gestures that were as antiquated as they were timeless, he tapped the cane against the topper one two three, causing a cloud of smoke to explode cannon-like from inside the hat, which shrouded out into white filaments that dissipated into a wondrous sight: a colorful parrot that fluttered up and perched on the Champ's forearm. The Champ smiled at her and she smiled.

Then the parrot spoke: Let me throw you a birthday party. Sweet sixteen.

You want to throw me a party?

Yes. Me and the Champ. Clowns, camels, corndogs, cotton candy, canapés, cannoli, Crush, and cable cars.

Was it a real parrot or some sort of ventriloquist dummy? She could see the Champ's lips move with the bird's mouth. Her question was answered when the bird took to the air and started flying about the room. She watched as it gained more and more height, rising above all the furniture until it reached the high ceiling. The Champ could not catch it. At one point it winged toward her. She ducked. Finally it settled on top of the coatrack.

The Champ looked at her. I'll get it later, he said.

The next morning at breakfast, her uncle asked her, What happened to you? His voice seemed oddly hard. He had seated himself opposite her.

She explained about the babysitting. Then she tried to smile but failed.

Her uncle saw her effort.

The moon woman—lip gloss today and rouge—brought her three slices of French toast then dusted them with cinnamon. She glanced at Laila; a flicker of communication passed between them. Just as quickly, Laila turned her thoughts away from the little woman serving them breakfast.

And what about today? Her uncle's cravat looked like a slug fastened onto his throat.

Would he want to sit quietly for most of the day? She lied: Belinda wants me to cornrow her hair.

I was thinking we could—he explained what he had in mind. Waited, but she did not answer.

She was talking to herself, trying to bolster her confidence. She had already decided not to tell him about the party. How could she?

First, he needed to do some work in the lab. The Original Asiatic Man had billions to be added to their numbers once the Nation could reverse the effects of the bovine curse. He had uncovered

DNA evidence that the Original Asiatic Man descended from the moon people or vice versa. Her uncle's eyes flashed. It was possible that—so he now believed—the moon people had sent an exploratory team to the earth a trillion years ago. Unfortunately, they kept no written records. Further tests were required.

Laila found her thoughts reaching into the brown strands of her hash browns that resembled upturned leaves on the ground. She looked around for the moon lady but did not see her. A portrait of her father watched over their conversation, her father a resplendent figure against an unwonted background, the stars and planets that populated the dining room wallpaper.

The past belongs to our great race, her uncle said. The future is another story.

She regarded him calmly.

Not only the strong but the weak have a legacy, he said.

How would the party take place without her uncle's knowledge? How would the Champ pull that off?

Other things were said that she didn't catch. Then something about a missed call.

What?

You were away, but I spoke to him. Her uncle glanced at her father's portrait. It has never been any man's total destiny to be both a father and a mother. To this, Allah may be the only exception. Looking forlorn, he started to say something else, perhaps repeat what he'd said. Then he covered his plate with his used napkin. I better see to my work. In his eagerness to leave the dining room he rose to his feet, forgetting that she was still eating breakfast.

On this Sunday, the day that God rested, the pictures were straightened, the curtains washed, the furniture polished anew, the entire mansion dusted and swept, the lush white carpeting shampooed. During this time the weather cleared, white mists of snow barely infiltrating the trees. Birds beyond the windows.

It came to pass that she found herself standing close to the moon woman, taking in her power, energy. No longer remembered when she'd first felt it, but now that she had she couldn't live without it. She saw but also sensed with her skin the steady stare of the pearl-gray eyes. Took in the girth of the thick torso. Although the moon woman was small, to touch her would be to touch a truly astronomical sum of cells.

She asked the moon woman about her planet. Certain things she thought she needed to glean.

The moon woman answered in her calm solemn way. What would you like to know?

A press of questions tumbled about her disordered mind. One passed through her mouth more random than selected.

I would like to tell you, the moon woman said, but it would be hard on you, finding the right words. It would take some time.

The doorbell rang, and it continued to ring, over and over, without pause like an alarm set off. Jarred, Laila went to answer it. Even before her eyes saw, she heard the voices of the men on the security detail.

How many rounds, Champ? How many rounds?

He ain't nothing to me, so he'll go in three. But should he refuse to go to the floor and want some more, he'll go in four. But if he's somehow still alive and full of jive, he'll go in five. If I had time for tricks, I'd take my time and clobber him in six. He snapped some punches into the air.

With eager eyes they noted the Champ's speed and his footwork (famous shuffle) in polished leather shoes. The Champ, always on display, his way of putting himself all out in front of himself. More so since there was no particular reason for him to put all his energy on. The fight wasn't until the end of the year.

The Champ asked them, How come you Negroes aren't wearing ties?

Each man brought his hands to his throat. Their bow ties had vanished.

Here, why don't you try these? The Champ pulled one tie from his pocket, then the second, and the third, finally the fourth.

They blew and sucked their faces into different shapes, flabbergasted at the Champ's sleight of hand, seemingly so easy for him. Her uncle entered the room, expressing surprise. Champ. They made some small talk, her uncle speaking in the breathless emotion-saturated voice of an admirer, another fan thankful to be afforded the opportunity to rub shoulders with the Champ, while the security detail made their way back to their respective posts.

Finding an opportune moment, the Champ said, We need to borrow your niece. Belinda wants her hair braided.

How had she and the Champ arrived at the same lie?

Watching, Laila could tell that the Champ's words and demeanor almost persuaded her uncle. But not quite. Seeing the expression on her uncle's face, the Champ leaned toward him.

Well, let me not detain you two. Then and there he decided he would go for evening prayers at the dutiful mosque.

Once her uncle had departed, Laila thanked the Champ for coming, and she meant it.

He said nothing in response, only roamed about the main parlor, with his hands in his pockets, looking at portraits of her father, taking his time before each one. Then: they needed to plan, the day was right around the corner (Saturday), certain details needed to be worked out, guests invited, arrangements made.

It took them some time to cross the street to his estate, moonlight volleying down the black air. Belinda and the toddlers were away. What opportunities were now afforded her? Decidedly, time was on their side, to plan for the party, yes, which they did, seated next to one another on a white couch made from soft Italian leather. She perceived that now was the moment to find out if the Champ would reveal what her father, her uncle, and other higher-ups in the Nation wouldn't with their strict, deeply embedded mores and their code of silence about the moon. The little she knew about her mother had come from the Champ. (Her poor mother, her lifetime ended by a strike of the sun. The Champ's exact words.)

The Champ heard her out.

Honoring her request, he spoke to her about the moon. First, he spoke of their ocean, then of the chain of floating islands inside the moon, then of the people on the islands, lastly of their ideas. As he talked, she visualized the interior of the moon—a live map unfolding in her mind—where the people lived, average lifespan one hundred and twenty years of age. The ocean, an elixir, helped keep them young.

Would you like to try some? His face was turned toward hers.

You've been there?

Once. I went there to relax after a fight.

She knew what that meant; he had gone there to heal.

You ain't missing much, he said.

Floating around on my own island all day sounds like fun to me. What's so bad about that?

The Champ thought about it. It's stuffy. The humidity. The sky is ugly. The clouds are black.

She said nothing.

And you wouldn't like the food.

He said the words half to himself as if he'd grown meditative, no longer conscious of her presence. She had to get him to continue.

All the butterflies were black. Like floating silhouettes. As on earth, many people disposed of their used sneakers by tossing them over a telephone or cable line, but on the moon, birds (all black) nested inside with their young.

Then the Champ said, I'm sure your father will bring you back a special birthday gift.

She expressed no surprise at the Champ's promise of a gift from the moon. Instead, she pushed the Champ for more, asked him about her father's mission. Her father had said it was an urgent calling with the survival of the race at stake, while her uncle had told her something different.

The Champ had not been made privy to the purpose of the mission. What he knew: Contact dated back until at least the turn of the twentieth century when the moon people had communicated with H. G. Wells to have him record the history of one of their failed conquests. A few years later they became concerned after the appearance of Georges Méliès's film *A Trip to the Moon*. The white devils were starting to get ideas. It took the moon people more than three decades—these things take time—to develop a plan of intervention and put it in motion. They made contact with Orson Welles, whose 1938 radio play of H. G. Wells's *The War of the Worlds* was a smoke screen for their first expedition to Earth. Welles was a light-skinned Original Asiatic, which was why he was so good at playing Othello. Through Welles they reached out to the Nation.

It was more than she'd had.

Back home, she overheard the four bodyguards—West, East, North, and South—engaging in conversation, shit-talking while they waited for the night detail to arrive and relieve them.

You ain't never seen the Leather Lady perform? Man, she can make her pussy burp.

You like them nasty women.

I'm just saying.

Now, the Champ's wife, that's my kind of woman.

Yeah. High butt pleasure.

You think you can handle that?

He can't handle nothing but his hand.

Yeah. The only sisters he dates are the Hand Sisters.

The men laughed.

To Laila, it was normal; she had lived like this always; she did not know any other existence. Like Upstairs and his security team, the four directions were more and more indistinguishable from one another, getting jumbled in her mind.

Quietly, she made her way to her room, the bay windows luminous with moonlight, her father reaching out to her, keeping tabs. Who knew all the things in the world that could get her in trouble with Allah? She dropped to her knees in prayer on her embroidered mat. Rather a slave of Allah than a free friend of Satan.

Underneath her she felt gravity push away. Soon she was hovering a few inches above the floor, an outgrowth of her faith. She had the Champ to credit for this phenomenon: on her birthday last year, he had shown her how to make a prayer mat levitate.

That night she had a dream that involved her father, but the memory of it disappeared with the sun.

Seated on two thick books—encyclopedias? Holy Bibles?—the moon man drove her to school. The brim of the hat he wore was broader than his shoulders, lending the impression of an upturned bowl. Now a measure of curiosity about the little man overcame her. She had tried to learn the names of the dozen who worked in the house, names that were all long, full of clicking sounds, and difficult to pronounce. In the rearview mirror he smiled at her, his eyes gray, intelligent, and penetrating. She smiled back.

She blinked as a dazzle of white illumination hurt her. Through the window she saw fleecy clouds specking the sky. A lasso of light circled the glass; the same light circled her head then her body. Wind rushing about gathered up a quantity of snow, swirled it into new flakes, blew them wet against trees that all looked to be under pressure, waiting to explode.

In the classroom, Mr. Levine revived his usual themes. On the anvils of experience, the structure of Greek society was hammered out. Their world was different from ours. Some might say better. Around the hero, everything becomes a tragedy. Around God, everything becomes what? A world?

Short (slightly taller than a moon person) with a long flat head, he looked like a walking hammer. Something tool-like about his hands as well, which he kept encased in purple surgical gloves, a color that clashed with the seersucker suit he wore every day over a white shirt and his brown shoes that curved up like tubers from the floor. He seemed to blend into this world not unlike the designs on the wall—roses, violets, and fleurs-de-lis.

Dante raised his hand to answer. The Greeks were right. At least about that. He sat in front of Laila, his eyes looking two ways at once, his body spilling over his seat like a weed searching for further places to grow.

Seated next to Laila, Erika listened, grunted, sighed, whispered. She was not short of admirers and made the most of her intelligent eyebrows, her small flat nose (cute), and her large friendly mouth kept half-open in a half smile.

Girl, what are you going to do for your birthday?

Probably not much, Laila said.

Isn't your pops away?

Yes.

So why can't the cat play? Erika asked.

Laila thought about it. I wish, she said. But I'm not like you.

Hurrying to leave her home for the Champ's, she lost her footing on the carpeted stairs and slid down on her bottom to the bottom of the staircase as if being released from the birth canal. Outside, moonlight floated in the air. She looked right through the night into nothing.

A few minutes later, Belinda bit down on a little wheel of red cheese, she and the Champ tense. Laila had come in the middle of an argument.

I have my own opinions, she said. She finished the cheese, her eyes cold and alert on her husband.

Could have fooled me.

So now you got jokes?

I know my business, the Champ said.

For a minute or more they faced each other under the chandelier, neither speaking.

I'm not worried about that chump. He used to be my sparring partner.

But he's the champion now.

Only because of the tomfoolery of these white devils.

And he's younger than you.

Time measures nothing but itself. He shook his head as if nullifying the effects of a punch. You know, you're starting to sound like—just forget it.

Belinda cleaned her hands on a towel, her floor-length skirt hugging the ample portions of her lower body, a cocoon trying to break open. She turned away from him and the Champ watched her leave the room.

Laila: it amazed her, the power of one argument.

At last, the Champ spun around her way and smiled, then smacked his abdomen with both hands, indicating that she should cross the room, stand under the lights of the chandelier, and punch him as hard as she could in the stomach. Not a boxer's thing but something he'd picked up in his reading about Houdini. She had it in her to do what he wanted.

He cheered himself on. Rumble, young man, rumble.

The next morning, Mr. Levine dove right back in. One wonders about incubation. How long? And under what circumstances?

Her thoughts were still packed down. A dream lingered that waking should have erased. She caught the key phrases of the lecture and jotted them down inside her notebook. Eurydice who guides . . . The Greeks are forever stepping on snakes . . . Orpheus who looks back . . . How can we have eyes to see? . . . Torn apart by women . . . Why can there only be reunification in death? . . . Or was that absolutely impossible after all? . . . Don't dance with naiads on your wedding day.

Dante said, Consider this: if X is true, then Y must be true. Or are we back to the original problem?

Everyone glanced at him. Was he mocking Mr. Levine or taking a serious shot at the propositions? After all, he had won the school's science fair competition with his anti-nigger machine.

Mr. Levine kept his voice deliberately patient. Go on, Mr. Michaux.

Dante could not go on.

Light orbited the lens of Mr. Levine's spectacles. You get extra credit for trying, he said. He picked up where he'd left off. The first myths are usually the worst. Not so for the Greeks . . . In this sense we are all, each and every one of us, storybook heroes. Every Greek myth contains all of human history.

Dante offered another idea, his voice inching out, word after slow word. There is another world inside this one.

Laila felt lucid now.

When the little moon lady came out from behind the curtain she seemed no longer a person. The evening light had disguised her as a basketball. Looking at her, Laila sensed the enormity of her own body.

She wanted to borrow one of Laila's head coverings. Was it an unusual request? No need to bite her tongue. Please say so. Together they searched through Laila's closet, the mundane noise of her trying one cloth after another before the full-length mirror until they agreed that a lavender shawl seemed to be the perfect match for her complexion. She took in the moon woman's scent. Could almost feel the enveloping presence of that other world.

After supper, she and her uncle sat in separate armchairs reading, his feet crossed. There had been a change in the condition of his patient, all he would say. She had a strange lingering intuition that they would not finish the evening this way.

The doorbell rang, over and over. Her uncle took a deep unsteady breath.

A few moments later the Champ appeared in the room wearing a fashionable brown leather jacket. (Did he ever dress for winter?) Her uncle stiffened up in his chair and eyed the Champ. What words would be spoken? He was afforded no time to get to his feet, the Champ bending down and embracing him, tight. Then putting himself straight again and giving Laila a playful slap on the chin.

What excuse would he use this time? Her uncle saved him from the need for one. The Champ's timing was perfect. Truth to tell, he needed to look in on a patient. Laila could explain. The Champ would be doing him a favor in seeing after his niece. Just for a few hours. Was it too much to ask?

The book that she was reading did not escape the Champ's notice. She knew the illusion that he wanted to perform so she took to her feet, crossed the room, and turned her back to him. Opened to a random passage in the book, selected a random sentence, then she closed the book, turned and faced the Champ. Warming up, he shook the kinks out of his body before bringing all ten fingers to the sides of his temple in concentration. He recited the sentence: "Dim light from the hall; fell pale and splintered on Regan's paintings; on Regan's sculptures; on more stuffed animals."

From the backseat she watched a flock of birds soaring in flight black against the white sky. Thinking that she had not fully appreciated the advantages of being the Champ's friend until now. Of course, the Champ had his own problems. Was everything fine with Belinda? She had not been able to tell last night during the preparations for her party. Belinda—

She made a thermos of coffee for you, the driver said telepathically. He was watching her in the rearview mirror, his eyes glinting as if polished, stone. She had been dimly conscious of him. He held up the thermos for her to see.

She did not drink coffee.

Don't think of it that way, the moon man said. It's perfectly acceptable. I drink it every morning. In fact, seven cups each day.

With some reluctance she accepted the thermos. To show the driver that she trusted him—his people, his kind—she unscrewed the lid, causing steam to erupt volcano-like, and took a sip. The coffee was already sweetened to taste just the way she imagined she would have prepared it. She poured a cup, already feeling a growing pleasure. Her mind deepened during the drive.

This statement by Zeus, taken in isolation from all the others, and from the rest of Greek reality, is wonderful and touching to think about.

But Zeus was a long time ago, someone said.

Yeah, he dead.

Zeus is not dead, Mr. Levine said.

What's it got to do with now?

Erika looked like some strange bird nested in the plumage of her brown wool sweater. She wanted to whisper to Laila about cute guys. Laila corrected her own visual assessment of Mr. Levine. She no longer felt that he looked like a tool; instead, his body came off as insubstantial, only so much batting for his clothing.

Loaves and fishes all over again? He gestured with his purple-gloved hands.

Yes, Laila said, loaves and fishes.

Mr. Levine sat down on his desk. Would you care to extrapolate?

She extrapolated. He nodded his approval. Resumed his lecture. For the remainder of the period she answered every question. She didn't want anyone else getting a word in before her, not in the least. What had taken her over? She could not say.

Mr. Levine gave her a long look, without expression, looked right through her. Miss Shabazz, I hope you don't mind my saying this. Please don't dominate class discussion. Give someone else a chance.

It was not lost on Laila that although her father believed white people were devils, he did not mind sending her to a school where she would be taught by devils.

Class over, Dante followed her down the hall. What a strange destiny it is to be followed. He followed her into her college-prep calculus class, a light and airy room, and took a seat quietly in the back row.

At the end of the period she sauntered forth, affording him the opportunity to talk to her. What class do you have next? Future studies. Hmmm. His eyes were as quick as pinballs, looking (pinging) here, there.

She wanted so badly to tell him about the moon people. Didn't know why. Took everything to keep from blurting out all she'd learned.

He started questioning the validity of Mr. Levine's class. What was it worth beyond the credits? Anything? Personally, he doubted it.

A fur-coat embrace, her birthday gift from Belinda and the Champ.

The snow melted for part of the next day and started to form into new shapes, bright visions in all the windows. Wet strange cars passed. She saw a river, the sky. Then it started to snow again. Was it to be cold forever? Her mind was full, every emotion, idea, sensation, all color, line, and shading, no blank spaces at all.

Myth is continuous, Mr. Levine said. Only daily life is intermittent.

Erika said, I wish he would rest his mouth. She was looking her best today, each strand of hair a black river. Full-length black boots emphasizing her long legs.

Think it through. Myth is like a finger pointing at the moon. Don't concentrate on the finger or you will miss all that heavenly glory.

Dante said, Mr. Levine, I got one for you.

The champ carried his toddlers on his shoulders.

Look at us, Aunt Laila. We're flying.

He bent his knees as if doing squats, heaved and launched them six feet into the air, spun his body one hundred and eighty degrees, his back now to Laila, and caught them on his shoulders again, their positions reversed, each toddler now on the opposite shoulder, smiling at her. (Who doesn't love flying?) He performed the feat again and again.

Magic (illusion) notwithstanding, around the Champ Laila carefully guarded her thoughts. Should she tell the Champ her fear? No reason to because her curiosity had become greater than her fear, yes? After all, the Champ had supplied an answer. Magic was like his bread and butter, boxing. How had he put it? Training is not just skipping rope and running roadwork and studying film. It's learning how to get into the mind of your opponent, think the way he thinks, become him. You start to feel him, anticipate how he thinks. By the time I'm in the ring I know when a punch is coming. Like I'm throwing a punch against myself. The art of defense.

Stop, husband, you'll give them gas. Now in the room, Belinda looked at Laila and said, The savage mind.

The Champ extended both arms and let the toddlers slide triumphant down his biceps and bounce to the floor. We can fly! Belinda had her own plans for them. She asked Laila to excuse her. Once she left the room with the subdued toddlers, the Champ made a motion so rapid toward Laila's face she might have easily overlooked it. Then he opened his hand. Inside, gold earrings in the form of the star and crescent, also a birthday gift, to be worn at the party on Saturday. How sweet, how thoughtful, but she failed to put forth the appropriate expression of heightened enthusiasm and gratitude since the pressing thing she wanted from the Champ cropped up in her mind and deflected her attention.

The Champ said, Belinda picked them out. He looked at her in such a way as if he were making quick mental notations, taking inventory.

They are just the right thing, she said.

That is good to know, he said, seeing her expression.

Why her reluctance to just come out with it? Why these feelings of embarrassment? If only she could communicate with him telepathically.

The Champ had an idea for the party. RAN should perform.

Not a bad idea. RAN (Real Ass Nigguhs) were popular, all of her guests would be impressed, floored, but she didn't care for that kind (political) of hip-hop. Would he be offended? Was he already offended? Perhaps she should put on the earrings now.

Then the words just came out of her: I've changed my mind. I would like to try some, the elixir.

Their gazes met. The Champ appeared to be rigidly attentive. She felt her heart vibrating in tension, alarm. Ill-concealed? In any case, she had said it.

Without a word, he walked over to an accent cabinet, stooped down before it, and getting out a common milk jug, brought the plastic container to the dining table. With care he unscrewed the lid, a swoosh of released pressure, vapors clouding the air.

In the car the next morning, the moon man said, Too many bad drivers today. Alert to his task, he glanced at her in the rearview mirror then turned his gaze back to the windshield. The moon man kept both hands on the steering wheel, his nine knuckles like a mountain range.

Who was she to agree or disagree? She had not noticed. Light angled through the windshield and struck his enormous hat, and for a moment he seeped out of focus.

How is the Champ?

She knew that the moon man was only being himself, courteous, trying to make conversation, not prying into her business or scratching around for scandal. Be that as it may, she had to keep silent because he'd asked a question that she could not answer. Could not tell him that last night she'd witnessed the Champ perform his greatest illusion. One where his art of diversion had fooled her into believing that he'd actually removed his head from his body and held it up on one palm before sliding it back into position on his neck.

Did you manage to ask about his coffee?

At last a question she could answer. No, she had not.

The presence of her classmates was comforting. Even Mr. Levine's voice. She told Erika about her birthday party on Saturday, which she supposed was a way of inviting her without inviting her. Withheld that the Champ was throwing it for her. None of her classmates knew that the Honorable Isaiah Shabazz was her father, and no one here knew anything about her friendship with the Champ, her secrets to keep. Erika asked her what cute guys she planned to invite, not an unimportant question. Before answering she took a deep shaky breath.

Dante voiced a certitude, agreeing with Mr. Levine. Yes, he too believed that this was so.

It's not enough to agree, Mr. Levine said. Do it backward.

She and Dante met outside the building after her last period for him to accompany her to her car. Bright sun, bright snow. The winter trees offered no shade, no shelter, Dante no longer wearing a coat but flickering pieces of sun. The wind pulled words from his mouth, nonstop chatter that she was not trying to hear. He only stopped talking to put his cupped hands together in front of his mouth and blow on them.

Your pops is Isaiah Shabazz, he said.

She turned away embarrassed.

When she came home, the moon lady threw herself everywhere, fluffed the curtains, scrubbed the bathrooms, dusted, vacuumed, made the beds (including her father's Dutch bed with curtains), cooked dinner, did the dishes, ate the cobwebs, ate the moonlight.

Her uncle decided he would help her with her homework: identifying the Greek elements in *Ancestors*—the limited series streaming on Remote—and *Hitler's Minions*—the limited series streaming on Woke. She said as little as possible; she did not want to talk but to hear. He was as certain as she was unassured, all his suggestions on the money. Both shows were committed to the idea that the thing you love the most is also the thing that will kill you. (Which Greek myth was that?)

The doorbell rang. Her uncle raised his head, studied her with large moon-darkened eyes. He did not move, leaving it to the security detail to respond, but something in her would not let her remain immobile. Feeling as if she were in a trance, she crossed the carpeted living room to answer the door. Upon arrival she found that the moon lady was already there.

The Champ had dropped off a package for her, a box not much larger than a mobile phone. Greeting cards? No. The opened box revealed ornate party invitations printed on hand-cut paper. The moon lady smiled up at Laila, lashes long, her gaze warm, inviting. Lending the sense that she thought Laila knew something or could do something. What? What was she after?

Now it was necessary to hide the box from her uncle.

The next morning, the driver carried Laila silently to school, every living and mechanical thing blasting into her awareness.

She thought she'd have to listen hard to take in Mr. Levine's analysis of the two TV shows. But it was as her uncle had said. At least in part. The love of bigotry bringing about the destruction of two societies, the slaveholding South and Hitler's Germany. She was beginning to regain her poise; she felt it seeping back, a little at first, then with a rush.

Erika had an opinion: Hitler was a pretty good painter.

You think so? Mr. Levine asked.

Yes.

Some would beg to differ.

Art is subjective.

A hand shot up. Teacher, why do we have to write a paper about the African Holocaust? I don't see why we have to write about something that happened hundreds of years ago.

Yeah. Let's write about something going on today.

Microaggressions.

Dismantling the forces that police our communities.

Anti-racism.

The New Jim Crow.

African Lives Matter.

The lack of cohesion among Black people.

Futurism.

Afrosurrealism.

Mr. Levine, our opinion has never at any time been asked.

I enjoyed watching the TV shows, Dante said. The horror. Did you see the way they killed that fat dude in the concentration camp? Today he wore an old-fashioned double-breasted pinstriped suit and pointed black shoes. Something spider-like in the lines and colors and his web of Afro.

Through his spectacles Mr. Levine eyed Dante with hard criticism. Be respectful, Mr. Michaux.

What do you mean?

How would you like it if I said, Did you see the way they whipped that fat dude in Africa?

Dante popped up out of his seat, hands tightened into fists. A noise started up in Laila's ears, went off inside her head. Mr. Levine looked Dante over carefully then inched toward him, slow, grim, and determined. Some of last night's chill returned, the moon lady bearing the box of invitations. Her teacher craned his head back looking up at Dante, his hair stiff as feathers, face to chest, Dante a foot taller and husky, fifty pounds heavier. The two studied each other with such intensity that Laila, sluggish, inept, and dizzy, felt compelled to get up out of her seat, put herself between the two combatants, and put an end to the conflict by the simple means of placing her hand on Dante's chest.

No, let him go, Mr. Levine said, his voice tight. Let him go. I'm not afraid. He seemed to mean it.

Still rocking the lavender headwrap, the moon lady went about her Saturday-morning chores with her little tool, looking vacant and bored. Sadness drawn across her mouth, no mistaking it. She peered into Laila's face, something there. Laila heard her attempting speech, the bubbles pinging inside her head but hollow, empty of words.

What was wrong? What could Laila do? Other than ask questions that were received with silence, only some tingling kinetic sensations.

For the whole day unmarked trucks arrived on the snow-wet street outside the Champ's house, uniformed men and women jumping out of them with bundles and packages or unloading boxes and crates, the tallest crates Laila had ever seen, towering in the icy air. The vehicles glimmered in the sun, a brilliance of the light she found pleasing.

The activity was not lost on her uncle. What in Allah's name was going on? What did she know about it? His eyes blazed, questioningly.

Laila took a deep expectant breath. Beats me, she said. Her uncle knew nothing about her party and she must keep it that way. Wait, she said, the Champ and Belinda mentioned something about a birthday party, for the toddlers. I had forgotten until now. I hope it's okay: they have requested my presence.

The first guest to appear, Erika arrived in a dress of stunning colors, nothing dim about it. For her part, Laila wore her new fur coat over a taffeta party dress that Belinda had purchased for her. A gloved attendant came to collect their coats, Laila careful in removing hers. She stood tautly waiting for Erika to praise her dress.

Girl, go ahead and pose.

Laila struck a pose. Then it was Erika's turn.

Pleasing expectation. They exclaimed in wonder at each new arrival. Jacinda! Jericho! Tashawn! Kenya! Bill! Buckley! Laquanda! Mandela! Gabrielle! Lumumba! Shaquira! Dante! Brown black yellow boys and girls striding past light-wrapped trees, down the red carpet into the basement of the mansion to a smiling Champ and Belinda, who greeted each guest, their hands out. Welcome to our home.

Soon a throng of hyperactive partygoers filled the basement served by a catering team who graciously held trays with ice-cold drinks (soda, juice, Gatorade, and punch) and hors d'oeuvres. The lights dimmed, and the DJ busted down on the turntable, throwing the room into dance.

Dante sought her out. Sorry about yesterday, he said. But Mr. Levine was out of pocket.

Right.

You know me, he said. I'm not a violent person.

Don't sweat it, she said. You may have done yourself a favor. He'll probably give you an A for the class. Aren't you glad about that?

He nodded slightly in the darkness. I earned it.

She said, Forget everything else. At least for tonight.

He forgot, sucked—whoosh!—into the whirlwind of dance. Possessing boundless energy, he was swiftly active, dancing with one girl after another, then even some of the boys, living it up.

Erika remained next to Laila, the two eyeing each other in the murky light. Talking about all the cute guys at the party, her arms got pulled out into incomprehensible shapes. It would be interesting to see what change, if any, overcame her tonight.

Girl, you got secrets. The Champ. He's fine.

He's my friend. I've known him all my life.

Dante moved toward her. He praised her clothing, her earrings, and her smile. Dance? Clopping up and down, his shoes looked like horse's hooves.

She staggered back, arms raised. (The following year, their final year of high school, she would come to think differently about him. And on the graduation trip to Europe—a trip that both her father and her uncle will welcome since it will afford her the opportunity to see and study the white devil in its place of origin—she and he will kiss.) He moved hurriedly away. The next song someone else asked her to dance and she accepted. Her feet felt easy moving in their shoes. Then with Erika again. Now in the dimness ninety-nine people eating catered food, ninety-nine people drinking Orangina and frappé that Belinda had made and served from a punch bowl. Vibrant knots of conversation beneath the booming music. So much energy in and around her.

The Champ gave a short speech, welcoming everyone to Laila Shabazz's sixteenth birthday celebration. He spoke glowing words about her, then he began to perform magic tricks.

I've been all over the world, he said. Boxing has taken me all over the world. I'm like a ball that bounces. Never bounces in the same place twice.

The Champ performed impersonations. Frederick Douglass, Brother Malcolm, Beyoncé, Denzel Washington, Will Smith, Oprah, Barack Obama, Future, Nicki Minaj, Lil Wayne, Snoop, Jay Z, Cardi B.

The partygoers screamed, More!

The Champ floated like a butterfly. Threw the fast punches that had made him the most famous man in the world. He said, People must not turn into bees who kill themselves in stinging others.

The Champ moved through curtains of light. Disappeared.

Then his voice coming through the ceiling, announcing that RAN would now perform. All ten members of the group exploded into view and started prowling about the stage in desert camouflage and bulletproof vests, rapping one hit song after the next, the unfolding flow of their reality. Soon everyone was swinging the new dance the Orbit, spinning about and clashing into each other's arms and shoulders, Laila swirling among the shoulders bare and proud (the women), angular and defiant (the men). Bodies now colliding into each other, bouncing off each other like bumper cars before forming into a circle, moving clockwise, then counterclockwise.

After the performance, the rapper with the best flow, B.C.E.—Before the Caucasian Era—hopped off the stage and introduced himself to Laila. Beside her Erika stirred restlessly, her ample shoulders tanned and freckled in the light of the room. Laila the center of attention—blown kisses, good wishes, shout-outs—but B.C.E. held an audience with her, his voice low and careful. She'd rather read his eyes than dance or talk to anybody else. He dreamily talked to her, much to say, while she stood next to him, quiet, feeling the silky texture of her dress, talking by listening, nodding agreement from time to time. Then he turned toward her, and she waited, her breath tightening around her. Would he try to kiss her? (Touch was too much.) Perhaps he was one of those people in the world you don't want to let go of, like the Champ. Soon breathing again. Many years later she can still remember the way his clothes smelled in the dark.

Some song playing, only five notes, slowly over and over, a little phrase, changing the air. Erika dancing with another rapper from RAN, getting to the music, hysterical gesticulation, shaking the air around her head, a lighted strangle of hair. Then several cute guys all wanting to dance with her, frantic in their urge. Erika like a bird fluttering in retreat from cats. Now the energy in the room flowed in another direction, to Dante. All at once lights flashed on and some huge blanket (or the Champ's magician's cape) came stifling down cutting off Laila's chance to breathe.

Time for Laila to take the stage and unwrap her presents: jewelry (bracelets, earrings, necklaces, anklets), books, a year's subscription to her favorite video game, an empathy box, fur-lined house slippers, The Wire: The Board Game, scented scrunchies, a kimono, a jewel (cosmetic)-encrusted pimp cup (Bitches Are Pimps Too), vitamin C–infused face peel masks (avocado, charcoal, and lemon), RAN merchandise, and two tickets to the smash musical *Girl, Do You Know What That Negro Said to Me?* Rivers of discarded gift paper on the stage.

Drop the lights and drop the music. New cadences rippled from the speakers, releasing a burst of emotion from the partygoers. That's my shit!

Laila stood and contemplated the splendor of this moment. Huge sounds in the dark. Tactile joy. People breathing hard from dance. One dynamic group blending into another. A word in everyone's mouth. None of it escaped her notice. Recognized. Laila breathing in all the life breathing around her. She felt all the doors inside her body fall down.

The first whisper of departure started in someone's nostrils, in someone else's groan, a sigh, a grunt, a flutter of the lips like an engine trying to turn over. A person left. Followed by another. Soon the party was over. No other way it could be.

The aftermath: Certain objects harden in the state they were left in. Other objects piled up in pleated shadows. Nothing left to do but thank Belinda and the Champ. She wanted to say something to the couple, tried to bring forth words from the enormous mass of verbiage lighting her mind, could not. Belinda hugged her, lay in her arms. And with her thoughts and emotions came sounds but no utterances. Already the Champ had set about to entertain the four bodyguards who were waiting to escort Laila back home. He demanded their bow ties, accepted each one by one, then—Abracadabra—he transformed the bow ties into a single length of colorful metal chain. Abracadabra changed them back. Astonished. Flabbergasted. Rattled. Nervous laughter the only suitable emotion. And Laila also laughed, moisture shining in her eyes.

Winter light and snow. Trees popping and creaking overhead. Everything looked like it was made of porcelain. The men in the contingent packed in wool and cashmere. Bedredged with blue of snow-glow, they seemed to be sporting robes of snow and ice. Nostrils pluming out different lengths of breath.

Unhurriedly, her father stood. He nodded at his brother, but they did not embrace. Earlier she'd revealed to her uncle that she now drank coffee so he'd prepared them some, spooned instant grinds into two identical mugs, sugar and milk spiraling in the boiling center of each, and as they sat across from one another she'd felt the dwindling of tension between them. What did it mean? Now he told her he felt cheated. Felt they had only just begun to talk, and here it was, time for him to go.

After a meditative pause, she said, I'm here, not going anywhere. Her breath crumbled like bread in the cold.

Her father was back. Still high from the party, questions speared what to why to who, her voice thickening in thinning air.

I will tell you, her father said, but not here. Let us talk inside.

The who involved a distinguished guest. She would be staying with them in their home for an extended period of time. He made the introduction to a portly moon woman bundled up in a patchwork coat of many colors and materials. (Furs were not an issue.) She looked up at Laila and smiled a nice smile, a questioning glow of wonder and concern in her large attractive eyes that gleamed with sudden light. Laila returned the smile.

The street moved with men from in the bounded-togetherness

of the Nation, their own dance groove, the snow recording their footprints black. Each man adding something to the other in the exhausted air, giving him what he lacked, completing him. One vision. The distinguished moon woman had her own concerns, glowed and smoldered darkly, bringing her hands to her ears. Apparently, she didn't like the sound of the car. Or was it the smoke coming from the muffler that she found bothersome? Now waving her hand in front of her face. She touched the fender and the engine stalled. Gazed at Laila's father with disappointment as if he had let her down, had failed her.

It seemed that the commotion in the street had drawn the Champ from inside his home. Laila saw him waving at her from a distance. She waved back, signaling him to come. Nothing slow about him, he hurried over. Her father embraced him. Champ. Introduced him to the distinguished moon woman although even he found her name too difficult to pronounce. For a few moments the two stood across from each other communicating telepathically while Laila, her uncle, and her father looked on.

He kissed Laila on the forehead. The moon woman eyed her impassively.

The Champ said, I kept my eye on her while you were away. She spent her birthday here with Belinda and the kids.

Okay, Champ, her father said. Many thanks. You always go out of your way to set an example for our youth.

The moon lady came from inside the mansion to welcome her father. Something less about her today, a kind of resigned inertia, not the usual energy. She did not acknowledge the dignitary. In fact, the two moon women gave no indication that they knew one another or had any interest in communicating with one another. The greater figure followed the lesser figure into her house.

Lingering behind, Laila took a moment to speak to her father. How was your trip?

We are making bold strides, he said, although we endure a peculiar dilemma. His aged face sat atop a web of wrinkles like a cat's cradle. To be ahead of everything and still to be behind. That is the condition of our great race. I have never found a solution. So other people's troubles are easy to bear.

She wished for more, but knew that was all; many years ago, she realized that she did not belong to him; he did not exist for her, only for the Nation, his millions of followers, and the moon people. She was herself.

Her father said, I hope you like the gift that I brought you for your birthday. I put a lot of thought into it. For you are now sixteen years of age, a milestone. He smiled at her.

She tried her best to return his smile.

In fact, now that you are a woman, I was thinking that we might send you on an important diplomatic mission. To the moon. We need to strengthen relations. The survival of the race is at stake.

They continued on inside the mansion where the two moon women waited in the great hall. Within moments one lightbulb blazed bright and burned out. Too much light for the moon dignitary. Laila had to keep her face composed, show no signs of fear or anger or concern, only skin. In the darkness already a plan was shining on the surface of her brain.

Once she was alone in her room, she sent the Champ a text. Surely he would help her.

Fornication Camp

"... Honey, behind the sun"
—Muddy Waters

Their suitcases were waiting for them beside the door of the villa, Dolores's polished expensive one and his own scuffed workaday bags. He studied the villa in the half light of dusk. He had not anticipated something so grand. The block-long two-story rectangular building with tile roof in a spectrum of shades from red to brown to gray, rows of doors and shuttered windows, and iron lamps mounted to the pastel-colored stone. A real Italian villa *here,* islanded among the cornfields, in twenty-first-century Illinois.

They'd pulled up into an arc (half circle) of graveled driveway and climbed out of the car to the sound of chanting frogs and under the eyes of a dozen curious white-clothed-gloved attendants, college-aged men and women.

Welcome to Villa Garibaldi.

Xavier tried not to show his doubtful surprise. He offered the best smile he could. Dolores spoke to them, but Xavier saw through the vague light of sundown the uncertain nod of one who had heard but not fully understood. An attendant held out refreshments on a silver butler's tray. Xavier took a glass and drained it.

Dolores did the same. She waited for his cue, then returned her empty glass to the tray next to his. The head attendant explained that their bags could remain here, by the door, to be brought into their rooms. They must hurry to the welcoming dinner. The attendant gave them a dry knowing smile.

Xavier followed Dolores into the villa, trying to take in every momentous detail. Bright-colored paint pulsing against the old walls, travertine floors, vases positioned on marble stands, and the Renaissance furniture (armchair, sofa, footstool) with little placards barring them from use. They stood inside the lengthy corridor just long enough for white gloves to come fluttering toward them, directing them into the dinner salon with tapestry on the walls (hunting scenes).

Dolores entered the salon greeting everyone with hugs and kisses. Xavier stood behind her determined to keep little distance between their bodies, establishing that they were together. Nothing but young people here, as far as he could tell, everyone in their twenties or thirties, making him easily the oldest. One person after the next sizing him up, this outsider, but he stayed himself, smiling, polite and reserved. He would take it all as it came. Dolores turned and began introducing him, looking at him in the way he loved, taking pride. The long drive here had pulled and dragged her beauty out of shape. Still, there she was, her hair held by ivory combs and drawn away from her face, her high cheekbones and ears reflected in the frail light from the chandeliers.

He and Dolores found their assigned seats, a fresco on the wall behind their table. Dolores held out her hand to take his glass and fill it from a bottle of red wine. Soon the congregants started to delight in the gathering, everyone interrupting everyone else, a crisscross of playful laughter, teasing, and arguing. He took offense at such backwardness but saw no point in expressing his objections to Dolores. One good thing, they weren't quoting biblical verses or trying to convert him. He was fascinated that his assumptions and expectations had been upended. What was he hoping to gain from coming here on this retreat? Was it only about appeasing Dolores? What were they reaching for together?

Early in their friendship, Dolores had told him, Look, I'm sorry but I'm married to my faith. That's the way it is with me until my Father gives me away.

Would their whole time together be spent in trying to free her from her beliefs? No. He would not pressure her or try to change her. Still, as whatever it was between them developed, much could befall an ordinary afternoon or evening when they were alone together. They would often sit close on his couch talking. He would hear something surface in her voice, and see her fix him with a bold stare, signal for him to push her hair to one side and start kissing her neck, slow and light at first, brushes and pecks. She would tilt her head, offering plenty of bare skin, a vampire move. Soon his hand was lifting whatever fabric covered her stomach, curving up her torso. She would cup one breast and lift her nipple toward his mouth. And so on, macking out.

A bell sounded somewhere in the room. Every woman stood up from her table. What was this? They shuffled around until one table marched off lockstep for some destination, then another fell in line, and the next and the next, as orderly as schoolchildren. What was this?

They left with tight formality, but they soon returned in a loose ebullient wave, cheering and laughing, each woman rushing forward with a plate of suckling pig in either hand. Dolores set one plate before Xavier and took the other for herself.

He ate, no questions asked.

The dinner was as splendidly prepared as it was lavish. Including the nourishing soup, it consisted of no fewer than six courses. The suckling pig followed by a gleaming flank of roast pork garnished with cherries and pineapple rings and set off with a bowl of raspberries and cream and a gooseberry tart, then a superb lamb roast with vegetables, followed by a salad (walnuts, cranberries, apples diced), then roast guinea fowl, a dumpling dessert, and finally cheese and fruit. Each time the bell rang

Dolores would get up from the table to retrieve the next course. Such was a woman's role as she understood it.

Move your mouth this way, Xavier said.

Hey, show some respect. Why did you come? She touched his knee.

A few tables away, a woman he recognized from photos as Madame Omocheke was explaining to someone that she knew how to prepare twenty-seven different sauces for fish. He couldn't place her accent, somewhere from the continent, the diaspora. She was attractive and curvy, her form encased in an ankle-length African dress and hair enclosed inside a beehive turban.

Now she was at their table.

Why, Sister Dolores, Madame Omocheke said, clean that frown from your face. Bring God with you. And then she turned her face toward Xavier. So it is you.

She gave Xavier a carefully measured smile and extended her hand in greeting, took his hand fully into her own with a flourish of affection then placed her other hand over the top of it.

He forced a smile at her and bowed his head in greeting. She did not relinquish her hold of him.

Glad to have you with us, she said.

Glad to be here, he said.

In the holding he tried to commit to memory her round face, smooth skin, her green eyes, bangled wrists, and—Enjoy, she said; Excuse me, she walked off, her hands dangling at her sides, bracelets slipping—heard the weight in her walk and the sound of fabric trying to give over her behind.

For an hour after supper people gathered informally in the parlor. Stood about chatting in little groups near the piano or in a corner. Green folding tables had been set up for devotees of games—dominos, backgammon, poker, Go Fish, and tunk. Some claimed that this group was a cult under the control of a charismatic leader. Xavier had been brought up in a secular household so, cult or no cult, organized religion was all the same to him. He was a nonbeliever. What he thought odd: they had organized a retreat for the purpose of denouncing the evils of fornication.

We can go outside, Dolores said.

Did she sense that he had suffered a disappointment, eager as he had been to meet the pastor?

He followed her through a set of glass doors that opened onto the end of the white driveway. The warmth had gone out of the air. She leaned against the building, watching him in the glow of a mounted lamp, radiant, holding his presence while he stood a few feet away, watching her back, feeling the gravel under his shoes and the reverberations of the frogs as a thing inside him. She will ask him what he thinks about this retreat so far. What words ought he to say?

She rubbed her palms against the side of her jeans, the cuffs of her shirt pinching the skin around her upper arms. Go ahead and smoke, she said. She was able to smile, having made the decision. No apparent risk for him, her.

He pulled his crumpled pack from an inner pocket of his blazer and was soon smoking steadily, drawing the cigarette half an inch from his mouth after each inhalation, the muscles in his face aching but the smoke seeming to expand in vast clouds with the frogs' exhalations. In the moonlight he took in the expansive grounds, could see the parterre garden and various other dwellings. Felt the stiffness starting to leave his body.

Done, he put the butt into his pocket for later disposal, affording Dolores the opportunity to take his hand and pull him into her, hold him as he held her, her head level with his chest; he kissed her neck, and she broke away, her fingers slipping from his, so awkwardly disentangled that he lost his balance and almost fell.

That's for coming here with me, she said. See you tomorrow.

Only after she had walked back through the glass doors did he enter the villa and seek out the room allotted for him. High-ceilinged, spacious, and perfectly furnished and arranged, writing table and chair before casement windows, a comfortable armchair and footstool tucked into one corner, a hand-painted armoire, a chest of drawers with a vase atop it like a dunce cap, a standing mirror, and a tapestry hung on the wall behind the bed. From what he could tell, the tapestry depicted a wedding ceremony, bride, groom, and other celebrants dressed in Renaissance garb. Half-conscious, he sat down on the mattress, bearing up under the long day.

A bright light flashed across the wall and disappeared, and flashed again, growing brighter, lines of illumination moving across the ceiling. And some vagrant sound. The arrival of more cars? He went over and stood at the window, put his palm on the glass, feeling the outer dark. Night dangling like a black apple.

Some bird woke the morning and set the sky bursting, broad rushing brightness that seemed to slow down everything else, the world waking around him and before his eyes, day sorting the landscape into distinct patches in each windowpane.

From somewhere in the middle distance Xavier heard a church bell sound the hour. Then in a confused moment of condensed time, Dolores was standing in the room with his breakfast on a tray. So it would go every morning. An ordinary thing, Dolores in a simple white knit shirt, jeans, and sandals. He sat down on the bed while she sat down at the writing desk, the chair turned around, facing him, the tall curtains behind her, him here, her there, not near, not far. While he ate, they exchanged chitchat about last night—How did you sleep?—and spoke about plans for the day, the tall curtains curling toward her in a listening posture. Comfortable now in her presence, he heard himself talking, nothing he couldn't say to her.

But before he had finished his coffee, Dolores started to tidy up the room, swift calculated movements, causing Xavier to get to his feet, the breakfast tray left behind on the bed like a ship deserted at sea, Dolores humming scraps of songs, Xavier still close. The awkwardness of his body. How would he keep himself out of her way? Now but also for an entire week? She turned the sheets back, tucked them in place—he turned away at the sight—took clothes from his wardrobe and arranged them on the bed. Drew his bath.

He was quickly in and out of the deep tub, elastic and efficient, fully dressed, fully groomed. When he returned to the bed, Dolores was on her way out the door with his used plates and utensils. She smiled. He thanked her for breakfast. She quit the room, only to put her head around the door and blow him a kiss, and when he blew one back at her, she stuck out her tongue.

They passed through rooms too fast for Xavier to take it all in, trying to remember what he could, no detail to be turned away from, Dolores speaking, excitement in her voice. Her clear knowledge of the history of this place. As part of a plot to woo Garibaldi to the Union cause, Abraham Lincoln had the entire villa moved, stone by stone and brick by brick, from northern Italy and reassembled here. (Who would have thought?) A feat best understood by studying this scale model of the villa constructed from cardboard, toothpicks, pebbles, broom straw, sand, plaster, and Popsicle sticks, the model so exact that it reproduced the cornfields outside stalk for stalk. (Could it be so?) Xavier circling the model, nothing else in the chamber, bare walls, no echoes of his footsteps or her voice.

They stepped outside the villa. Much more for her to tell him in the time it took them to reach the top of the plateau, Dolores alert as they went, watching where she stepped, so careful, so serious, his mood quickly matching hers. She ended her narration, and they stopped and stood for a while staring at the valley beyond. Xavier let out a burst of breath. He saw the villa rising black from the cornfields like a breaching sea monster. The hills squatting on the horizon seemed to be vacuums sucking up all color and light from the air.

Working a field was a surefire way of humbling oneself before the Creator, a burden Xavier was willing to bear to impress Dolores. The way to the field seemed slowly gained. Lumbering through a copse of trees with huge bright leaves like peacock feathers. Did Dolores take his slow pace as hesitation, reluctance? And his cigarettes? He could smoke in the presence of the two men accompanying them, their chaperones Taylor and Milk, who looked like flying squirrels in their baggy jumpsuits. He found them companionable enough, unobtrusive. (Something between him and Dolores that shut out everyone else.) Both men possessed distinctive features that for Xavier illustrated their respective sufferings. The younger of the two, Taylor spoke with a stutter that troubled the steady set of his face and that didn't seem to match his whimsical scalp-close haircut etched into geometric figures and arabesques. Taller darker older, Milk possessed the kind of vanity that made him sport a full-blown Afro simply to show to the world that he still had all his hair. Good for him since no telling what he'd been through. He was missing his right earlobe and one finger below the knuckle on the left hand. What was left of him appeared ordinary, half-gray goatee shaped onto a puffy face above a lean body, a man of stunning form, broad shoulders and long limbs, a swimmer's shape. He tried to set Xavier at ease with a good-natured smile.

Lined up three paces apart, they began to work their way across the plot, bending, chopping, and gathering, taking half steps forward in a rhythm that soon had Xavier hot and dizzy. A cloud rotated heat overhead like a clothes dryer. Not an easy job for the four of them, but they worked quietly and efficiently, brown-bodied in the spring heat, their scissoring shadows cutting across the stalks. They finished the plot without exchanging a word. How many hours had gone by? Would tomorrow be more of the same?

They dried the sweat from their faces with heavy towels and left them behind on the ground, white flags of surrender. Straggled along to a shady hill and flopped down onto the grass, knees raised, lethargic, the two men between Xavier and Dolores. Xavier could smell the pine and hear the whipping of the branches and beyond that the sound of a river. Somewhere close in the trees behind, a bird gave a curious trilling call. He glanced around but saw only pine cones like little brown claws. Comfortably quiet together, they enjoyed a simple lunch from a picnic basket. With the food and drink he could see the gradual reappearance of their energy in the brightening of the landscape. Then Milk tossed the empty basket down into the field, but the others didn't react. Was Xavier the only one to notice?

The largest bird he had ever seen materialized in the sky above, huge wings working like ungainly oars. The feathers colorless, translucent.

You see the kind of man I have here, Dolores said. Her hand reached over the bodies of the other two men to grasp his. Xavier did not know what to say, looked at the way her neck and shoulders emerged from her blouse. Looked at the turquoise nail polish on her dark toes.

Milk turned toward Xavier, nodded, mouthed something silently in the air—*You know what to do*; was that it? *I'll show you what to do*—winked, smiled, but Taylor seemed not to hear Dolores, remained hunched over next to him, silent. Reticent to speak for fear of stuttering? No. Xavier sensed that something more had crossed his mind.

He's different, Dolores said.

Oh, I noted that, Taylor said. I'm also different. So what does that really mean?

Dolores released Xavier's hand.

Taylor broke off his complaint to turn and look at Xavier, a questioning brightness in his face. I'm very touchy about these things, he said, the insult all the worse for the time it took him to get the words out, so much noise in him.

Xavier resisted the urge to strike back. *Different.* Clearly this fool didn't know the meaning of the word. Xavier lit a cigarette. Took the smoke in deep. Exhaled hard. Taylor took the stream full on in his face.

Taylor slid up one pants leg then the other, revealing bony pale ankles and calves that seemed to be full of vibrant tension, twitching with hidden life. He asked Xavier something, waited for Xavier to answer, only to have his voice echoed by the bird in the hard sky above them.

Xavier glanced at Dolores, saw that she was watching Taylor with an expression he didn't recognize.

A child is born with no state of mind, Taylor said. That's why I needed the church before I knew there was a church. Why I needed the prophet before I'd even heard of him.

His words like a fast sketch in the air. Xavier continued to smoke, barely looking.

Let me tell you about my home life, Taylor said. This woman who raised me. He gave Xavier a private little smile. My mother, she has demons.

She's just sick, Milk said. His soft almost shy voice. Some harmony seemed to exist between the two men.

I saw them, Taylor said.

You saw them? Xavier blew a haze of smoke behind the question, imaginary demons filtering through into the present day.

Many times. Taylor looked away for a moment as if something had been forgotten.

Xavier knew better than to say more. He stubbed out his cigarette in the dirt then flicked the butt away, the taste of smoke lingering in his mouth.

Milk raised his head in a firm gesture, put a reassuring hand on Taylor's shoulder. Brother, he said, ease up. We should be grateful to have this rare man among us. We should be thanking him.

So thank him, Taylor said. He gave a dismissive wave. This was Taylor, so much to say, so many wobbly, rattling words.

Birds broke in over their voices.

You two have said enough. Dolores lifted and dropped her shoulders, stirring her breasts. Let him be. She used a different voice to speak to the men, one Xavier had never heard, although he knew that she always strove to be decisive, knew her casual sarcasm and affronts. (Wow, will you look at that booty. Amazing. Stop pretending. Go ahead and look.)

She looked at Xavier, releasing Milk and Taylor from her

watchful gaze. We're tiring you out, she said. A small awareness between them. She shaped her hair, patting loose strands into place, then heaved up from her sprawl, slapped loose grass off her jeans, helped Xavier up and put an arm around his waist, Milk doing the same for Taylor.

The day unraveled quickly, a yellow-red-black thread. Bats taking to the sky like ink spurted from a pen. They walked through the warm darkness of the cornfields into early-evening light, untranslatable sounds around them. No decrease in the speed at which Dolores moved through the slushing leaves. From time to time, she half turned to make sure Xavier did not miss his footing, although for his part he trusted each step he took with her. Dolores held Xavier's hand as if afraid she might lose him. No words passed between them.

Another meat-heavy meal for lunch the next day.

Hitler was a vegetarian, Dolores said. Her thrilling smile.

She excused herself from his company, freeing him to spend most of the afternoon with Milk inside a windowless marble-walled room, the two men surrounded by other members of the church sharing their individual beliefs about the world and reconstructing the shards of their respective histories, no pause within their conversations, endless talk. The other men seemed to watch Xavier's face for any reaction. So casual with what they revealed to him he was prepared to hear anything. Too much closeness but he yielded to it all. Carried along. Saying little. (Who was he in comparison to all that experience?) Although it was clear that they wanted him to share some intimacies, secrets, about himself. Even thought he heard someone ask, How many women have you fornicated with? To avoid opening that Pandora's box, he would have to give them something. He did. When he spoke, his voice felt loud to him in this room where light had a strange way of moving against the walls, growing then diminishing as with the rise and fall of voices. Squiggly striations in the marble like snakes caught in amber.

The hours slid into each other, his mind drifting at times. Then, gradually, the room began to empty out, leaving Xavier wobbly, full of uncertain feelings, unable to assimilate all he'd heard. Had he given away something of himself? Milk was quick to arouse his attention. Leaving the room, Xavier noticed new striations in the marble, as if the stone had absorbed the conversations, recorded them. For his part, Xavier had his own questions, what Milk seemed to sense. Taylor.

I'm sure he would have talked your ear off. Milk smiled. But I think his misfortune exceeds his hopes, so he made the wise decision to leave. Me, I don't need a babysitter. Me, I want to serve God.

Milk led him through double doors into an immense and brightly lit salon alive with dozens of voices, a loud gathering of church members either seated on or ambulating about rows of folding chairs, adapting themselves, trying to get comfortable. He and Milk waded through the preperformance racket and established themselves on either side of Dolores. She turned toward him as if hoping to catch a look or thought, but he did not let his eyes meet hers. That was when he first took in the grand arrangement displayed at the front of the room, a hundred or more polished wooden musical instruments, many that he recognized, some he had never seen. They were all string instruments, the one commonality, a repeating universe. A tribe of luminous beings.

Then a man slipped onto the scene. The congregation pulled away from their chairs and encircled him in an effort to greet him. Xavier had not been expecting Omocheke to appear, there, at that moment. This man nothing like the image in his head, despite the many videos he'd seen of the pastor in his element, someone other than this short dark guy with curly close-cut hair dressed plainly in matching black pants and shirt like a delivery driver, nondescript no-nonsense clothing except for green crocodile shoes. It was difficult to see him now, Xavier forced to observe the pastor down to his small dimensions, the way his pointed sideburns changed color at the tips, graying, the lower part of his face clean-shaven like a politician's. And the all-mighty purpose of his stance, the proud lift of his head, his repertoire of gestures, including the sideways tilt to his mouth when he answered a question, the way he smiled when he offered advice, the way he could place his hand on someone's shoulder, back, or arm, and sway the person into laughter.

Then Omocheke brought them out of their revelry, implored them to return to their seats. The room began to quiet down. Apart from the noise made by the movement of hands and feet, squeaking chairs, and coughs and throats being cleared there was silence. The pastor leaned back on his heels and watched his audience.

We all know the story of the animals meeting to choose their chief. They chose the leopard, who began to use a big chair and to wear clothes.

Omocheke started moving loudly along the parquet floor, throwing everything into his body when he walked, force, energy, prowling crocodile shoes.

At night the chief, with his court, went out to hunt other animals.

The pastor stopped, took up an instrument, tucked it into his chin, and fingered a short riff.

One by one, the children started to disappear, devoured by some creature. Relatives of the children came to complain to the chief, who would always ask: "Did you notice the characteristics of the animal that ate your child?" The complainant would retort: "The only characteristic we saw was that the animal had a tail." But the chief kept his tail hidden inside his trousers and remained seated all the time, so it was impossible to identify him.

Omocheke took up another instrument. Plucked a variation of the earlier riff.

Brothers and sisters, we are children of God, and what we will be has not yet been made known.

Now as he talked, he began to move from instrument to instrument, playing a riff on one then repeating it on another, the little phrase made new each time as words continued to fall in place.

But we know that when Christ appears, we shall be like him, for we shall see him as he is. The earthly paradise will bestow on us a new perspective, and indeed a new history and a new future.

The slight gnawing sound Xavier heard did not seem to come from the bulky instrument held in the pastor's arms.

All who have this hope in Christ purify themselves, just as he is pure. But the path to purity is no simple matter of abstinence and affliction. In ancient days, men guilty of every crime abandoned the world, shut themselves up in monasteries, macerated their bodies, lashed their backs with scourges, fed on coarse food, dressed in sackcloth, and died believing they were the embodiment of piety and holiness. And yet must we not say that these supposedly holy men began in the flesh and ended in the flesh? Where was Christ in all of this deprivation and suffering?

Strummed strings broke the cadence of language.

We have a saying where I come from, "A starving belly has no ears." Brothers and sisters, are you starving?

The congregants answered in a single voice.

Do you have ears?

Again.

Brothers and sisters, we are gathered here to indict the body, with its longings, its lusts, its pleasures, its pains, its ruses, machinations, and games. Its plot to unseat the spirit from the holy vessel that carries each one of us through this world. Understand when I tell you that you will never come to the end of things the body can do. But, brothers and sisters, instead of being afraid I encourage you all to use this retreat to meditate on the evils of fornication and other acts of lust that encamp in the body.

At this commandment the entire room shimmered into murmuring. Xavier beheld. And, still holding the instrument, Pastor Omocheke let his followers converse for a minute, two minutes, three, his face empty of expression.

Now, brothers and sisters, please prick up your ears and listen to what I am about to say to you.

He set the instrument down.

Don't focus all your attention on the body. Instead, seek the work of grace upon your hearts. Do not leave here without obtaining what you've come for. Let us pray.

The lights dimmed. Now every person in the room was sliding into the light of prayer, every head bowed, every eye closed, except for Xavier. For him the body was just the body.

Oh Lord—

The pastor's voice carrying across the room to Xavier, low, murmuring, elliptical. He tried to concentrate on the spacing between syllables, only to hear other prayers around him, variations of the pastor's words growing in volume, rising to the ceiling to hang like bats above him.

Let us pray for the downtrodden, the hopeless, the missing and the disappeared. Let us pray for our African leaders, that they give up corruption and embrace concern. Amen.

Amen.

The ceiling lights snapped bright, causing people to pop up from their seats as if snatched. Several women became all ajangle with tambourines. Everyone else waved hands of praise at Pastor Omocheke, who was already drawing away from them, intent on leaving the room. He took a moment to nod his head and fling his hands in the air, smiling and swaying a little, signaling his satisfaction.

Xavier remained seated, gazing away at the congregation, who were giddy with the force of spent emotion. Muscle by muscle and limb by limb, his whole body felt tightened upon him as it had after the afternoon in the cornfields. (That day he had been spared.) He turned to see Dolores still seated next to him secretly watching him, her face flickering. They were one to one, each waiting for the other to say something.

The whole formation of congregants moved out of the room. Unhurried, Milk and Dolores accompanied Xavier to the driveway for him to satisfy his want for a cigarette. They stood and waited a few feet away while he smoked, looking neither at him nor at each other. Smoke swam across his vision, revealing Dolores's bare calves and feet below cuffed jeans. After some time, Dolores released herself from her silence, moved closer and put a hand on his arm. They would see him at supper. With that, she and Milk excused themselves. He smiled thanks.

Walking back for dinner, he waved whenever he encountered a member of the church, feeling his function as an outsider, knowing that they were suspicious of him. Turned a corner and heard voices breaking the air. He saw Madame Omocheke standing before the door to the dining salon with a great display of being in a conical head wrap, a string of bright wooden beads around her neck, and a long dress spilling across the floor. Eyes wide, she met his gaze and at once signaled to him not to move, then started to come toward him with inescapable intention. She took him familiarly by the hand. He surmised she'd been watching out for his arrival. They entered a dining room pulsed like a hive with talk and consumption. A flutter of napkins alight in the room, doves. Everyone proceeded to slow their meals to watch Madame Omocheke walk hand in hand in greeting with Xavier from table to table.

Spokenly together, they made their way patiently around the entire room, picking up deferential exclamations until they reached the table where Dolores and Milk were seated. No sooner had Xavier settled himself between them—side by side again—than Madame Omocheke drew away, leaving him to find his way into a conversation—something about frogs—but never quite doing so, since she returned a short time later with his food. She slid the plate to him with a glance, half smile. He thanked her. She brought her hands together, gave a slight bow, her head steady under its turban.

During the meal Dolores had the chance to look at Xavier closely in every interval of his attention. And he was there to look at her when she said something. Then the sound of eating gave way to a group entering the salon, a circle of women dressed in black blouses and ankle-length skirts, their faces painted white. Heavy women with huge hands and hats, wielding thatch purses shaped like Noah's ark. Ten women. No—counting—twelve. The pastor suddenly recognizable at the center of the circle, a bend of black sunglasses draped over his face. A clear song audible in the silent gestures the women mimed and the unspoken words they shaped with their mouths—*Jesus on the mainline, tell him what you want*—dancing in broken rhythms, a few steps front then one back, a few steps right then one left, again and again, steadily advancing forward, the pastor dancing in the center, and Madame Omocheke holding orbit a few feet away, the pastor's movements extensions of her own. At one point, he gave a quick signal to the women and the circle began to move in determined concentration toward Xavier's table. Xavier looked to Dolores, but her expression was closed to him.

Madame Omocheke waved him forward, and so summoned, he found himself leaving the table—feeling what?—to enter the circle through a space created for him and that placed him before the pastor amid the press of mimes around them. The pastor quick now to remove his sunglasses and smile up broadly with good feeling at the taller man, presenting himself to Xavier.

So good to finally meet you. He quickly put out his hand and Xavier took it, the flesh a little too warm, too clumsily large for the modest body. Something in Xavier lifted under the pastor's enthusiasm and acceptance of him, the smaller man expansive with ease and hospitality. Xavier felt his skin relax, loosen.

Not to disappoint you, Pastor Omocheke said, but you see, this is how we are. He introduced the congregation with a collective sweep of his hand, watching Xavier, his head to one side. Demanding something? Speaking as the little circle moved about the room, the air shuddering with the heavy cadences of the women surrounding them . . . The pastor leaned close, his mouth almost against Xavier's ear and whispered, You are important to me. I want to know you better than the rest. But for now you should eat. A full stomach always chases away sorrow. He looped the sunglasses back onto his face.

He did not come out with anything else unexpected, only

danced, throwing his weight too far this way, then that way, and too far again, reestablishing his balance in a set rhythm but disrupting Xavier's own sense of equilibrium, gravity, until the circle opened, allowing Xavier to plod out.

—

The next morning, Madame Omocheke showed up in full splendor outside his bedroom door. Face-to-face again. They exchanged a few words, preparing him for a special sort of generosity. She let her gaze steer him toward the desk, where she laid out his breakfast, starched napkin folded into a triangle, then swung around to the other side and placed herself before the window, her turban hovering behind her. Once he was seated, Xavier sought out knife and fork and began to eat stolidly, self-conscious and silent, wondering what thoughts were buzzing inside that beehive-like head garment. What must he say? What would be all right?

She must have felt him thinking about her, because her face came around full upon him, her small nose and mouth made smaller by the surrounding plumpness. The pastor will see you in his office, she said. Once you're done. I will take you there.

He did not know what expression to wear on his face, so he accepted her words with a sense of inevitability.

Now was the time to finish his breakfast. Digestion could wait.

She swiveled around and took his astonished hand into her own. They went out of the room, through a series of corridors and out of the villa. A beautiful day. By way of the landscaped garden and posed statues, they set out for a distant branch of the compound, encountering glances, whispers, people in conversation—voices flying about—and reached a turret-like structure down an approach hidden behind a shrubbery of bright flowers. She rapped on the door, waited a moment, pushed the wood open and held it wide. In silence, she presented her husband with the presence of this other man, Xavier. The pastor's voice sprang out bright and clear from where he sat in a tall leather chair with his back to Xavier, who entered the office with its deep armchairs and standing lamps and patterns swirling in the dark grain of the wood-paneled walls. The framed black-and-white photographs (trees, beaches, houses, empty streets) and lavish plants rising out of ceramic pots, their leaves pointing upward as if trying to direct Xavier's attention to the ceiling.

She took him straight to a chair at room center to the right of Omocheke and facing the single window overlooking a fountain. He sat down in the chair grandly pulled out for him with the effect of making the pastor swivel around. The pastor did not stand up, only thrust his hand out for Xavier to take it, his touch the same as before. Xavier flexed his shoulders against the seat back and got settled. Husband and wife did not seem to see each other.

Madame Omocheke left the two men alone, shutting the door behind her. The world went up a notch, morning sun flooding through the window, touching them. They sat in this intimacy of the light, the pastor watching Xavier with wide-spaced eyes, the full contour of his face shining hairless, his shaped hair holding atop his head like a roused cobra. The green crocodile loafers asleep on his feet.

He spread his legs and put a hand on each knee. What do you think about my wife? A gesture of his head toward the door.

Xavier searched for words, had in his mind exactly how to put it.

That's not the half of it, the pastor said. She has done a beautiful thing to me. Perhaps you and Dolores will have what we have. I am hopeful about that possibility. More than hopeful.

The pastor's look held, Xavier incapable of responding. He had no need to think about the possibility, unwelcome knowledge, no way he and Dolores would ever jump the broom. Smiled to put up a good front.

I am in awe of your professional accomplishments. Our church could use a man like you, a man with your talents, experience. Truly. I'm not one given to hyperbole. So do consider us. But I try not to speak more than I have to. He popped a smile. As you know, so much of religious life is about building upon what we can't see but what we know is there because we feel it. Our bones are ghosts inside us. That is the surprise of living.

Relayed casually as if these suppositions were all fact. The pastor weighing him up perhaps? No way to tell.

The pastor remained silent for a while, his chair creaking in a satisfying way whenever he stirred. No doubt he was circling around to something, time that allowed Xavier to peep at the fine stripe of dark green fabric in his trousers that harmonized with the green line in his socks. Bending his neck slightly in Xavier's direction, he said, You asked to see me.

What was this? A mistake or something more? Anybody's guess. A space in his thinking: keep cool, don't oppose him, just go with it.

Shall I tell you something, Xavier? I've come to understand that discretion is the better part of wisdom. My father was all talk talk talk. The pastor pulled a face of tasting something bitter. Now my mother wasn't one for talk. We would eat, and then she'd say, "Here, take this yam to that man over there." She knew he was poor, he was hungry, but that he was also a powerful man in certain ways, dangerous. She was skilled in the art of protection, you understand?

Xavier nodded his head, set on remaining respectful of the conversation.

I'm not sure what some people think they can achieve here. The sick can only serve their affliction, not God. They should first take the time to get better, to heal, as lonely as that is. Be that as it may, we have a responsibility to those we love. All he shows us are his faults so we must remind ourselves about his good qualities, his talents, his affectionate ways.

Now Xavier knew. Taylor. Water flashed. Xavier, seeing the fountain outside the window, trying to build up the image of the pastor's wife in his mind.

Thank you for your concern. Pastor Omocheke looked at Xavier, half breath, half grin, pushing Xavier to smile.

The pastor leaned forward, using his hands. You appear before us as your own witness. Not many men would do that. I like you. I want to go on liking you.

Shoulders hunched, Xavier followed the thought across Omocheke's face. He stared into Xavier's eyes, a genuine look. The quality of his presence had changed. They could talk about other things.

In the light, the cows changed color, going from brown to white to red and yellow and back. Face crooked with effort, Milk wavered from one bovine to the next squeezing swollen udders, a giant among lesser creatures. Buckets and bottles filled, Xavier and Dolores sat watching on the grass a short distance away, detached. The air alive with the unseen, flies, gnats, winged ants, midges and mosquitoes. Insects that Xavier spat from his mouth. The ground beneath him brutal and hard, the grass hairs standing away from skin. And moving waves of heat as if they were mounted on the back of some heaving ancient monster.

He recognized the humor in the scene, the animals grazing on scorched grass while lifting their ears, alert to threat.

Imagine how you appear to them, Dolores said. They smell you before they hear you before they see you.

Nothing he could say to that. Dolores before his eyes again.

Come here, he said.

What?

Just come here.

She watched him, her eyes holding the enjoyment of his attention. You just stay over there, she said.

Amused, he let the matter sink down under silence between them. Studied her fashioned eyebrows on her thick-skinned face. Was she sunburned around the eyes? On her cheeks, neck, and bosom? And also asking himself this: Were they referring to the same things when they talked together? The question bubbled into a force field around him.

Milk started to put a sagging fence in order. Watching, Xavier's thoughts spaced, slowing his breathing into straight lines.

When she thought it time, Dolores looped the strap of her

handbag over her shoulder and took to her feet, causing Milk to give up on the fence, tools thudding to the earth. The three left buckets and bottles in the field and made their way to the lake, a good little hike, her hand in his. The shimmering lake came to life under his eyes. Leaping fish made the water tremble. He could hear their mouths snapping in the air. His gaze carried on as Milk tramped past him and Dolores until the water accepted him and gave him shape.

Dolores sidled up close to Xavier on the ground. Placed her handbag near her feet.

We should go in, Xavier said.

No way, she said. That water will dry out your skin and turn you white.

But it's fresh water, no salt or chlorine.

She looked at him. So you go in.

He went in.

Today, brothers and sisters, the House of Jacob.

The pastor's announcement brought a swarming in the air, a thickening of sound and action, an exhortation of yelling and handclapping. Xavier feeling the momentum in his body, withstanding the moment when Milk leaned his long torso across him to slap Dolores high five. Throughout the salon, congregants were doing likewise, beaming, embracing one another, clutching hands.

Dolores slid round on her chair in one easy movement and turned her legs toward him, then placed her handbag in his lap. Holding her arms across her body to still her excitement. Once again, Xavier felt the stirrings of a shameful curiosity. The House of Jacob?

A kind of alert, then, row after row, people retook their seats, more tentative than settled like birds on telephone wire.

Pastor Omocheke moved from left to right lacing across vision, his crocodile loafers going silently over the polished floorboards, the musical instruments untouched behind him. He stopped in place and looked out over his congregants. Yelled,

Misery, come forward!

A woman left her seat, advanced, and presented herself before the pastor. They squared off, she to the left, he to the right. She put praying hands in the middle of her solar plexus and bowed slightly at the waist as if she were about to engage in a kung fu match.

In so many words, she explained that her husband was addicted to porn.

Pastor Omocheke sucked his teeth. People, do you hear this? He faced the audience and began to pace again. How do you eat food? One has to sprinkle salt into the palm then pinch some onto the food. You don't just grab the shaker and let it rain all over your plate.

In motion, the pastor shifted dark against the light. Then he stopped before the woman and removed a glass vial from his pocket.

I anoint you with this saliva extracted from the mouth of a lion and in so doing release your husband from his affliction.

Feet balanced wide apart, the pastor snapped the vial forward and flung lashes of liquid across the woman's face. She made a clear leap straight up. Xavier tipped his head back, outraged witness. So this is what he does.

The woman hung about a moment thanking the pastor again and again until she felt sufficiently satisfied to return to her seat, where she passed remarks with those around her and received congratulatory pats on the back.

Misery, come forward!

A man sprang forth as if ejected from his chair. The pastor turned a challenging face on the supplicant, who proceeded to explain that he worked three jobs but still faced foreclosure and having his car repossessed.

Xavier thought he saw someone smiling sideways at him from a back row. He felt compelled to look. Observed Madame Omocheke. Something in the set of her mouth. A second glance. Did anyone else notice? They now had this between them.

Did you hear that, brothers and sisters? I ask you, is this world not wicked?

The room sounded loud affirmative noises.

I have another question. Tell me, who was the serpent that spoke to Eve in the Garden of Eden? Think carefully. You have heard it said that it was Satan. But can that be right? No, it cannot because God had not yet made Satan. In fact, he had not made any of his angels. So listen closely and I will tell you. It pains me to inform you that this serpent was some tax collector, some bureaucrat, some politician. This serpent was your neighbor your cousin your brother your sister your father your mother acting in concert with some lawyer or banker or policeman or judge to take possession of your inheritance.

Slumped, lopsided, the man looked on, his hands clasped in front of him, waiting, full of concern.

Brother, fear not. You now have money. You come and work for me. We shall make it so with this saliva extracted from a lion's mouth.

The pastor flung the liquid once again. The man burst into a dance, arms over his head and knees comically bent like an athlete celebrating a touchdown. The pastor let him have his moment then gestured for him to return to his chair. He complied but with no reduction in enthusiasm, taking his own good time, scrambling along on dancing feet.

Xavier had been so busy studying this spectacle that he thought nothing when Dolores retrieved her handbag from his lap and passed it to Milk, but he was conscious of the movements involved in her taking his own hand and pulling him up and out of his chair, and pulling him forward toward Pastor Omocheke. Astonished. Standing there, hand in hand with Dolores, overcome by the sensation of knowing that everyone was watching him, causing him to be slow in looking out over the audience, no easy matter to restore his concentration, composure. He was unbelieving to see her kneel down on the floor next to him, her body tilted sideways, her legs angled behind her like those of someone seated at a picnic.

Pastor Omocheke's face widened in surprise, beckoning. Sister Dolores. Omocheke staring down at Dolores, speaking with that ring of voice, the habit of authority.

Prophet, I would have this man for my husband. She kept her head bowed, speaking to the floor.

You love this man?

Yes, Prophet.

Has he asked for your hand in marriage?

No, Prophet.

So why taste the soup if you can't drink the full bowl? Omocheke's look went from Dolores to Xavier then back again.

Head bowed, Dolores said nothing. She stayed like that in a moment when not one of the three moved. Then the pastor turned and faced his congregation.

People, look at her. Isn't she pretty?

The room confirmed that she was.

She has such a pretty face. And look at him, Mr. Big City. He's so cool. Isn't he cool? Refined. The embodiment of style. Good looks. Nice clothes. Educated. Clean cut. Clean words. Great job. Perhaps Dolores has made the right decision in choosing him. They may well have things to say to each other.

He turned once again to Dolores. Sister Dolores, is he a man of God?

No, Prophet.

I did not hear you.

No, Prophet.

Omocheke turned and looked at Xavier. Sir, are you a man of God? The question lit his darkened throat. Sir, did you hear my question? His defiant eyes. Xavier felt his indignation rising. You see, even he knows. So then, why all this talk about love? See, this is what happens when you speak words to people. Talk talk talk. Love love love. Baby baby baby.

The pastor blew a puckered kiss. The congregation laughed.

Omocheke turned away from Xavier and Dolores and started to pace again, now here, now there, a physical expansion of being.

You can ache and ache and ache for a lost limb, but you will never grow another.

The pastor shook his head, shook his head.

I wish I could lie to you. Then my job would be easy. But you see, the burden I carry is that all my words must come from God. And it takes a lot of courage to get down on your hands and knees in the dark and wait patiently and try to hear what God has to say to you. So when you see me up here, don't think that it's easy for me. It's not easy. No. But let me show you what I can do for you.

Omocheke leaned over and reached elbow deep into the hollow insides of a musical instrument, searching for something. After a moment he pulled forth a straw basket fitted with a lid. Removed the lid then held the basket up for all to see that it was empty inside.

You people with all of your secrets, put them in here.

Omocheke presented the basket to Milk, who slipped his hand inside, then passed it to the next person. And so on, the basket circulating from seat to seat, row by row, Xavier waiting in confused impatience at the center of the room with Dolores while everyone else deposited an invisible secret.

Depositing completed, Omocheke retrieved the basket and fitted the lid back on. Then he looked out at his audience, waited two beats, three, and lifted the lid. Serpents slithered up from inside the basket, several spiraling around his forearms. Voices rose, piercing notes and cries, but Omocheke showed no fear or concern at the reptiles, simply forced them back inside the basket and secured the lid. Working the audience, he looked out at them, his head hanging forward on his shoulders, and started walking again but slower than before, taking his time, drifting across vision, making every moment count.

He stopped. Behold! Lifted the lid. The basket was empty once again.

Shouts of amazement and declarations of holiness: Praise the Lord! God is good! Hallelujah! Amen!

Pastor Omocheke kept the mood. You people, here are your secrets. He opened his mouth. A bird flew out. It flew a few inches into the air above his head and evaporated.

Xavier watching, the sight rousing an angry revulsion. He may have spoken aloud to himself, cursed. The pastor may have heard him, but the fake miracle brought a fresh surge of celebration from the assembled, many leaping off the floor into the air like aquarium-trained dolphins catching fish. Dolores focused on him too, believing, enraptured.

Omocheke broke in when he saw the advantage in doing so, anger in his face. You two, he said. An intake of breath. You connect with nothing. Go. Go. He waved at Xavier and Dolores then turned and walked away. Xavier had it in him to take the pastor's annoyance with enjoyment, his pleasure lessened by seeing small movements in Dolores's body, a purely physical awareness. He felt a strange embarrassment. Looked into her face to see what he should do. Saw trust expressed there. Trust in him. Perhaps something more too. Before everyone present, she'd been chastised by the pastor, rebuffed. And, in a way, she'd also been rebuffed by him. Still, she trusted him. That fact surged in his body.

Dolores waited a full minute and stood up. Clutched his upper arm and together they started back for their seats in the humming room, Dolores pushing past members of the church as if they were insignificant, not there at all. Xavier witness to those around him, seeing them arise and drop and sway, Omocheke's words and miracles released in the movements of their bodies. Omocheke among them. They were all around him now, laying their hands on his shoulders and back and chest.

Xavier saw a woman off to herself gesticulating, bottled up, striking one hand into the other, stomping her foot. And now Madame Omocheke was whispering, pleading with her. Sister, can I help? What can I do? Let me help. Madame embraced her and held her still.

The woman's hair fell across her cheeks, flew back. Her face in her hands now, making it difficult to hear what she was saying between the wet choking noises her mouth made. What am I going to do? What am I going to do? What must I do?

Xavier saw another woman sitting in a corner weeping, hunched shoulders supporting her tiny head, locks covering her face. He released himself from Dolores and pressed forward. Sought her out and touched her, feeling the shape of her skull in his hand, a distinct object. She looked up at him, unblinking eyes magnified with tears. When was the last time he'd faced such emotional excitation?

A surge of movement, a break in the circle of congregants making it possible for Pastor Omocheke to find Xavier with his unavoidable gaze from where he stood on the other side of the room, his congregation radiating around him in concentric rings. He reasserted himself, his voice clear and forceful.

You people, do you know who I am? I will show you. He made a sweeping gesture. Anyone here today who is sick is cured.

A burst of response.

Do you know who I am? My mother and father and sister and brother cut down before my eyes. Their lives coming off the bones while I watched. Do you know? A hundred times kicked out hungry and naked. In every house turned away. My palms cupped and begging but they fed me not. What did I have to eat? Plodding on like an unwilling animal. Carrying my shame like a gallstone I could not pass. And I came to a wretched field with broken fence and skinny buffalo. Was that meat for my mouth? Was that milk for my tongue? Plodding on until I found myself in a mangrove at low tide. Was there water I could drink? Fish I could eat? No, just the red earth drinking. The black earth eating. I plodded on. Marching in mud, silence, and rain. Through unresolved darkness. But you see me now.

Once you do that, you can say, I am God, because you know who God is. No separation. I am the place where everything occurred. I am the body that felt it all. I gave salt and pepper to the table. I gave meat to the forest. I gave salt to the oceans. I made the bread rise to give it shape. I put milk in the cow. Out of this mouth came the oxygen of birth and all that is just and good.

A short time later, Xavier moving through corridors bound for his room, encountering at random members of the congregation in small groups or alone, their testimonies—Did you see? Is there anything he cannot do?—breaking the sequence of his progress. Took advantage once he could, relieved to escape them, so much so that, approaching his room, he slowed his pace to savor the quiet. That was when he heard Dolores's voice behind him. He inserted the key into the door.

Tugging as hard as she could on his arm, she stopped him.

You heard me calling you.

He did not answer her. Moved and placed himself before the high window in the corridor, dwelling there, the sun a thickening blur of radiance through the glass.

Okay. So you gonna do me like that?

Why did you kneel? He could hardly speak, an arch of emptiness under his diaphragm.

Something proclaimed itself in the change of her manner, his question not what she'd been expecting. That? she said. I just wanted to show proper respect. She looked at him, looked away.

As long as we are together, don't ever kneel before another man.

She leaned her whole body against him, belly to belly, breast to chest. He put her away from him. She smiled, unconvinced, her mouth full again.

The octopus seized his tongue. For the moment, fascination at the first meatless meal distracted him from the unpleasant taste and from the shock of wine at supper, Namaqua, new to his tongue, bottled here on the estate, according to Dolores. After several glasses, he'd grown languid and easygoing, patient. Felt drugged.

If you let yourself, you could feel like that, Dolores said.

Looking, listening, smelling, tasting, his attention racing between Milk and Dolores, he had lost the thread of the conversation. He said, Like an octopus?

What? Dolores tucked her head back to her shoulder. The Namaqua set flowing some tipsy laughter. She was not alone, Xavier fully aware that he was also feeling wine.

He pondered the food on Milk's plate, tentacles intertwined in seeming motion, seeking a resumption of liquid life in a sauce of olive oil and butter. Milk watching him with responsive eyes and not hiding it. For this dinner he had chosen a turtleneck sweater underneath a suede blazer with leather patches at the elbows. A bib hanging across his broad relaxed chest. What could he be interested in that Xavier could tell him?

He said, Octopus makes a man strong. He bent his arms in a Mr. Universe pose, biceps bulging like eggs.

Xavier gave no consideration to the boneheaded statement.

Halfway through dinner the circle of women entered the room, and the room went silent. Dolores shifted her chair nearer Xavier. An orchestration of bodies, bobbing their heads on long slender necks, a flock of swans swaying in unison, each adorned in a pleated black skirt and white blouse fitted with a black bow tie. They broke the circle, and Pastor Omocheke danced out, dark glasses on his face and wineglass in hand. Danced over to a table and raised his glass in toast. A man and woman met his toast with raised glasses. He danced over to another table and repeated the ritual.

See, Milk said. We are rejoicing.

Dolores stared into her wine.

Soon Pastor Omocheke stood dancing before their table. The stare of sunglasses. Xavier raised his glass.

Omocheke did the same. Drink more, he said. More. Enjoy.

Sometime later, Xavier stood at the window in his room, the red eye of his cigarette glowing into brightness at set intervals, tracing his consciousness, his thinking blurred, unshapely like octopus ink and the smoke escaping out into the night. He heard a low whine then something fleeting invaded his sight, and he leaned back into the room and shut and locked the window. Night close to his face. He began to push about the dark. Sensed something floating by and reached up and touched it, soft and mushy, black gelatin.

Much was happening in his stomach, the muscles of his abdomen knotting up against his ribs. He had the fanciful feeling that he would barf.

That night he dreamed himself in a body heavy with second skin. With both hands he grabbed at the waist and pulled the skin upward, only to have it get caught around his forehead. Heard himself breathing muffled beneath it. Once the skin was freed from his body, he dropped it into a brown puddle at his feet.

Woke before dawn. The sun came up slow and stubborn. For some time, he listened to his breathing echoing off the pillow. He felt like he had been beaten up, but at least the smell of octopus and Namaqua had cleared from the room. Despite his body's refusal, he managed to prop himself upright on the bed, and there in the stillness was Dolores sitting at the computer desk, watching him.

You were sick, she said. I had to stay with you.

She stood up, the chair cushion recovering shape. Now the slap of her sandals against the floor.

Something else to her. Always something new. Xavier breathing her in.

Xavier stood there for some time after everyone else had gone inside the villa. Looking. Smoking. The sky flashed, wild bursts of light. Birds flapping like the cascading pages of a book, a trick of perspective. Watched as the birds pushed farther into the sky.

The dead weight of heat in the air. Xavier suspended between the night before and some night in the future, his comings and goings mangled in bits and chunks of time, Xavier aware of not knowing where he was in the order of a day as he had always known it. Found himself standing unblinking in a cornfield of overpowering light, a harvest of illumination above and beneath him.

Milk smiled at him. He was able to smile back. What was Milk trying to draw out of him? There was so much to say, so much to find out and understand.

A hard rain fell that night as he settled into sleep. He heard water beating like wings against the window glass, pummeling the building, the trees, the ground, perhaps washing away the heat.

The next morning the whole estate glistened in a glaze of polished brilliance, although the air was still heavy and humid. Everyone stood outside the villa under the heat-soaked sky in a loose gathering around Pastor Omocheke, who stood on a little round swelling of earth like a pitcher's mound.

Now we go, he said. He pulled a prim face then started walking, Madame Omocheke hanging on his arm with animated affection, the first time Xavier had seen them touch.

The congregation followed the couple in a loose procession. The rain had stripped the trees, bare swaying branches. And the ground torn up, floating in brown and green fragments. They walked with grass stroking their ankles and thick brush scratching at their clothes. One good thing, the certainty of Dolores in the flesh again, walking next to him, Milk tagging along behind, a disembodied presence. Dolores. Responsive, excited, her limbs loose and dangling. Looking at him. Gazed at by her. The glisten of her eyes. How well did she see into him?

When they reached the cemetery, she hung back—one beat, two—but willed herself to continue. Moved quickly around the sunken and leaning gravestones as if on an obstacle course. To where?

That question answered when Omocheke sat down on a stone and Madame seated herself on a second stone near him, each person in the group following suit, a tumble of humanity atop gravestones. Facing the assembly, the pastor lifted his throat.

If I may speak please say Yes agree.

Yes agree.

He spread his hands.

Have you heard the latest news? An earthquake in Haiti. A terrorist bombing in Barcelona. Unarmed man shot seventy-five times by cops. An honor killing in Pakistan. Singapore declaring war on Japan. A massacre of protesters in Chile. A tiger eating a toddler at a zoo in Maryland. A dozen teenagers incinerated in a vaping fire. Is what I say not true? You've heard? Yes agree?

Yes agree!

Brothers and sisters, we must not become superstitious about disaster and tragedy and injustice. It doesn't necessarily mean that the days of the world are numbered. In fact, they are not. Each day Christ is resurrected in our hearts, or at least he should be. Everything needs changing, but don't let the world turn you around. Don't let anybody or any situation stand in the way of your relationship with God. That relationship matters more than anything else. Yes agree?

Yes agree.

Omocheke's eyes absorbed all their gazes.

Stay the course.

He stopped himself.

Be until that day when Jesus returns and we enter the earthly paradise together. Let us pray.

Heads fell forward. Eyes shut. With the murmuring and blur of voices, Xavier's concentration wandered, tripped, recovered.

Tools were produced and they set about beautifying the cemetery, whitewashing stone, laying down wreaths, pulling up and tugging out weeds, raking up undergrowth, and replanting, Pastor and Madame hard at work too, carrying out the expected labor, husband in a black suit and the imposing crocodile shoes, wife elegant in a turban, a pearl necklace, and colorful dress of plenty. Dolores's clothing plain by comparison, flair in her mannerisms, the way she held and utilized a brush, trowel, pruning shears. Xavier could tell that she enjoyed the activity, Xavier feeling the hard work going on in his body. Exertion. A half hour later they were done. Pleased with the restoration, the group uproared into a volubility of high spirits and fluttering hands. Exhilaration. Dolores too. Xavier watched her sweaty face swim from solemnity to laughter with an intense fixing of her eyes upon him. In his weariness, Xavier sat down on his tombstone, free to have a cigarette and enjoy the grassy scents of bleach, disinfectant, fertilizer, and fresh soil. Smoke drew down all through his body. Feeling Dolores too, her warmth and liveliness, that aura of closeness. And everyone else. Here he was, installed among them in a graveyard, considering the interpretive meanings of their differences.

They moved on to the parterre garden, walking on wide cement paths among geometric structures that seemed undamaged by the rain. Bent around fortresses of green. Long tables had been set up with snacks and refreshments. Dolores let him choose her cold drink. Moved through streams of celebrations. Turns of talk. Splutters of laughter. Sharing in high emotion. There was no mistaking it. These were happy people. Surely all this friendship, all this affection (love?) must endure beyond this shared occurrence.

The sun sank and flung colors up into the sky. Fading light sprinkled down like golden dust. Lamps flashed on. Dolores drew close to him and although she did not touch him with her hands, her body caressed his side and thighs.

Uninterrupted squawking pulled everyone over to a crop of low hedges sculptured into a square, a green cage where chickens posed inside a trampled plot. Wet with rain they looked ceramic, ready to shatter. Absent up until now, the silent circle of women materialized and produced machetes and cleavers from their black clothing. Attentive, careful, the chickens scrambled about.

The pastor spoke to the group. Don't pity them. We were all once winged creatures. We share their memory of flight. We suffer together.

He seemed to say it all with satisfaction.

Xavier turned once again to admire the chickens although they were nothing special to see. The seemed larger in their mystery as they strained to assert themselves against death. The rhythm now their coming and going.

Everyone was animated by the thought of meat and wanted to get on with the feather-plucking and cleaning so the cooking could begin. Serving trays in hand, Pastor and Madame went about distributing glasses of thick cloudy liquid to everyone present, whetting appetites. When the pastor reached Xavier, Xavier pretended to consider the offer, only to wave his hand and decline.

Omocheke smiled at him. It's lion's milk. Tastes better than it looks. His smile deepened.

For the first time, Xavier saw that Omocheke found him amusing, saw that his rival had anticipated his refusal, his decision to be different, remain other. No choice then but to accept the glass and down it, easy as that. No telling Omocheke's true feelings, only that he waxed proud and delighted at Xavier's acquiescence.

Tonight, we have a special dish. I think you will be pleased. He walked away, crocodile shoes.

Once the pastor was out of earshot, Dolores made a bad face, pretended to gag, choke, hoping to get Xavier to let go and participate in the joke. And so he did, although later he would be hard put to describe what the milk tasted like.

He turned and looked at her, silenced by what he saw. Her open gaze contracted and dilated, holding him, that concentration in herself that kept him. He understood now why she'd brought him here. They were identified with each other. This might have been a kindness. What had not been put in words found its way into consciousness. With Dolores he could put off suffering and prolong life, knowing what his mind would do to him again and again. The vile thoughts, the old sorrows and fears, the shame of wanting, the weighing and the longing, the hoping and the hurting. Had it really been impossible to see her this way before? An immense gratitude moved him.

Without stooping or kneeling, Omocheke stepped out of his crocodile shoes, barefoot now in a broad stance. Each member of the group did their best to reproduce this action. Then a mime dressed in black came and took Xavier's hand, hard. Another seized Dolores. Soon they were being pulled and pushed and jostled along with the gaiety of the group in the cool cozy dark, Xavier carrying away earth and grass on his toes. At the desired location in the garden, they were made to stand side by side, everyone looking on. The woman who had dragged him there spoke something to him that he did not catch, but he did not ask questions, only behaved as if he knew everything that was to come.

Calm, quiet, stillness. Xavier felt that each second, each minute, was something gained. Pastor and Madame present now before him and Dolores, face-to-face, man to man, woman to woman. Omocheke speaking, statements running together, words and phrases overlapping. Omocheke reaching out to thumb lion's saliva warm and greasy like oil on his forehead.

His turn to speak. When the words left him, he could feel his body lighten, by five pounds, ten. Something wet taking shape near his feet. All the weight in his life sinking down into the soil. He kissed Dolores on the mouth. Madame Omocheke unclasped the pearls from around her neck and encircled and secured them around Dolores's. Pastor and Madame stepped away and a little straggle of mimes came forward pulling some animal, an ugly goat with a rope tethered to each leg and around its head. The women tugged on their respective ropes in five different directions, causing the animal to flatten against the grass as if caught in a web. A mime held out a machete and Xavier accepted it. Dolores accepted a second machete. Without being instructed, she hacked into the goat's shoulder. Xavier saw the brilliance of coloring released. Sheen on the grass but no sound. Could the animal have been killed with the first blow? He aimed his machete and hacked into flesh at the same location.

Mouths intoned ululations. Corks popped from bottles. And everything else that had opened. They allowed the machetes to slip from their hands, and the blades stuck into the ground at their feet, two sails riding red streams of blood. People came forward. Kept rushing up to touch Dolores, make a show of congratulating her and wishing her well, laughing and teasing her. She laughed and teased back.

Everyone dropped to the ground cross-legged. Then the simple sight of the meat being readied. The butchering done expertly by Madame Omocheke in a cloth apron and rain boots. A fire was prepared and meat placed for slow roast on the grill. Fatty liquids sizzled, white blobs caught between glowing coals that congealed into black button-like knots.

Someone brought a bowl of warm water for Xavier and Dolores to wash their hands. This body blotted against his body. Cleaning done, they received a single platter of food to share. Using their fingers to bring pinch portions into their mouths while flourishing a circle of onlookers waiting in anticipation. And so the feast commenced. More plates circulated and all began to partake. Dolores ate with appetite, signaling with her lips that she enjoyed the chicken and the goat. Xavier let rich cold milk wash down the potatoes, vegetables, cornmeal, and meat.

After some time, Omocheke came and squatted down before Xavier in an awkward posture. He clasped his hands before him, a gesture that seemed to help him maintain his balance. What would he want to know?

Sweet, yes?

Xavier nodded.

That's the bird pepper. Omocheke's gaze expressed everything and spared nothing. At the same time, it spoke acceptance. Their business was done. He stood and walked off, making himself available to the celebrants.

The blare of music. People began to dance. Laughter and singing and chatter flying through the air. Xavier and Dolores too, pulled body to body, sweat to sweat, into the circle. Challenged. Encouraged. Putting on their best moves. Gathering up the life of this place.

April 7, 2020
Johannesburg, South Africa

The Next Flight

He mounts the shaking platform, lays the weight of his fingers on the delicate wings. No more red-eye. No more standby or baggage or weight restrictions. From now on he will go wherever he wants whenever he wants and take along whatever he wishes to, one carry-on bag or ten, one suitcase or a thousand. And he will remain airborne to his long heart's content. For his best ideas come to him forty thousand feet aboveground while strapped in an aisle seat with a cup of coffee steaming up from the slim rectangle of his tray table and strings of cloud framed in a little square of window. Frequent flyer. Always on the go.

When he was seven years old, his grandmother told him the story of the Flying Africans, the earliest known transatlantic flight, causing him to understand aerodynamics as a thing to live by. He began to thread his way through passages of Leonardo, Newton, and Liang, mull over the treatises of Cayley, Francesco Lana de Terzi, and Wernher von Braun, review and improve the schematics of the Montgolfier and Wright brothers, Zeppelin, and Langley, putting their thoughts into his own language, a tireless record stretching across several decades and filling twenty notebooks the size of folios.

Heading out into the world, he examined firsthand ancient instrument panels unearthed in the jungles of Peru, surveyed precolonial airfields in the Congo, and cataloged magical carpets on three continents. Gazed through the slot of his diver's helmet (his own personal pressurized cockpit) into inky ocean depths to chart the crash sites of downed fighter jets.

Many such exploratory missions, necessary groundwork for the numerous vehicles he has engineered over the years: a kite sliced from linoleum, a mobile pieced together from flypaper and Popsicle sticks, a crude dirigible ballasted from condoms (latex more preferable than rubber), a helicopter spun from wire and string, a glider constructed of mangrove, bamboo, and banana leaf (an object lesson in objects), and his singular achievement, a prototype for a single-person flying apparatus.

Bearing his history, he checks his gauges, adjusts his belts and straps, and takes to the sky, already thinking ahead to his next flight in a craft indistinguishable from air, made of air itself.

Acknowledgments

The love, encouragement, and support of many friends made this book possible. I wish to thank Kalisha Buchannan, John Casteen Jr., LaForrest Cope, John Keene, Lore Segal, John Edgar Wideman, Nana-Ama Danquah, Tyehimba Jess, Morowa Yejide, David Henderson, Shelley Marlowe, Micheline Aharonian Marcom, Sterling Plumpp, René Steinke, Michael Anania, Bayo Ojikutu, Karen Martin, Reginald Scott Young, Peter Trachtenberg, Jacqueline Johnson, Josip Novakovich, Kim Coleman Foote, Caryl Phillips, Daaim Shabazz, Chiseche Salomé Mbenge, Ishmael Reed, Terese Svoboda, Marc Zimmerman, Myrtle Jones, Joseph Cuomo, Judith van Praag, Gary Davis, Josephine Ishmon, David Daniel, Najah Webb, Ethelbert Miller, Mary Gaitskill, Dan Buckman, Ken Buhler, and Rebecca Chace.

Sincere gratitude to the following musical forces for invoking the spiritual and showing me how to make a way out of no-way: Sade, Young Thug, Jorja Smith, Future, Summer Walker, JID, Tems, DVSN, Jazmine Sullivan, Drake, SZA, Dawda Jobareth, Oumou Sangaré, Brent Faiyaz, Burna Boy, Teyana Taylor, Kendrick Lamar, H.E.R., Earl Sweatshirt, and Erykah Badu.

Special thanks to my agent, Cynthia Cannell, and to Fiona McCrae, Ethan Nosowsky, and everyone at Graywolf Press.

Special thanks to Martha Sanhayi. Always and forever.

With gratitude for the love and support of my children, Elijah, Jewel, James, and Jacob, who will always be first in my heart.

I am grateful for the support of the John Simon Guggenheim Foundation, the Bellagio Center of the Rockefeller Brothers Fund, the Schomburg Center for Research in Black Culture, Jentel Arts, and the Johannesburg Institute of Advanced Studies.

And in memory of Binyavanga Wainana, Randall Kenan, Keorapetse Kgositsile, Grandmaster Masese, and Greg Tate. Until we meet again . . .

Permission Acknowledgments

"Louisiana Blues." Words and Music by McKinley Morganfield. Copyright © 1959 Watertoons Music. Copyright Renewed. All Rights Administered by BMG Rights Management (US) LLC. All Rights Reserved. Used by Permission. *Reprinted by Permission of Hal Leonard LLC.*

"Work." Words and Music by Robyn Fenty, Jahron Brathwaite, Allen Ritter, Aubrey Graham, Matthew Samuels, Monte S. Moir and Richard Stephenson. © 2015, 2016 MONICA FENTY MUSIC PUBLISHING, WC MUSIC CORP., SONY MUSIC PUBLISHING (US) LLC, EMI APRIL MUSIC INC., RITTER BOY, SANDRA GALE, 1DAMENTIONAL PUBLISHING LLC, NEW PERSPECTIVE PUBLISHING, AVANT-GARDE- MUSIC PUBLISHING, INC. and GREENSLEEVES PUBLISHING LTD. All Rights for MONICA FENTY MUSIC PUBLISHING Administered by WARNER-TAMERLANE PUBLISHING CORP. All Rights for SONY MUSIC PUBLISHING (US) LLC, EMI APRIL MUSIC INC., RITTER BOY, SANDRA GALE, 1DAMENTIONAL PUBLISHING LLC and NEW PERSPECTIVE PUBLISHING Administered by SONY MUSIC PUBLISHING (US) LLC, 424 Church Street, Suite 1200, Nashville, TN 37219. All Rights for AVANT-GARDE-MUSIC PUBLISHING, INC. Administered by UNIVERSAL MUSIC CORP. All Rights Reserved. Used by Permission. *Reprinted by Permission of Hal Leonard LLC.*

"Consideration." Words and Music by Robyn Fenty, Solana Rowe and Tyron Donaldson. Copyright © 2020 Monica Fenty Music Publishing, Songs Of Universal, Inc., WC Music Corp. and Antydote. All Rights on behalf of Monica Fenty Music Publishing Administered by Sony Music Publishing (US) LLC, 424 Church Street, Suite 1200, Nashville, TN 37219. All Rights on behalf of Antydote Administered by WC Music Corp. International Copyright Secured. All Rights Reserved. *Reprinted by Permission of Hal Leonard LLC.*

"Oceans." Words and Music by Shawn Carter, Pharrell Williams and Christopher Breaux. Copyright © 2013 Carter Boys Music, EMI Pop Music Publishing, More Water From Nazareth and Heavens Research. All Rights on behalf of Carter Boys Music, EMI Pop Music Publishing and More Water From Nazareth Administered by Sony Music Publishing (US) LLC, 424 Church Street, Suite 1200, Nashville, TN 37219. All Rights on behalf of Heavens Research Administered by BMG Rights Management (US) LLC. International Copyright Secured. All Rights Reserved. *Reprinted by Permission of Hal Leonard LLC.*

"The Healer" by Malcolm Robert McLaren, Daniel Vangarde, Erica Wright, Otis Jackson. Copyright © 2008 by Peermusic (UK) Ltd. All Rights Reserved. Used by Permission.

Jeffery Renard Allen is the award-winning author of six books of fiction and poetry. He has received many accolades for his work, including the *Chicago Tribune*'s Heartland Prize for Fiction, the Ernest J. Gaines Award for Literary Excellence, a grant from the Creative Capital Foundation, a Whiting Award, a Guggenheim Fellowship, a residency at the Bellagio Center, and fellowships at the Center for Scholars and Writers, the Johannesburg Institute for Advanced Studies, and the Schomburg Center for Research in Black Culture. Allen is the founder and publisher of *Taint Taint Taint* magazine. He was raised in Chicago and divides his time between Johannesburg and the United States. Find out more about him at www.authorjefferyrenardallen.com.

The text of *Fat Time and Other Stories* is set in Source Serif Pro.
Book design by Rachel Holscher.
Composition by Bookmobile Design and Digital
Publisher Services, Minneapolis, Minnesota.
Manufactured by McNaughton & Gunn on acid-free,
100 percent postconsumer wastepaper.